LADIES INVITED

A JACK OATMON THRILLER

TJ REILLY

This book is a work of fiction. Any resemblance to actual places, events, or persons living or dead is entirely coincidental. Historical personages portrayed are used fictitiously and their actions are products of the author's imagination.

ISBN (Print): 978-0-9972426-0-7
ISBN (Ebook): 978-0-9972426-1-4

Cover, interior, and ebook design by Steven W. Booth,
www.GeniusBookServices.com

Author Photograph: Adam Reilly

Dedication

For Bill, Becky, and Ali

Acknowledgments

Many people say writing a book is a solitary process, and in certain ways that is true. However, this novel would never have been completed if it wasn't for the generous support and encouragement from a lot of people. I want to thank those who took the time to read and comment on the early drafts: Phyllis Frank, Jim and Irene Dorsey, Tim Kelly, Clarke Howatt, Dr. Anna Sarabian, Robert, Linda, and Emily Porr, Tom DeMars, Tom Johnsen, Larry Rolapp, Dan Morgan, Jim McCullough, Dennis Ballam, Reverend Joseph Gaglione, Kathryn Field, Bettina Breckenfeld, JoAnn Cornelius, Becky Stilwell, Michelle Durgy, Lisa Brandl, Rick Clark, Denise Milton, Sue Hartman, and Corinne Atwood. Your efforts made this a much better book.

I would also like to thank authors Cara Black, Sheldon Siegel, D.P Lyle, and everyone at Book Passage in Corte

Madera, CA. I will always be grateful for your interest, help and encouragement.

Thanks to Steven Booth and Sam Barry for guiding me through the self-publishing maze, and to copyeditor Mark Burstein for his attention to detail.

Finally, I must thank author Catherine Coulter, and her anonymous senior reader. The generous gift of their time and insight will never be forgotten.

PART ONE

CHAPTER ONE

Los Angeles

Her name was Katarina.

Long legs, blonde, big breasted, and dirt poor.

And perfect.

No one would miss her.

No one would look for her.

Kidnapped at seventeen from Moscow, she willed herself to survive for the past two years, and always looked for an opportunity to escape.

That chance might be tonight.

Her "date" for the evening, a grossly overweight, foul-smelling, drunk German named Horst Wolpert, decided to leave the hotel and sample the club scene. The limousine dropped them off at a loud, crowded club on the Sunset Strip that catered to men like Horst. The curtained booths in the back offered a semblance of privacy, and were used for everything imaginable.

Horst led Katarina to the booth furthest away from the front door and the pounding music. The club was packed with sweaty, drug-crazed wannabes oblivious to everything and everyone but themselves. He flagged down an overly endowed, silicone-enhanced cocktail waitress, ordered two bottles of champagne on ice, and followed Katarina into the booth. He leered at her with bloodshot eyes, and roughly pawed her with his large, fat hands.

"I give you a night you will never forget," he said, slurring his words in heavily accented English. He pulled off his blue blazer, sat on the small sofa next to her, and planted a sloppy kiss on her painted lips. Katarina did her best to accommodate his bulk as he clumsily maneuvered on top of her. She was saved by the waitress knocking on the wood frame holding the curtains.

"Champagne as ordered, sir; would you like me to open it?"

"*Nein*, I do it myself."

"Very well, sir, will that be cash or charge?"

Horst handed her a gold American Express card, told her to start a tab and not come back for an hour. He stood up and opened the first bottle.

"I treat you well, no? We enjoy the luxuries only Western society can provide. Much better than those incompetent peasants where you come from."

The champagne bubbled out when he popped the cork. He brought the bottle to his lips and drank, but more of the liquid ended up on his chin and shirt than down his throat.

Katarina had endured countless similar evenings. She encouraged him to drink because it increased the odds he'd get too drunk to perform, but she'd still get paid.

Horst offered her a glass.

"We must dance," he said.

He pulled her to her feet with his free hand, the other still clutching the bottle. He continued to drink, his large frame looking ridiculous moving about the small area. In a very short time, Horst was breathing heavily.

He stopped.

"Now the best part!" he said as he pushed her down on the sofa. He took another long gulp, emptied the bottle, and shoved it neck-first into the silver ice bucket. He began to undress her.

"Off with the clothes, woman; I show you how a real man treats a woman."

He reached his hand up her skirt, lurched on top of her, and gasped for breath. His hand came off her thigh and reached for his chest. Katarina thought he was trying to take off his shirt, but his face turned blue as he choked for air.

He was having a heart attack!

Many things went through Katarina's mind in the next few minutes, but summoning help for the fat slob was not one of them. He died quickly, most likely before she was able to get out from underneath his weight.

She had to act quickly.

Someone from the syndicate was surely outside, waiting to escort her back to the house in the hills where the girls were held.

The club's rear exit was next to the booth and might offer her an escape route. She was terrified, but she might not get another chance. There was several thousand dollars in hundreds, fifties, and twenties, and half a dozen credit cards in Horst's wallet. She took it all, crammed it into her small purse, and put the wallet back in his pocket.

Easing out of the booth, she bumped into the waitress. It took all her self-control not to panic.

"Is everything okay?" the waitress asked, concerned.

"Oh, yes, thank you. I need the ladies room."

"Right over there in the corner past the bar."

"I see it, thank you."

Katarina scanned the room for the familiar brutal faces, but found none. She got to the bathroom, astounded she could function, actually used the facilities, washed her face, and fixed her makeup.

She returned to the booth.

Horst was there, still very dead. She calmly sat on the sofa facing him and made the decision. She got up, and in an attempt to cover her scantily clad body, put on Horst's much too large blazer. She slipped through the curtains, took a few steps, and went out the back door into the cool Southern California night.

She found herself in a small parking lot that opened into a wide alley between the back of the club and the office buildings on the other side. There was a six-foot block retaining wall on the far side of the alley, so Katarina was forced to go either left or right along the back of the club. She had no idea which way might be safer, so she went right, simply because it looked darker and might hide her better.

She quickly reached a side street. Going left would take her by the empty office buildings, and to her right was Sunset Boulevard, where she saw a line of people on the sidewalk, presumably waiting to get into the club. There were other people milling around, so rather than take a chance in the empty spaces to the left, she decided there would be safety in numbers and turned right. She would always wonder what would have happened if she had turned left.

She reached Sunset and tried to be casual, just another young woman out for the evening. Heading east, she tried desperately not to run and draw attention to herself, but it was too late.

She didn't get far.

CHAPTER TWO

Alexei Persoff, stationed on the south side of Sunset facing the club, was trained to look for anything out of the ordinary. A tall, blonde woman in an oversized blue blazer emerged from the shadows behind the club and caught his eye. He called his man inside the club, the one Katarina obviously missed.

"Where is the client?" he snapped without preamble.

"A booth in back," replied the goon named Gorky.

"Check him, now! And don't hang up."

Gorky wasted no time getting to the booth.

"Herr Wolpert?"

He pulled back the curtains, and knew immediately something was very wrong and he was in a lot of trouble for letting it happen right under his nose. He stepped inside, hoping no one from the club had seen inside the small room. He checked for a pulse on the cold, blue mass of flesh sprawled on the sofa.

There was no doubt he was dead.

"What is it?" Alexei screamed in his ear.

"The man is dead and the girl is gone."

"Is his blue blazer there?"

"No."

"Get out now, and stay on the phone."

ꕥ

The further Katarina got away from the club, the more terrified she became, and the faster she moved. It was lunacy to think she could get away, especially in a strange city, but she had to try. If she could find a hotel room and hide for a day or two, she might pull it off.

She thought her prayers were answered when she saw the sign for the Hyatt Sunset. She quickened her pace, and never looked back to see Gorky and Alexei gaining on her.

Only fifty yards to go!

Twenty!

When she reached the ramp leading down to the underground parking she started to run.

"Now!" Alexei said into his cell phone.

Gorky sprinted the last twenty yards to grasp Katarina as she started up the walkway to the entrance.

"There you are, darling, I thought we lost you." He leaned down close to her ear and whispered in Russian so there was no doubt she would understand. "Don't even think about screaming."

Alexei arrived from the other side of the street and sandwiched Katrina between their two much stronger bodies. "Come quietly or you will regret it," he said.

There were a few people near the entrance to the hotel, but they paid the three of them no notice. The two men reversed course and started back toward the club. They passed the wall bordering the ramp to the garage when Katarina finally snapped. She had come too close to freedom, and would rather die than return to the degrading life controlled by men like these two.

She screamed.

"Get your fucking hands off me, you pigs!"

Alexei and Gorky were momentarily stunned. They had no idea she spoke English, one of the few things she had kept hidden from her captors. Katarina used the precious seconds to try to break free. She struggled mightily, but they only squeezed harder and inflicted more pain, infuriating her even more.

"I will not go back!" she screamed. "You treat me like an animal!"

She would take it no longer. Her life was worthless if she allowed herself to be taken back. She kicked, trying to reach their groins, but the best she could do was the sides of their legs. She punched them to no avail. She couldn't get her fingers close enough to gouge at their eyes, so she screamed at the top of her lungs.

"No! No! Help, please God somebody help me!"

Alexei had had enough. He moved in front of Katarina and slapped her hard, stunning her into momentary silence. They needed to get her off the sidewalk and away from the curious eyes of any bystanders or motorists.

There was a narrow walkway, bordered on one side by large shrubs and on the other side by the parking ramp wall that led to a patio off the side of the hotel. They dragged her there as she continued to scream. Alexei had no choice now. He punched her as hard as he could in the stomach. She collapsed to her knees, out of breath.

"Get up, bitch," said Gorky, "or we kill you here."

"Go ahead, asshole, I WILL NOT go back. EVER!"

Now Gorky had had enough. He grabbed a handful of her hair, pulled her head back, and smashed his fist into her face, breaking her nose and loosening a few teeth.

"Get up now or you die!"

"Fuck you," Katarina rasped. Blood poured from her nose and mouth.

"Last chance, Katarina; come quietly, or we kill you here. It is your choice."

"Go to hell."

Katarina was almost able to stand by leaning against the brick wall. She didn't see another vicious blow coming as Alexei crashed his fist into her temple. She went down again.

Then the miracle happened.

A window on the second floor of the hotel opened. "Is everything all right down there?"

To Katarina, the young man's voice sounded like an angel from heaven. Deep down in her soul, she knew this was her last chance. She summoned every ounce of energy she had left in her battered body, stood, and screamed.

"They are going to kill me!"

She looked up to the window, her face caught in the muted, yellow light of the streetlamp. The young man in the window could see the horrible damage.

"You motherfuckers!" he yelled as he punched 911 on his cell phone.

Alexei and Gorky now had no chance to get Katarina back to the car, but they also couldn't leave her here alive. She knew too much. They dragged her to the darkest spot against the wall, and out of the view from the hotel window. Alexei pulled a silenced Beretta from his shoulder holster and placed it against the back of Katarina's head.

Katarina was vaguely aware of the cold steel.

She was about to die.

What a waste, she thought. She wanted to do so many things with her life, and now she wasn't going to get the chance. But a small part of her brain was still functioning, and flashed a spark of defiance. She remembered from her studies as a child that the skull was very hard, and could withstand amazing force. If she anticipated Alexei pulling the trigger, she would turn her head and the bullet might not kill her.

"*Au revoir, ma chérie,*" Alexei said.

He was distracted by the wail of sirens in the distance, which slightly changed the angle of the gun against Katarina's head. He pulled the trigger.

Katarina's upper body twisted and she slumped to the concrete pathway, bleeding profusely from the head wound. Alexei saw blood and didn't think to fire a second time.

CHAPTER THREE

Adam Reeves felt helpless two floors above the dark walkway. The cops were on the way, but he didn't know if they would be in time. His spirits sank further when he heard the spit of the silenced gun.

He had to do something. He grabbed towels and a pillow, raced down the stairs, and burst out the side emergency exit that opened onto the back patio above the ramp to the parking garage. The woman was around the corner. He was about to move when a piece of the wall behind him exploded in a rain of stucco. He dove under one of the metal outdoor tables, upended it, and used it as a barrier. He was terrified and defenseless in the dark, with no idea what to do. The hotel door closed automatically behind him and the keyed security lock blocked a retreat back into the hotel and safety. The sirens were close now, no more than two blocks away. Surely the gunman wouldn't stick around any longer.

Adam was right.

He waited until the cops rolled up, sirens screaming, to the front of the hotel, then scurried around the corner to see if the girl was okay. He stayed close to the brick wall and, thankfully, no more bullets whizzed by his head. He reached the crumpled form in a few seconds and was gratified to hear her breathing. It was shallow and raspy, but at least she was alive. In the darkness he could not see the extent of her injuries, but he did notice the blood. He didn't want to move her, and as his eyes adjusted to the dim light, he saw the wound to her head. Responding totally on instinct, he placed a rolled up towel against the head wound, then braced it with the pillow against the wall. He took a second towel and dabbed at the blood on her face. He couldn't see or feel anything major, but her face was badly swollen and already starting to bruise.

He didn't know what else to do.

His cell phone buzzed in his jacket pocket. He didn't recognize the number on the display.

"Yes?" he said.

"Are you the one who just called 911?" a calm female voice asked.

"Yes."

"Where are you now?"

"The walkway on the west side of the hotel, above the ramp to the parking garage. Hurry, the woman has been shot and severely beaten. She's alive, but barely."

"Okay. Stay right there, and don't hang up the phone this time!" the female voice insisted. "The police detective will be there in a few seconds. His name is Jack Oatmon. What's yours?"

"Adam Reeves."

"Okay, Adam, stay with me and everything will be fine."

Adam looked up toward the front of the hotel and saw a gun coming around the end of the block wall. It was followed by a tall, slender man in civilian clothes, crouching low.

"Move away from the girl, now!" he said firmly.

"Do exactly as he says," the voice in his ear told him.

Adam held onto the phone, lifted his other hand away from the fallen girl, and slowly crawled away.

"Are you Oatmon?"

"How did you know my name?"

"I'm on the line with 911 right now. She told me."

Jack Oatmon moved closer and motioned for Adam to give him the phone.

"This is Detective Jack Oatmon, who's this?"

"It's Gwen, Jack. The kid called it in."

"Thanks, we got it from here." He handed the phone back to Adam, pulled a small flashlight from his belt, and examined the damaged woman. "Well, she's still alive."

He used his shoulder mike to call for an ambulance and fire off requests for backup.

"Are you the one who put the towel on the wound?" he asked.

"Yes, did I do the right thing?"

"If you stopped the bleeding you probably saved her life."

ഗ

The paramedics showed up, worked quickly, got the woman into the ambulance, and sped off. Other police officers showed up, including Oatmon's detective partner, Eric Schroeder. There were quick discussions with Oatmon, and they fanned out to canvass the area.

Jack Oatmon took Adam aside and guided him through the events of the last half hour. "Start from the beginning and tell me everything about the incident, no matter how trivial."

They went over it several times, but Adam had only heard the noise on the walkway and never got a good look at the two men.

"She gonna be okay?" Adam asked.

"I don't know. Listen, you can't continue to stay here. We'll put you up somewhere else for a few days because we might need you as a witness. You weren't planning on leaving town, were you?"

"No, I don't have to be back in Sacramento for another week. I'm here looking for a bartender's job, trying to get into some acting classes and find an agent. I want to be an actor."

You and ten thousand other guys like you, Oatmon thought.

"Go get your stuff, check out, and meet me in the lobby in a few minutes. We'll get you someplace safe, and then we both might be able to get some rest."

Oatmon finished up with the technicians on the walkway, now cordoned off with yellow police tape. A crowd had gathered on the sidewalk and the media jackals would be there soon.

He would be long gone by then.

CHAPTER FOUR

Detective Jack Oatmon walked quietly into the dark hospital room. The soft beeping and the greenish glow from the machines hooked up to the unidentified woman gave the room a decidedly eerie feeling. The doctor said her chances were improving by the hour, but wouldn't know the extent of the damage until the swelling went down. Her last bit of defiance, and Alexei's momentary distraction, had saved her life.

Jack was appalled at the destruction to the woman's face. Her eyes were swollen shut, a deep gash was surrounded by a huge bruise on her left cheek, and her lower lip looked like hamburger. There were tubes running into her arms, mouth, and nose, and her breathing was shallow and raspy, but steady. The grimace on her face spoke volumes. Jack couldn't imagine the pain she endured.

He stayed into the early hours of the morning, contorting his lean, athletic, six-foot-four-inch, two-hundred-and-ten-pound frame into a quasi-horizontal position on a small waiting room couch. Sometimes being tall was a disadvantage, but at thirty-one, Jack weighed only six pounds more than when he graduated from college. He still played basketball three mornings a week, and held his own against the young bucks trying to show him up.

Roused from his uncomfortable dozing by the activity of the morning shift change, he needed to move. He stood, stretched, and went to check on the woman again. She was still unconscious, but breathing steadily. He walked over to the window and peeked out at the morning. A weak shaft of yellow sunlight broke through the blinds and spilled into the room near the head of the bed. Jack wasn't sure, but it seemed she reacted to the light, and he trusted that was a good sign. He closed the blinds, left the room, and went downstairs, hoping the cafeteria would be open this early for some much needed coffee.

He was on a second cup when Sue, one of the night nurses, rushed into the cafeteria looking for him. She was a short, slightly overweight Hawaiian woman in her mid-thirties, but she moved with unmistakable grace and efficiency. Jack had been impressed by her kindness and compassion toward the woman throughout the night.

"Detective Oatmon, we have some good news upstairs. The doctor would like to see you immediately."

The two moved quickly to the elevators and rode back up to the Critical Care Unit. They entered the room and watched the doctor carefully inspect the woman's wounds. The tube had been removed from her mouth, and she moaned quietly.

The doctor, a tall, blond, Nordic type named Endquist, noticed them and smiled.

"Well, detective, it seems we have a very strong, resilient patient here. She woke up for a few minutes, but all I could ascertain was her name apparently is Katarina, and she is from Moscow. I gave her medication for the pain and a sedative to help her rest, but she should be awake again later this afternoon. Her vital signs are much improved, and the ice packs have significantly reduced the swelling."

"Is she going to make it?" Jack asked.

"I can't be certain at this point, but after seeing so much improvement in the last few hours, we can be cautiously optimistic. Go home and get some sleep. Come back this evening and you might be able to talk to her for a short time. If anything happens in the meantime we'll call your cell phone."

CHAPTER FIVE

Jack and Eric had registered Adam Reeves into the Travelodge in Santa Monica and told him to call in every day. The hotel was a safe distance from Hollywood, and right down the street from Eric's condo. Jack was pretty sure Katarina's attackers didn't get a good look at the young man, but he wasn't taking any chances.

On the drive back to his bungalow in Los Feliz, Jack checked in with his partner. "Sorry to leave you with all the paperwork."

"No worries," Eric said. "I was doing it before you got here and I'll be doing it after you leave. Go home and get some sleep; I'll meet you back here tonight."

"Thanks, partner," Jack said.

Jack was grateful. He got lucky when Eric Schroeder agreed to be his partner, even though the assignment was temporary and Jack was considered by most to be an outsider. Eric had been gracious and accommodating, and helped ease Jack's transition to life in Los Angeles.

Jack Oatmon's situation was unique. Technically, he wasn't a detective, but it was easier for everyone to call him that. His true title was Special Field Agent, and his paychecks came from Langley, Virginia. He'd been recruited by the CIA straight out of college, first working as an analyst, then as a field agent in the Middle East. After 9/11 and the consolidation of many agencies into the behemoth Homeland Security Agency, Jack was assigned to a newly formed group called the Interdepartmental Cooperation Unit, or ICU. Their mission statement was simple: stop the bureaucratic intransigence and turf wars, find ways to increase communication, share information in a timely manner, and actually get things done. Jack had seen numerous reports suggesting that 9/11 could possibly have been prevented if the governmental agencies charged with protecting the United States had simply been talking to, and trying to help, each other. Jack shuddered to think how many investigations were stalled, abandoned, and unsolved over the years. His job was to improve the situation.

Classified as a "rover," he pulled duty at both local and federal agencies in an effort to maximize efficiency. It was a position ideally suited to his personality. The idea of going to work every day at the same place, possibly for years at a time, gave him the screaming heebie-jeebies. Jack constantly looked for new challenges, and the opportunity to work all over the United States, and eventually all over the world, intrigued and motivated him.

He'd been sent to Los Angeles six months ago to assist in the investigation of the Russian mafia and the trafficking of Eastern European women as sex slaves. So far, they'd had minimal success, busting very uncooperative, small-time pimps and low-level operatives. Most of the time they were back on the street before Eric could finish the paperwork.

The early morning sun exposed the smog-ridden skyline as Jack pulled into his driveway, retrieved the morning paper, and let himself in. He was glad to have an empty house for a few days. His significant other for the past few months, Maria Acosta, was out of town. He'd met her a few weeks after his arrival, and she'd moved in before he fully unpacked. The sex was enthusiastic and fun, but the whirlwind romance had moved much too quickly and was showing the strain of unfamiliarity. Maria didn't understand his crazy schedule, and because of her culture of family and tradition, couldn't fathom why Jack would agree to the frequency and uncertainty of his geographical postings. Maria was a creature who craved the comfort of routine, while Jack was always antsy in anticipation of adventure. Maria wouldn't, or couldn't, buy into Jack's outlook.

She complained his was a pursuit of the impossible, because there would always be bad guys. Jack argued that someone had to keep the peace, or what kind of world would we leave to our children and grandchildren? Which Jack knew was the real bone of contention, and the true source of Maria's unhappiness. Her biological clock was ticking like a time bomb, and the unrelenting parental pressure for her to stop living in sin and start a family made for more than a few heated discussions.

Jack's repeated insistence that he didn't ever want children had fallen on deaf ears. He was convinced Maria had stuck it out for the last month hoping she could change his mind.

The phone rang.

"Oatmon."

"It's me," Maria said. "Are you just getting home?"

"Yeah, it was a bad night." He didn't give her any details.

"I called to tell you I'm going to stay in Seattle for a little while longer."

"How long?" Jack asked.

"I don't know, maybe a few months, maybe for good."

Jack said nothing.

"I'm sorry, Jack, but I can't do it anymore. I won't jeopardize my chance for a real family, or play second fiddle to your career. I've decided to start over from here."

Jack still said nothing.

"Are you there?"

"Yes, I am, and you're not. I guess I'll have to get used to that now."

"I'll come down later to get my things."

"That won't be necessary," Jack said. "I have extra suitcases in the garage. I'll send everything to you when I get a chance."

"Thanks, Jack. I'm really sorry."

"Me too," Jack said, although he really didn't mean it. His relationship with Maria had laid bare a basic disconnection. He always thought he could figure things out and make it work, even if he knew the circumstances were not ideal. That attitude served him well in his professional life, but in his personal life, not so much.

He wandered to the kitchen, gulped orange juice straight from the container, then went into the second bedroom he had set up as his office. He punched the button on his iPod docking station and Kirk Whalum's melodious saxophone filled the room. He went through his mail, paid bills, and returned phone calls for some of his other cases. It was almost noon when he finally made it to his bedroom. He picked up the half-finished *New York Times Magazine* crossword puzzle, grabbed a pen, and spent the next half hour completing it.

He fell asleep, fully clothed, on the bedspread of his king-sized bed.

When he woke up, the bedroom was dark and the green LCD light on the clock radio read 5:45. With the heavy drapes blocking any potential natural light, he momentarily panicked, not sure whether it was 5:45 a.m. or p.m.

Had he slept straight through the night? Or was it still the same day?

His cell phone vibrated on the nightstand.

"Oatmon."

"Detective, I'm glad I caught you this evening."

At least that answered the a.m. or p.m. question.

"This is Dr. Endquist. Katarina's improved enough for you to talk to her for a few minutes. How soon can you be here?"

ᔓ

He was on his way twenty minutes later and made good time to the hospital. Dr. Endquist had his back to him when he entered the room.

"How's she doing, Doc?" Jack whispered.

"I must say, she is a very strong young woman," he remarked with true admiration. "She has a long way to go, but there doesn't seem to be any permanent damage, other than she might lose a few teeth. The wound to her head is serious, but not life-threatening. She's a very lucky girl."

Jack gazed at Katarina. She looked awful. The swelling had subsided a bit, but her entire face was bruised almost beyond recognition.

"She certainly doesn't look like a lucky girl," Jack said.

"The human body is an amazing thing, Detective. It has recuperative powers that even in this day and age we don't fully comprehend."

Katarina reacted to the soft voices.

"Where am I?" she asked slowly, careful to minimize the movement of her lips.

"Hollywood Presbyterian Hospital. You're safe now; no one can hurt you here," Endquist said. "Now, Katarina, I don't want you to talk too much, but Detective Oatmon here would like to ask you a few questions." He turned to Jack. "Four or five minutes tops, so make your questions simple and make them count. I'll be right back."

"Thanks, Doc." Jack was impressed with his bedside manner.

Jack pulled a plastic chair to the bedside, put his hand on top of Katarina's, and gave it a gentle squeeze. At this point, all he knew was that she was probably Russian. He started simply. "Do you understand English?"

"Yes."

"You put up a hell of a fight, Katarina. I'm glad you're going to be all right."

Katarina looked at him with a hint of a smile. "Thanks."

"Listen, I'll make this easy tonight and then we can talk more later. Is that okay?"

She nodded slightly.

"Do you have any family we can call? Here or anywhere else?"

"No," she said.

"Were the men that did this to you Americans?"

She shook her head slightly. "No. Russian."

"Did you know them?"

She nodded.

Jack had seen his share of prostitutes roughed up. He didn't know for sure, but this looked like a particularly bad example. Katarina had been dressed in a halter top and short skirt, and overly made up. This didn't necessarily make her a working girl, but it did seem to tip the scales in that direction. He pressed on delicately.

"Were you trying to get away from these men?"

"Yes."

"Do you know where we can find them?"

"Maybe. I don't know. Always in cars … dark windows … mostly at night."

"Did they force you to do things you didn't want to do."

"Yes." Katarina closed her eyes and recoiled slightly.

"Do you want to help me find these men?"

Katarina hesitated. Jack could only imagine the horrific things this poor young girl had gone through.

He pressed on.

"Are there other girls like you?"

"Yes. Maybe ten or twelve."

"And they are being forced to do things too?"

"Yes."

"Then we have to find them and help them."

"I'm … scared."

"I'm sure you are, Katarina. But no one is going to hurt you anymore, I promise." He squeezed her hand again as a silent tear rolled down her cheek. "Get some rest now. I'll be back later and we'll figure out how to help the other girls."

"Okay." It was obvious the short conversation took a lot out of Katarina. She closed her eyes and drifted away.

Jack found Dr. Endquist outside the door. "Well, detective, I see you took my instructions seriously. I'm impressed."

"I got enough to start my research. I appreciate you taking an interest in this case; I'm sure she feels all alone in a strange country."

"I have worked here for a decade, and I'm continually amazed at the inexcusable cruelty shown to vulnerable people, especially the working girls in this area. I'll use all my medical expertise to help this woman so she can help you find the animals who did this to her."

Jack was shocked by the passion in Dr. Endquist's voice. "I appreciate that, Doc, and I'm sure Katarina is grateful, too."

"It's the least I can do," he said. "Just nail the bastards."

"I will," Jack said.

CHAPTER SIX

Jack knew if Katarina really could help, it might be the break they'd been waiting for. Human trafficking for the purposes of prostitution was a multibillion dollar industry, and the numbers were staggering. Since the fall of the Iron Curtain and the breakup of the USSR, the percentage of Eastern European women trafficked increased from *less than one percent to twenty-five percent* of the worldwide total. Estimates ran as high as 40,000 women per year. If the figure was even close to accurate, that meant thousands of Eastern European women were brought to the United States as sex slaves.

Every year.

The Russian mafia realized right away that along with their stealing oil, gold, and other natural resources, young women could be exploited for huge profits. They were smuggled mostly to countries where they couldn't speak the language, and therefore even more dependent on their brutal captors. One young female body, either kidnapped or bought for a few hundred dollars, could generate a profit up to $250,000 in the first year.

Jack and Eric spent the next week continuing their research and, after several brief visits to the hospital, pieced together the sequence of events that ended up with Katarina's beating.

She had worked as a maid in one of Moscow's Western hotels, where she learned to speak English. She used her meager earnings to keep her mother supplied in vodka and pay for a rat-infested tenement apartment near Red Square. She had been kidnapped outside the hotel, smuggled first to Bulgaria, then on to Prague, and finally to Los Angeles. It was a horrifying and chilling tale of rape, brutality, and degradation.

They did basic police work and tracked down the dead German, Horst Wolpert. A search of the phone records from his hotel room and cell phone led to the phone number of an escort service called "Ladies Invited," run by Russians. It was a prepaid cell phone, but in the spirit of homeland security, the credit card company provided them an address in the Hollywood Hills.

ঞ

The house was huge, even by the opulent standards of an overindulgent show-business town, on a gated property of several acres off Coldwater Canyon. They had done reconnaissance over the past two nights. Big, dark SUVs and limos with blacked-out windows were seen coming and going from what they assumed were the garages at the back of the mansion. None of the drivers looked like typical chauffeurs; they were big, mean-looking men.

Jack and Eric enlisted the help of others in their department and followed the vehicles to numerous upscale hotels and mansions from Palos Verdes to Malibu, even out to Palm Springs. At each destination, the vehicle would discharge a young woman, sometimes several young women, who were quickly whisked away to a hotel suite or the interior of a large private residence. An hour or two later, the process would reverse, and the drivers would reload their cargo and return to the house.

They ran the license plate numbers. The SUVs were leased to a Russian company called Dante International, the limos registered to Paulette's Limo Service in Sherman Oaks. Jack was not surprised to find that Paulette's Limo Service was owned by another firm, Sigorsky International, which in turn was owned by Dante International.

The house was leased to Victor Ischenko, the current CEO of Dante International. After consultations with Jack's contacts at the CIA, the FBI, and the U.S. Embassy in Moscow, they confirmed Ischenko was a former KGB agent, spoke English, and had leased the house for over a year. Ischenko was suspected of widespread bribery and misdeeds in Moscow, and had left the country under suspicious circumstances. Jack and Eric reviewed the research with their boss, Tom Dorsey, and convinced him to set up a meeting with Ischenko.

With the help of Dr. Endquist, they released a statement confirming the death of the unidentified woman. In truth, Katarina was secretly transferred to a private room at Cedars Sinai, which, due to its many famous patients over the years, had developed a sophisticated system of deception and secrecy to protect the privacy of its clientele.

Jack and Eric worked with two other LAPD detectives, Dave Ketcham and Pablo Perez. Most of their experience had been with smugglers and pimps from Mexico, Central America, and the Far East, but over the last two years they too had heard references to an Eastern European operation. Their resources were severely diminished due to budget cuts (one of the reasons Jack was there and being paid by the ICU), and they didn't have the opportunity to pursue many of the leads. Katarina's misfortune might be the catalyst to make some headway, and they were excited to help.

The plan was to call Ischenko, explain that one of his company's phones was linked to a murder case, and assure him it was probably all a misunderstanding—but could they come by this morning and talk to him for a few minutes to clear it all up?

Jack and Eric, in the lead car, were the designated team for the interview, with Tom, Dave, Pablo, and several other officers from the department as backup. If there were up to a dozen other girls being held captive, they wanted to make sure Ischenko and his associates didn't have the opportunity to get them off the premises and disappear.

Jack made the call from his cell phone. They were surprised when Ischenko's assistant assured them his boss would surely cooperate with the local police to clear up the matter. Jack informed the helpful assistant they were in the area and could be there in a few minutes.

Jack pulled up to the security gate, pushed the call button, and waited.

"Yes?" came the scratchy response on the voice box.

"Detectives Oatmon and Schroeder to see Mr. Ischenko."

"Please show your badges to the camera on top of the box."

Jack complied.

The ornate, black wrought-iron gate slowly opened, allowing them to enter. The brick-bordered concrete driveway was shaded from the late morning sun by large mulberry trees, and led up the hill in a semicircle to the front doors of the massive edifice. The double doors were eight-foot-tall solid oak with leaded glass inserts, beautifully stained and lacquered to a high sheen.

They were met by a fastidious, balding man of about forty, wearing fashionable rimless glasses, a suit costing at least two weeks of Jack's salary, and a red silk tie worth more than any suit Jack owned. He spoke English with a slight French accent.

"Please come in. I am Frank DeMarchand, Mr. Ischenko's chief of staff." He did not offer to shake hands. "Follow me, please."

He led them into a large entryway. To the left was a huge step-down living room with bay windows providing a spectacular view from downtown to Santa Monica. To the right, down more steps, was a long, wide hallway with several closed doors on both sides. DeMarchand led them straight ahead, up a marble stairway to a landing. On the right was a formal dining room, and on the left, more oak doors led into a library with floor-to-ceiling bookcases. A large, rectangular glass table was in front of French doors that opened to a lush interior courtyard with potted palms, wood park benches, and comfortable outdoor lounge chairs surrounding a pyramid-shaped granite water fountain. In one of the lounge chairs was a beautiful, tall, dark-haired woman in her late twenties or early thirties, wearing white shorts and a red bikini top.

Jack and Eric were invited to sit in the two black-leather-and-chrome director chairs in front of the glass table.

"May I offer you something to drink?" Mr. DeMarchand asked formally.

"No, thanks," they both said.

"Mr. Ischenko will be with you momentarily." He left through a side door and they were left to gaze at the woman by the fountain.

"Sorry to keep you waiting, gentlemen."

Jack and Eric started to rise. "No, no, please don't get up. I know how comfortable those chairs are, and the scenery isn't too bad either," he said as he glanced into the courtyard. "She is beautiful, no?"

"Yes," they both agreed.

Ischenko was a big man, at least 6'3", over 250 pounds, and carried himself like a former athlete gradually falling out of shape. He was in his early fifties, a full head of hair gone completely white, but stylishly cut. He looked tanned, either by artificial means or from weekends at the beach or Palm Springs. He wore an immaculately pressed charcoal gray suit with a powder blue dress shirt, and a red silk tie similar to DeMarchand's. Jack's first impression was of a man comfortable with himself, and who liked being the boss.

"Ah, but you didn't come here to admire the surroundings, did you? How can I help you?" he asked as he settled himself comfortably into the plush executive chair behind the glass table.

"Well, Mr. Ischenko ..."

"Please call me Victor."

"Okay, Victor. I'm Detective Oatmon of the LAPD, Hollywood division, and this is my partner, Detective Schroeder."

Ischenko nodded to Schroeder and looked back to Jack. "Welcome to my home, gentlemen."

"Thank you," Jack replied, trying not to get disarmed by Ischenko's hospitable manner. "Ten nights ago, a young Russian woman was murdered outside the Sunset Hyatt hotel in Hollywood. Earlier that evening she was seen in the company of a German gentleman, Horst Wolpert, an unfortunate victim of a heart attack in a club down the street from the hotel.

He made several calls to a cell phone paid for by one of your company's credit cards, and Dante International charged one of his credit cards $3,000. Do you know how we could find out about this transaction, Victor?"

"As I am sure you are aware, Dante International is a very large, diverse company with offices around the globe. I can't be aware of every cell phone and credit card charge. Furthermore, I have spent the last two years preparing to retire. I am not really involved in the day-to-day operations of the company anymore; Mr. DeMarchand handles that now."

"Where are the records kept that might shed some light on the charges and whose cell phone was called?" Eric chimed in.

"I don't know that either," Ischenko replied, as he punched the intercom button on the desk phone. DeMarchand reentered the room immediately.

"Frank, where do we keep the records of phone and credit card charges to Dante International?"

"All those paper and electronic files are kept in our offices in West LA, on Bundy Avenue. I usually have computer access from here, but our Internet connection is down today."

"So the only way to see them would be at those offices?" Ischenko asked.

"Today, yes. If the detectives would like to come back tomorrow, or meet at the offices tomorrow, I could help then."

"Tomorrow is Saturday. Why not later today or this evening?" Jack asked politely.

"I am afraid that would be impossible. Mr. Ischenko has several important meetings in Santa Barbara today and dinner tonight with some diplomats from the French Embassy. In fact, we are already late. This can all be cleared up easily tomorrow morning. Why don't we meet at the Bundy office, shall we say nine o'clock tomorrow morning?" He handed them each a business card.

"There's nobody there to help us today?" Jack tried again.

"We have given the entire staff the day off because we are repainting the office. I will have to meet you there tomorrow."

"That seems like a reasonable request to me," Ischenko said.

"Do you have anyone in your employ here in LA named Gorky or Alexei?" Eric persisted. Katarina had given them the names of the two men who had tried to kill her.

"We have thousands of employees, I am sure some with those names. Do you have last names?" asked DeMarchand.

"Sorry, I don't," Jack said.

"That's a shame, it would make it much simpler with last names," DeMarchand said, his voice dripping with condescension. "We really are late now, sir," he said to Ischenko.

"I guess it's tomorrow at nine then," Jack said. "We'll let ourselves out."

As Jack and Eric got up to leave, there was movement in the courtyard. All four men turned to see several scantily clad young women with towels, suntan lotion, and magazines get situated on the other lounge chairs around the woman in the red bikini top.

"One more question, Victor," said Jack. "How many people live here?"

"Well, that depends on the time of year. Usually, it is only me and my girlfriend, Sasha." He pointed to the tall, dark-haired woman. "But the winters in Moscow are long, and bitter cold. How can I deny my dear Sasha when her girlfriends want to visit sunny California?"

A mischievous grin spread over Victor's face. "Have a nice day, gentlemen. I am sure Mr. DeMarchand will resolve your questions tomorrow morning."

Jack and Eric made their way down the steps to the car. "I should have worn boots today, with so much bullshit in there," Eric said.

"I know," Jack said. "But there's nothing else we can do right now. We need a plan to watch these people around the clock, and a search warrant in case DeMarchand stonewalls us tomorrow morning. Then we can put some pressure on them."

Jack phoned Dorsey in another car down the block to call off the other teams. "Right now we need bodies to follow these people, not firepower," he explained. "I don't think they'll do anything suspicious until later tonight, so why don't Eric and I go get some sleep and be back on at ten tonight." Dorsey agreed to get the search warrant and committed several teams of detectives for the next twenty-four hours.

"Tell the guys to follow these people and not engage them," Jack said. "We're dealing with a nasty group here, boss." He ended the call and headed back to the office to drop off his partner.

CHAPTER SEVEN

Inside the mansion, DeMarchand and Ischenko were in full damage control mode. Plans were in motion to get out of the country immediately. Ischenko, several bodyguards, and Sasha, with a few of the other women, would leave on the corporate jet from the Santa Barbara airport late in the afternoon. Their sudden departure would be explained by urgent business in France, a result of their conversation with the French diplomats. If all went well, they would be in Paris by midday tomorrow.

DeMarchand would skip the trip to Santa Barbara, stay an extra day, and deal with the two detectives. He wasn't worried about the phone and credit card records—there was minimal evidence on the computers in the West LA offices—and he could delete anything damaging in a matter of minutes. He would tell the detectives that the suspect cell phone had been stolen, when in fact he had smashed it himself and thrown the various pieces down several storm drains. Horst Wolpert's credit card charge to Dante International was also easily explained away. DeMarchand had set up a subsidiary company that promised top quality pornography, which was in fact never delivered. He had warehouses full of it though, just in case. Alexei and Gorky were paid in cash, and both were already back in Paris anyway. After satisfying the detectives, he would board a commercial flight and regroup with everyone in Paris.

The rest of the women would slip away to other Dante International safe houses in Las Vegas, San Francisco, Dallas, Palm Springs, Palos Verdes, and Santa Barbara. They would dye and restyle their hair to match their new bogus passports and, one by one, would be flown to another city and another company-controlled escort service outside the United States until the heat was off. If they survived, some would eventually make it back to LA, but time and more fake documents would leave the original trail ice cold.

DeMarchand and Ischenko had been through the drill many times before in other major cities around the world. They were fully aware the LAPD did not have enough manpower to follow all the individuals for more than a few days, and with a few well-placed bribes and a little time, the whole thing would blow over and it would soon be business as usual.

CHAPTER EIGHT

Jack was exhausted. After dropping Eric off at his car, he headed straight home. He could catch a few hours of sleep before going back on at 10 p.m. The recent switch to nights had prompted Jack to hang heavy dark curtains over his bedroom windows to block the ever present Southern California sunlight. The cool darkness came in handy on days like this. At least this time he was able to undress before climbing under the covers to the Egyptian cotton sheets that still smelled of Maria's expensive perfume. He drifted off into a fitful sleep.

The buzz of his cell phone jolted him awake. "Oatmon," he answered in a groggy voice.

"Detective Oatmon, this is Adam Reeves. Did I wake you up?"

"It's okay; I have to get up anyway. Notice anything suspicious in the last couple of days?"

"Not at all. I've been out running around, making good use of my time. You're not going to believe this, but I got an agent already and I have my first audition on Monday. Isn't that great?"

"Sounds good," Jack said as enthusiastically as possible.

"Listen to me," Adam said. "In town less than two weeks and already so self-absorbed all I can talk about is myself. How's Katarina?"

"It looks like she's going to make it. Maybe lose a few teeth." Adam had been so helpful, and literally could have saved her life, so Jack had told him the truth about Katarina, and sworn him to secrecy. "She should be able to leave the hospital in the next couple of days."

"That's great. I'm glad we got there in time."

"Me, too," Jack said. "Listen, you're only going to be here a few more days, right?"

"That was the original plan, but who knows, I could get lucky and land this commercial on Monday. Got to think positive, right?"

Jack couldn't help but laugh at his enthusiasm. "It's already Friday, so why don't you stay where you are through the weekend, on the Department. Starting Monday you're back on your own, but call my voice mail at work and let me know where you end up."

"That's more than fine with me," Adam said. "You guys putting me up here saved most of my budget, so I'm ahead of the game. Which reminds me, how is Katarina going to deal with everything? She obviously doesn't have insurance, money, or a place to live, does she? Maybe I could help out with some of the money I saved by staying here."

"That's a nice gesture, Adam, but we still want to keep everything quiet for now. We've taken some money from a task force budget for the time being. Keep in touch, if there's a way for you to help, I'll let you know. I'll tell Katarina you offered."

Jack was fully awake now and still had an hour before meeting Eric back at the station. He wandered into the kitchen for something to eat. As he sat at the counter munching a cinnamon raisin bagel, he picked up the card Frank DeMarchand had given him. The Dante International offices were literally two blocks from Eric's condo. He called Eric and convinced him to reconnoiter the Dante International premises on his way back to the station. Eric didn't like the idea of doing it alone, but finally relented when Jack promised to be available at the first sign of anything suspicious. Jack would head to the station early and monitor the other teams.

❧

Eric Schroeder showered and dressed completely in black: jeans, turtleneck, windbreaker, and running shoes. He didn't know what the night would bring, but he wanted to be prepared for action. He was in great shape due to a disciplined workout regimen, and occasionally joined Jack at the morning basketball games in the gym. They shared a passion for putting criminals in jail, especially those who preyed on the weak and vulnerable. They complemented each other in a variation of the good cop/bad cop scenario, with Jack masking his intensity behind a reasoned, thoughtful demeanor and Eric being more emotional.

He tucked the department issue Smith and Wesson in his shoulder holster and set out on the short walk. It was a comfortable evening, and he was there in less than five minutes.

The building was one of the several modern office towers built in the area in the mid-eighties. The security was more for show than effectiveness and Eric walked unimpeded through the lobby to the elevator bank. The guard behind the desk noticed him, but was more focused on a small TV tuned in to an early season Dodger game against the hated San Francisco Giants.

Whisked quietly up nineteen floors to the penthouse suite, Eric was greeted by an eerie quiet. He imagined the daytime activity behind the doors, with accountants and insurance people slaving away for their piece of the American dream, living completely different lives than a detective working graveyard shifts. He looked right and saw the etched glass doors of Dante International. Through the embossed lettering he saw no sign the small office was being painted. Looking more closely, he noticed the walls were adorned with subtly lined wallpaper. Eric wasn't surprised DeMarchand had lied to him, and it might give him a slight advantage in the morning. He was about to knock on doors to see if there was someone in the other offices, when a light went on behind the Dante International doors. Immediately suspicious, he put his back to the wall by the glass doors so he couldn't be seen from the office interior.

The person inside was not concerned about noise, and Eric could hear a chair rolling on hardwood floors and a briefcase landing heavily on a desk. He peeked around the corner of the glass door. The line of sight was down an angled interior hallway, leading to a window office. He had a three-quarter view of the hunched figure of none other than Frank DeMarchand himself, booting up a computer. He could see the computer screen as DeMarchand brought up different information. Eric wasn't a whiz with computers, but he knew enough to know DeMarchand was probably running a program designed to make information disappear into cyberspace. He wondered if the LAPD or FBI computer wizards would be able to recover the information later.

DeMarchand abruptly stood, pulled papers from a printer and his briefcase, and walked out of sight. Eric heard the soft whirring of a shredder in an interior room. He took the opportunity to quietly get back to the elevator and push the call button.

PING!

It sounded like a church bell in the silence.

He was out of sight unless DeMarchand stood directly inside Dante International's glass doors. Eric hit the "door close" button and then the one for the garage. The doors swooshed closed and he was safe.

He exited on the first level of the underground garage, circled the elevator shafts, and checked out the cars remaining on a Friday night. He rounded the last corner. To the left was the door to a private elevator. A black SUV was parked right in front, possibly one from the house in Coldwater Canyon. He didn't know what to do next. He didn't want to confront DeMarchand here, and he didn't have his car to follow him when he left, either.

The decision was made for him.

"Don't move, Detective." The silenced muzzle of DeMarchand's automatic pistol was pressed firmly against the back of his neck. DeMarchand reached around and took Eric's gun from his holster.

"You won't need this for a while," DeMarchand said. "Any other hidden weapons?"

"No," Eric answered honestly. "I'm curious, though, how could you possibly know I was here?"

"Very simple, I saw your reflection in the darkened window of my office."

Eric silently cursed his stupidity.

"No doubt deleting all the incriminating files. I'm sure our lab guys will be able to recover them."

"I sincerely doubt that, Detective. Put your hands behind you, slowly," he demanded. Eric complied and DeMarchand expertly used Eric's own handcuffs to shackle his wrists. The keyless remote beeped to unlock the doors to the SUV. DeMarchand kept the gun at the base of Eric's neck, and reached around to open the rear door. "Get in, lie on your stomach along the back seat, and don't look up. Be still or I will kill you right now."

In a matter of seconds, a strong rope and duct tape were wrapped around Eric's ankles. DeMarchand used the seat belts to further restrain Eric and added duct tape over Eric's mouth for good measure. When he was satisfied with his work, he shut the back door and got behind the wheel.

Eric had been in tough spots before, but he had a bad feeling about this one. He was defenseless, and only Jack knew where he was right now. He was wedged uncomfortably against the back of the bench seat and something was pushing against his right side. He first thought it was the buckle of the seat belt, but he realized it was his cell phone tucked into the pocket of his windbreaker. If there was a way to maneuver his hands around he might be able to somehow get it open and hit his speed dial to the station.

DeMarchand started the SUV and exited the garage using a plastic card to open the gate. Eric spent the next few minutes twisting and turning, pretending he was trying to get comfortable. He was able to get his right hand to the outside of the windbreaker's pocket, but unable to get inside to retrieve the phone. Over the top of the front seat, Eric could see DeMarchand concentrating on the road with occasional glimpses in the rear view mirror. It seemed like he wasn't familiar with driving such a large vehicle.

"I know you are uncomfortable, Detective, but not for much longer," he said. He had taken his eye off the road for a few seconds to check Eric's reaction, and as he tried to make a right turn onto Pico Boulevard, the right rear wheel hit the curb and severely jostled the car. Eric was thrown against his restraints. DeMarchand immediately regained control, straightened out, and accelerated west on Pico.

The mishap worked in Eric's favor. His cell phone was knocked completely out of his pocket. It landed between him and the seat back, very close to the back of his right hand. To get it, he would need to inch toward the passenger-side door while lifting his cuffed hands so they wouldn't push it out of reach. He tried once, but the phone moved with him.

He relaxed, tried again.

This time it worked, and he now had the phone in his hand. The question still remained, how was this going to save him?

"Goddammit!"

Eric froze. Concentrating so hard on getting the phone, he forgot to pay attention to DeMarchand. He could hear a soft pinging from what appeared to be the dashboard.

"Idiots. They all have cash and company credit cards! I can't believe they don't keep the tank full. I need to stop for gas, Detective. Nobody can see you with the blacked-out windows, so sit tight and we will be on our way soon. If you try anything I swear I will kill you."

Eric thought he was going to kill him anyway, so he had to try something soon. DeMarchand pulled into a gas station, and after another warning, got out of the car and started filling the tank. Eric knew this was probably his last chance. He tilted his head enough to see the face of the phone, punched in his security code and hit speed dial #1. He had thankfully left it in silent mode, so DeMarchand heard nothing.

"Oatmon," Jack answered.

Eric knew the desk phones had caller ID so Jack knew it was him. He moaned as quietly as he could without arousing DeMarchand's suspicion. With the tape over his mouth and the phone down by his waist it was a long shot to pull this off.

"Eric, is that you?"

Eric moaned a little louder, hoping it sounded like an affirmative grunt. He didn't have much time. DeMarchand had finished pumping gas and was already on the side of the car near the driver's door.

"Eric? What the hell is ..." Eric cut off his partner again with a loud moan, hoping Jack was smart enough to figure it out, stay on the line and listen, or use the GPS system to track the call. Eric had no choice but to leave the line open and hope for the best.

DeMarchand got back in the car, started it up, and eased back into traffic. He made his way to Lincoln Boulevard and turned south. Ten minutes later, he pulled into the deserted Dockweiler Beach parking lot off Vista del Mar in Playa del Rey, near the end of the runways at LAX. He parked, turned, and leaned over to Eric in the back seat and ripped off the duct tape covering his mouth. It hurt like hell, but Eric didn't make a sound.

"A tough guy, eh? We shall see." He pulled out the gun and pointed it at Eric's groin. "Tell me what you know or you die."

"You're going to kill me anyway."

"You underestimate my compassion, Detective. I have no intention of harming you further as long as you tell me what I want to know."

Eric didn't believe him. If he was going to die he should make every effort to get something on the record. He spoke for a few minutes, briefly outlined what he knew, using DeMarchand's and Ischenko's names frequently, and hoped Jack was recording it back at the station.

"Very good, Detective, but you can prove nothing. We have every contingency covered, and it will only be a matter of time before it will be business as usual. You are wasting your time."

He turned back toward the front and got out. The driver's side back door opened and DeMarchand unhooked the seat belts and cut the duct tape and rope around Eric's feet. He placed the gun in the small of Eric's back.

"Work your way slowly back until you get your feet on the ground."

DeMarchand actually helped by grabbing Eric's belt and pulling, making it a little easier. It was awkward with his wrists cuffed behind him. Thank God he had dropped the cell phone onto the back seat while DeMarchand was outside the car. Eric did his best to shield DeMarchand's view of the back seat so he wouldn't see the phone.

Eric thought he had gotten away with it, but as they started away from the car, his cell phone chirped. It was the sound it made when the battery was low. DeMarchand looked back in the car, saw the phone and sighed.

"You were so close, Detective."

"It's only the sound it makes when the battery is low," Eric explained, hoping he would get away with it.

DeMarchand had parked the SUV next to a dumpster enclosed on three sides by brick walls and double metal doors on the fourth side. He instructed Eric to lie down on his side facing one of the brick walls, covered him with the silenced weapon, went back to the SUV, and picked up the phone. "Who is this?"

"It's Detective Oatmon, you asshole. We've got everything on tape, including your threat to kill a Los Angeles police detective."

Even with his face to the wall and several yards away, Eric could hear his partner's voice. He didn't know now if he was going to live or die, but he had to do something. He rolled away from the brick wall and struggled to his feet. He couldn't hear any more because a plane taking off drowned out all other sound.

As the plane roared west into the night, DeMarchand lowered the phone slowly, a sad look on his face, the gun still pointing at Eric. "I told you not to try anything." He raised the pistol, aiming for Eric's torso.

"You can't kill an LAPD detective in cold blood and get away with it, DeMarchand. Give yourself up and cooperate and I'll see they go easy on you."

"You fool. You will never understand the people I work for. If I betray them, there is nothing you can do to protect me, there is no place on earth you can hide me where they won't find me."

"Then leave me here, get in the car, and take your chances. You solve nothing by killing me. They've probably done a GPS search on the phone and are on their way already. You don't have much time."

In the faded light cast by the distant streetlight on Vista del Mar, Eric noticed DeMarchand's eyes momentarily lose focus. He had to make a break for it *now*. He backed away from the dumpster, seeing nothing but the expanse of beach in both directions.

"Stop!" There was resignation and emptiness in DeMarchand's chilling voice.

"Sorry, can't do that," Eric said as he continued to back away. They were the last words he ever spoke.

DeMarchand fired three shots in succession, all three finding their mark around Eric's heart.

"I'm sorry too," said DeMarchand simply. "I almost liked you."

He threw the cell phone to the ground, got into the SUV, and sped away.

CHAPTER NINE

Jack Oatmon was inconsolable. He had tracked Eric's cell phone, sent the nearest units to assist, and raced to the parking lot in Playa del Rey.

They were all too late.

They found Eric's body slumped in the sand next to the dumpster. The damage to Eric's chest was massive, and there was no doubt he was dead. Jack's only thought at the time was that he probably didn't suffer.

After they removed the body and scoured the scene for clues, it started to sink in. The long hours, the busts, the sharing of countless meals, the mutual support and respect they had for one another. It wasn't supposed to end this way; Eric deserved better than to die next to a dumpster.

Hours later, Jack was the only one left in the parking lot. He listened on the scanner to the raid on the Coldwater Canyon house. Not surprisingly, it was empty with no sign of its former inhabitants. The officers on the scene found a disguised path behind the mansion that led to another large house further down Coldwater Canyon. DeMarchand and the women had eluded capture and escaped from the second house. Ischenko was followed to Santa Barbara but had slipped away too, most likely in a private jet from the small local airport.

Jack felt the darkness surround him. He tried to fight it, but then gave in to his anger and grief.

And wept.

ઌ

The sky turned from black to deep blue as the sun rose behind him. Jack knew it was his responsibility to notify next of kin. Eric's only living relative was his brother, Tim, who lived in Moscow and worked for a relocation firm that helped executives find housing. Jack had met him once on one of his trips back to the States. Jack didn't understand why anyone would *choose* to live in Russia, but who was he to judge?

He called the sergeant on duty and got patched through to the number pulled from Eric's personnel file. Jack didn't know the time difference, but it had to be at least ten hours, so it was late afternoon or early evening in Moscow.

"Hello?"

"Is this Tim Schroeder?" Jack asked, and waited for the inevitable delay as his voice bounced to satellites and then to Tim's cell phone, ten thousand miles away.

"Yes," Tim replied. "Who is this?"

"It's Jack Oatmon, Tim. I have some really bad news."

Jack heard Tim choke back tears when told of his brother's murder.

"I'll be on the next plane out of here," Tim said, his voice breaking. "Probably be there tomorrow sometime. I'll call you when I arrive."

"I'm so sorry," Jack said.

"Thanks," Tim said. "Me too."

He hung up.

❧

The next few days were awful. Jack knew everyone was trying to be considerate, but he quickly tired of the condolences and wished people would just leave him alone.

Tim Schroeder arrived late Sunday afternoon and called from his room at the Westwood Marquis Hotel.

"I've been contacted by the Police Association," Tim said. "They want a funeral with full honors. I don't know if that's what Eric would have wanted."

"I really don't know either," Jack said. "But the advantage of doing it their way is they have people to take care of everything. You sign the paperwork and follow their instructions and timetable."

"They want to do it on Thursday," Tim said.

"Is that okay with you?" Jack asked.

"Yeah, I guess so."

Even with the Police Association handling the show, there were endless details to keep both Jack and Tim too busy to deal with their grief. On Wednesday night they found themselves sharing a few minutes and a good brandy in Jack's back yard.

"When are you going back to Moscow?" Jack asked.

"I leave next week with a stop in Paris," Tim said. "Eric and I inherited a ton of money when our mother died, so I invested in a new American restaurant near the Champs Élysées called L'Avenue Bar & Grill. It's scheduled to open this summer. I'll eventually move to Paris, but for now I've hired an old friend from college to manage it and an American woman living in Paris to help him. I want to stop and check on their progress."

"Sounds like you've got a lot on your plate," Jack said.

"I like keeping busy. I've already been to Eric's condo and gone through his things. It was strange to sift through old family photographs and the memorabilia of a brother I hadn't been close to as an adult. I have no interest in keeping the condo, so I'll hire a real estate agent and put it up for sale. I boxed up all the personal papers and things I want to keep; the rest of the furnishings will stay with the condo. Is there anything you would want?"

"As a matter of fact, there is," Jack said. "Eric has a forty-year-old bottle of Irish Mist whiskey. We were going to open it the night before I left for my next assignment."

"I'll make sure you get it," Tim said.

"Thanks. Let me know if you need any help with anything else."

"I'll probably take you up on that," Tim said. "I still need to file all the paperwork for the two life insurance policies. I didn't realize Eric had them and named me the beneficiary. We were close growing up, but not for the last fifteen years. After Mom died there was even less reason to stay in touch, especially with me living on the other side of the world. The two of you spent more time together the last few months than we did in fifteen years."

"It wasn't just the job," Jack said. "It was us against the world. If it takes the rest of my life, I'm going to find DeMarchand and the bastards who beat up Katarina."

"Do you have a plan?"

"Not yet, but I will."

ꟸ

The funeral was well attended, with an impressive show of solidarity from the LAPD and other law enforcement agencies paying tribute to one of their fallen brethren. The state attorney general and Mayor Garcetti were present, along with other politicians taking advantage of the media coverage.

Tim did his best to hold it together during his eulogy but, understandably, there were times he stopped to compose himself. He finished with a story about how Eric helped their ailing mother in her final days, and even the macho cops had tears in their eyes. There were other speakers, mostly colleagues from the department and local LAPD brass, praising Eric's dedication and promising to bring his killer to justice.

Jack sat in the back and listened to the musically challenged vocalist/organist sing off-key and miss notes entirely. If anybody else noticed, they were too polite to show it. An hour and a half later, it mercifully ended with the honor guard leading the flag-draped casket down the aisle and out to the waiting hearse.

Tim came over to Jack, Pablo, Dave, and Tom on the church steps. He looked shaken, the burden plainly weighing on his broad shoulders. "Is there anything we can do?" Jack asked.

"No, thanks. Right now I need to get through today. I don't mean to sound ungracious, but the last few days have been difficult, with all the formality and bureaucratic involvement. I want it to be over."

The funeral officer came over and touched Tim's shoulder. "It's time to move to the cemetery, Mr. Schroeder," he said solemnly. "You're in the car directly behind the hearse, with the mayor." He expertly maneuvered Tim toward the waiting limousine.

"I'll talk to you later," Tim said. He allowed himself to be led away.

"Isn't the car behind the hearse usually reserved for family?" Pablo asked.

"Yes," Jack said. "But, there are no other siblings or close relatives. Tim's all alone now."

CHAPTER TEN

Tom Dorsey wanted Jack to take time off, but he refused. Jack's plan to find Eric's killer, and the goons who beat up-Katarina, took on a life of its own. The Monday after the funeral, he was sitting at his desk viewing the interior photos of the Coldwater Canyon houses when he got a call from Bill Seacrest of the Los Angeles FBI office.

"Meet me for dinner," Bill insisted.

Jack had worked with Bill on a kidnapping case a few years ago and they got along well, despite Jack's working-class upbringing and Seacrest's Ivy League pedigree. Neither embraced the cliché of the Feds not working well with the locals.

Bill was six-five and had played basketball at Princeton before joining the FBI. On several occasions, Bill had participated in the morning basketball games, and a few other times he and Jack played very competitive one-on-one games.

Jack pulled up to the valet in front of Bill's favorite spot, an Italian restaurant on Wilshire Boulevard less than a mile from the Federal Building in Westwood where he was stationed. He found Seacrest at his usual table against the far left wall with a man Jack had never seen before.

"Jack, it's nice to see you again," Bill said as he stood and gave Jack a firm handshake. His well-tailored, dark blue Brooks Brother's suit and powder blue, French-cuffed dress shirt screamed Ivy League, but Jack didn't hold that against him. "I'd like you to meet Chief Inspector Daniel Covyeau from the Paris bureau of Interpol."

Jack shook hands with Covyeau, a slight, compact man with a thick, neatly trimmed mustache and delicate hands. He looked even smaller standing next to the two tall peace officers.

"Good, here's our final guest," Bill said, looking back toward the entryway.

Jack turned, surprised to see Tim Schroeder striding toward the table. What the hell did Bill have up his sleeve?

Introductions were repeated and they all sat down.

As if by magic a waiter appeared and took their drink order.

"I am very sorry to hear about your brother," Inspector Covyeau said to Tim. "And your partner," he said to Jack.

"Thanks," they both mumbled.

"Any news on DeMarchand?" Tim asked.

"We think he's back in Paris, but at this point it's only a guess," said Seacrest.

"Why Paris?" Jack asked.

"We looked at the surveillance tapes from the international terminal at LAX the night Eric was killed," Bill began. "We found nothing. On a hunch I had them check tapes and records from San Francisco International for the twenty-four hours after the shooting. A man fitting DeMarchand's description, using a Belgian passport in the name of François Marchand, boarded the afternoon Air France flight to Paris. I showed the tape to Inspector Covyeau, and he's certain the man is DeMarchand. We also found a black SUV in short term parking; the license plates match one registered to Dante International's limo service. We assume that after killing Eric, DeMarchand drove all night to San Francisco, dumped the SUV, and fled the country."

The conversation was momentarily interrupted by the efficient waiter returning with the drinks and taking their dinner orders.

"We suspect Dante International and Mr. DeMarchand of many illegalities in my country, but have never been able to prove anything," Inspector Covyeau said.

"That's one of the reasons I wanted you to meet Inspector Covyeau today," Bill said. "He's asked us to participate in a small, elite task force in Paris. I'm going on temporary assignment in Washington D.C. to take advantage of the combined resources of the FBI and Interpol. We might have a window of opportunity with these guys on the run. We want to build a real solid case against DeMarchand and, by extension, Victor Ischenko and Dante International, then put them out of business permanently, not only in LA but the rest of the United States and Western Europe."

"We'd all like to see that, and we'd like to help," Jack said as Tim nodded in agreement. "But, how effective can we be with me in LA and Tim in Moscow?"

"That's the point, Jack," Bill said. "You won't be here, but in Paris working directly with Inspector Covyeau."

"Whoa, slow down. I don't speak French, don't know my way around Paris, and have my job here."

"I've already talked to Dorsey and the brass at ICU," Bill said with a sly grin. "They are willing to loan you out to the task force for six months."

"I have an interpreter for you, and Paris is an easy city to know and navigate," Covyeau said. "I value your expertise and instincts in dealing with your American Embassy people. It is a delicate situation, because it is not possible to have operations like Dante International without some complicity, not only with the local police, but with conspirators in the diplomatic corps. We suspect the involvement of Russian, French, and American embassy personnel in several major European cities, including Paris. Many have been compromised by Dante International and others. We need someone like you to bring a fresh view on the situation, someone none of these people will know."

"We also have ideas how Tim can help us both in Moscow and Paris," Bill said. "I interviewed Katarina several times and read the notes on your conversations with her. She mentioned a friend, Magda, several times, an independent high-class call girl. We tracked her down in Moscow and put her in contact with Katarina. At first, she was grateful to hear Katarina was alive, but, as she heard more of the story, she got angry and offered to help. She speaks English and French, so she could be invaluable to the task force."

"That is where you can help, Tim," Covyeau said. "We would like you to meet with Magda in Moscow; you will draw less attention than me or Bill. We want you to convince her to come to Paris, go undercover, and infiltrate the Dante International escort service. A significant amount of cash will be available to fund her activities, and maybe you could use her at your restaurant as a cover."

"If I can convince her, it won't be a problem with my partners to use her at the restaurant, especially because of her language skills," Tim said.

"We have another favor to ask," Covyeau said. "This task force is top secret—only a few people in my department are aware of its existence—and coordination with the local Paris police is equally restricted. We need a place to meet away from the suspicious eyes around us. I was hoping we could use your restaurant."

"Sure, there's a back room with a rear entrance we can use."

"We'll work out the logistics later," Bill said. "Now we eat!"

The waiter arrived with their meals, and conversation stopped as all four men began to eat.

"Is there a name for this task force?" Jack asked.

"Yes," Bill said. "Operation Mary Magdalene."

CHAPTER ELEVEN

The following evening, Jack, Tim, Bill, and Inspector Covyeau reconvened in Jack's living room, sharing a bottle of wine Covyeau had brought with him. After yesterday's dinner they decided to meet in a less public setting.

"It is a small vineyard in Burgundy called Gevrey-Chambertin," Covyeau said. "A university friend of mine and his wife manage it, and send me a few bottles of private reserve every year. I brought a bottle to officially launch Operation Mary Magdalene. *À votre santé!*"

They all drank.

"Our adversaries are formidable, gentlemen," Covyeau began. "They don't play by any rules, are ruthless, manipulative, and have resources embedded in the legitimate bureaucracies and law enforcement agencies of many countries. The various smuggling operations are probably aware of each other, but work independently, so there is no central operation to target. This task force will concentrate on the Russian operations smuggling women to the European Union and the United States. We will start in Paris, but I assure you it will lead to many other places.

"The smuggling and escort operations are quite fluid, utilizing fake passports, constantly changing personnel, and the residences and private clubs they operate from, as evidenced by the recent activities here. It makes them extremely difficult to track and make a case against them. The prosecutions against the traffickers are a joke and a disgrace; even when we catch them red-handed, they are given the equivalent of a slap on the wrist.

"The women are usually uneducated and most likely in the country illegally, so there is no recourse but to deport them, sometimes right back into the hands of their kidnappers. Many of these women end up in insane asylums or commit suicide."

Covyeau's comments sobered the men in the room.

"This time, however," he continued, "we will take our time building a case by allowing certain activities to continue until we get a better grasp of the whole operation. We will know when the time is right to make our move."

"How tough do you think it will be to bring Magda on board?" Tim asked.

"She's open to helping us," Bill said. "If necessary, I'm authorized to offer her asylum in the witness protection program, like we plan to do with Katarina. How exactly she uses her experience and contacts is up to her. For her own protection, she should have no direct contact with Jack or Inspector Covyeau; we want her to pass on information only to you at the restaurant."

"This sounds dangerous for a civilian like Tim," Jack said. "How do you plan to protect him and the restaurant staff?"

"Tim and the staff shouldn't be in any danger if we handle it right. He's simply the conduit for information and the bank for Magda," Bill said.

"Are you sure you want to do this, Tim?" Jack asked.

"I'm sure. I couldn't live with myself if I didn't do something to avenge Eric's death. Once we get started, I'll be doing my job, with a little additional responsibility to help the task force. I'll be fine. But, we need to protect Greg Irvine, my American manager, and Nikki Dunn, his assistant."

"There are two vacant apartments left over from a previous operation," said Covyeau. "You can offer them as part of their compensation so we can keep an eye on them; they'll never have to know what we are doing."

"What about my living arrangements?" Jack asked.

"I have already thought of that, too," Covyeau said. "My family owns a large apartment in the 16th—we use it for visiting relatives and as a rental property—but I will keep it empty for the next few months. We will use it as our command center and your living quarters. Interpol will pay a nominal fee to me for the utilities and such. Consider it a perk for being a founding member of the task force."

"Sounds like you have everything all figured out," Jack said.

"This is the simple part. The hard part comes when we all get to Paris."

CHAPTER TWELVE

Moscow, Russia

Tim Schroeder walked into the Night Flight bar on Tverskaya Street, the contact point Magda suggested. The phone conversation to set up the meeting had been brief: he should wear an expensive tie, sit at the bar, and she would find him.

The place was noisy, smoky, and crowded with people from all over the world. He blended in, moved through the crush of people, found a place at the bar, ordered a beer, and surveyed the clientele of mostly European and Arabian men. They were there to get drunk and find female companionship, not necessarily in that order. He observed several negotiations playing out at the bar, the provocatively dressed women plying their trade like true professionals.

When he was almost through his first beer, a girl who couldn't have been more than eighteen approached him. Her hair was bleached blonde, she had on too much makeup, wore a halter top that concealed very little, and spoke with a heavy accent.

"Buy me drink?" she asked. She leaned close to his ear to be heard over the din.

Tim knew right away it wasn't Magda. "I'm sorry, I'm waiting for someone else," he said.

She leaned close again. "Please help, if I no get someone to buy me drink soon, I in big trouble with boss," she pleaded.

Tim relented, stood, and gave up his seat for her.

"What is your name?"

"I am Sonja, pleased to meet you," she said as she held out her hand.

Tim shook it.

"I'm Tim. What would you like to drink, Sonja?"

"The bartender will know," she said. She made herself comfortable on the barstool, retrieved her cigarettes from a small purse, and lit one.

The bartender delivered her drink quickly, and Tim paid the exorbitant tab without complaint. He lifted his drink in a modest toast.

"Good luck, Sonja."

"Thank you," she said, leaning close again while blowing smoke out the side of her mouth. "I am on feet for many hours; it is nice to sit down. Pretend to talk with me, please."

Tim obliged. "Where are you from, Sonja?"

"Moldova."

"How long have you been in Moscow?"

"Four years."

The last was said with a sigh of resignation. Tim looked closer; even through the makeup he could see the dark circles under her eyes. Her lifestyle was taking its toll.

"Do you want to be here?" he asked.

"Sometimes there is no choice. One must survive," she said. "And you? Do you want to be here?"

"Yes. I'm here because it's different and more interesting than where I was living. When that changes, I'll go someplace else."

"Nice to have choices."

"There are always choices, Sonja."

"If you say so," she said.

They were silent for a few minutes, both aware of the huge gulf separating their life experiences. The noise from the crowd was louder, making it harder to talk without shouting. Tim scanned the crowd to see if he could identify Magda, while Sonja sat and nursed her watered-down Scotch.

※

Magda's vantage point allowed her to watch Tim and the young girl without being seen. She recognized the expensive tie right away, but would wait a few more minutes before making contact. She wanted to make sure Tim wasn't being followed. She recognized some clients and did her best to avoid them as she moved through the throng of sweaty men and women. Her experienced eye caught nothing too suspicious in the usual midweek crowd of international businessmen, American expatriates, and Eurotrash.

She was dressed more conservatively than the other women and girls because, at least for tonight, she was not interested in attracting attention. The management of Night Flight allowed her to work here occasionally, as long as she didn't cut into the house action. She paid a hefty percentage for the accommodation, but for the most part it worked, plus she kept her independence.

After Sonja left, another girl immediately moved in on Tim, stayed for one drink, and left. Now Magda could make contact without fear of reprisal.

"Is this seat taken?" she asked.

"It's for my friend Magda, if she ever gets here," Tim said.

"It is your lucky day, Mr. Schroeder," she said.

"About time! The waiting was getting expensive," Tim kidded.

"The cost of doing business, no?"

"I guess you're right. May I buy you a drink?"

"Of course. The bartender will know."

"That's the third time I've heard that in forty-five minutes. The bartender must have a good memory."

This time, the bartender brought Tim's beer, but instead of a tall, watered-down drink, he placed a tumbler of Scotch, neat, in front of Magda. Tim looked at Magda with respect and again paid the tab without complaint.

"The privileges of seniority," she said. "Leave him a nice tip, and let's find a quieter place to talk."

Tim did as instructed and followed Magda to a sheltered corner table away from the main crush of patrons. The noise noticeably reduced and allowed for a more normal conversation.

"This is much better, don't you think?" she began.

"Yes," Tim said, not sure how to start the conversation. "Thanks for agreeing to meet me."

"I would do anything to help Katarina," she replied. "How is she?"

"Improving rapidly," Tim said. "She might lose a few teeth, but the doctor expects a full recovery. She's lucky to be alive."

"Considering she was shot in the head and viciously attacked by two large men?"

"Yes."

"What are the plans for her future? Is she to be deported back to Russia and start the whole nonsense over again?" Magda asked sharply.

"Wait," Tim said. "Let's not start on the wrong foot. Why don't I tell you our plan, and you can ask any question you want when I'm finished? Does that sound fair?"

"All right, as you Americans say, it's your dime," Magda said, but in a softer tone.

Tim spent the next ten minutes explaining his brother's murder, the plan to place Katarina in the witness protection program, the task force, and what they thought Magda's role would be in Paris.

"Will you help us?" he asked.

Magda was silent for a long time. Her first question surprised Tim. "You are a civilian, aren't you?"

"If you mean not in the military, then yes," he replied.

"Not just the military, but other than helping the task force to get revenge for your brother's death, you are not part of the police force or the intelligence community?"

"No, I'm only involved with the task force. My role is strictly to ask you to help us, fund your activities, and use L'Avenue Bar & Grill as a meeting place. I'm not qualified for anything else," Tim said. "But, if you help us, I would really appreciate it."

Magda was silent again, weighing her options as she sipped her Scotch.

Tim excused himself and went to the men's room to give Magda time to consider his offer. He lingered, taking the long way back to the table through the crowd. Magda looked different when he arrived at the table.

"I will help you, but there are conditions," she said.

"Of course," Tim said trying to keep it light.

Magda was all business now, though.

"I deal only with you. I will never meet with the task force or be seen with any of them at any time. I work on my own timetable, all expenses are paid, in cash, up front. No one will know where I stay or who I see, and I pass information to you as I get it. No cell phones or set meetings."

"What about working in the restaurant as a cover?"

"Maybe one day a week; it will facilitate the exchange of information without causing suspicion. I will need my nights free."

"We can work all that out," Tim said. "When can you be in Paris?"

"A week, maybe less. There are things to do here in Moscow first. I need the address of the restaurant and cash before I leave: 25,000 Euros now and another 25,000 once I get to Paris. If I need more, I will tell you."

Tim had been authorized by the task force to pay up to 20,000 Euros to recruit Magda. The cash was in an envelope in his jacket pocket.

"Is it hot in here?" he said as he took off the jacket and placed it on the table between them. "Give me your hands."

Magda complied and they leaned close together.

"I only have 20,000 Euros," he said as he guided her hands into the fold of the jacket. "It's in the pocket."

"Are you sure you are a civilian?" She found the envelope and quickly slid it under the table and into her purse.

"Will you trust me for the balance when you get to Paris?" Tim asked.

"Of course."

CHAPTER THIRTEEN

Jack sat across from Tom Dorsey, and sighed. "Maybe we should let the French and Interpol handle this, with me working here in LA?" he said.

"No way, José," Dorsey said. "All the leads in this case point to Paris, and you can't be effective working eight time zones away. Your expertise and street sense are more valuable there, even if you don't speak the language. Besides, you need a break; you haven't taken a day off since the night Eric died, and you look like you haven't slept in a week. Everything around here is going to remind you of him, so a change of scenery will do you good."

Jack always knew his status as a rover would move him around a lot, but he felt responsible for Eric's death, and guilty to be going to Paris as a result. "I guess you're right," he said.

"Damn straight! Now I have another idea I need to run by you."

"What's that?"

"Bill Seacrest is still working on the witness protection program for Katarina. In the meantime, she needs a lot of recuperation time and we want her close by to continue her debriefing. I've pulled some strings and found some money to pay her expenses for a few months. If you'll let me, I'd like to put her up at your house."

Jack didn't need to think about it. "I was going to leave it empty, but that's a much better solution. There's even some of Maria's clothes there she can use. I was going to take them to Goodwill, but this works out even better."

"Great, I'm glad you feel that way," Dorsey said. "Get me a set of keys and the household information and I'll take care of the details. I don't want you distracted in Paris."

"Thanks," Jack said.

"Turn over your cases to Pablo and Dave, then get out of here. Go home, get some sleep, go to the movies or the beach, or do whatever it takes to get your mind off things for a few days. That's an order. Covyeau and Seacrest need you in Paris next week."

Jack did as he was told. The meeting with Pablo and Dave went smoothly, as he brought them up to date on his cases and the task force plan. He was putting a few personal items from his desk into a box when his phone rang. He debated whether to answer it now that he was officially not assigned to a case. The caller ID flashed a vaguely familiar number, so he picked up the receiver.

"Oatmon."

"Detective Oatmon, I'm glad I caught you. It's Adam Reeves."

Jack momentarily couldn't place the name. "Oh yeah, Katarina's good Samaritan. Is everything okay?"

"Everything's fine. Sorry to hear about Detective Schroeder; he seemed like a nice guy."

"Thanks, he was the best."

"I promised to keep in touch if you need me as a witness or something. I talked to a Detective Ketcham early this week and he told me to call today. His line was busy, so I asked for you. I hope that's okay?"

"It's fine, but I'm leaving for Europe in a few days and won't be working from this office. Call Ketcham back in a few minutes; I'm sure he'll help you."

"All right. Again, I'm real sorry about Detective Schroeder. Good luck finding who did it."

"We'll find him," Jack said.

Jack hung up and walked over to Dave's cubicle. Dave had the receiver hooked over his shoulder and pressed against his ear while he typed notes on his computer. He saw Jack, and waved him into the tiny space. "I'll get back to you tomorrow," he said and then hung up. "What's up, Jack, something wrong?"

"No, I don't think so. I just got a call from Adam Reeves. He said he talked to you earlier in the week and you asked him to call back today. Your line was busy so he called me."

"Yeah, so?" Dave said.

"My question is why was he calling you earlier this week and not me? I was still on the case then."

"Nothing sinister or underhanded, Jack," Dave said. "Dorsey had your calls routed to Pablo and me for the last few days. You wouldn't take any time off so he figured it was the least he could do. He was looking out for you, Jack, so don't get all riled up."

"It was the right thing to do," Jack said. "What bothers me is I didn't notice it, and that's not a good sign. Maybe I do need a few days off."

"That's what we've been telling you, but you wouldn't listen. Now, as a friend and coworker I'm asking you to follow orders. We'll hold the fort until you're up and running in gay Paree."

"Thanks, Dave. You're the best."

"Damn straight!"

Jack laughed despite his mood. Life already would be drastically different now that Maria and Eric were gone. Maybe the gods were trying to tell him something. Maybe the unexpected change of scenery to Paris was meant to be.

Jack went to his desk, picked up a box of personal items, and walked out the door without looking back.

PART TWO

CHAPTER FOURTEEN

Paris

Time went by quickly as Jack settled in to the palatial digs provided by Inspector Covyeau. The apartment had three bedrooms, three baths, a formal dining room, and a living room with an alcove that Covyeau had set up as his task force office. The master bedroom was large, with a four-poster bed the size of a small bus. The master bath was big enough to sport a two-person Jacuzzi tub, a large tiled shower, dual sinks, and several warming towel racks. The kitchen was larger than Jack's bedroom back in Los Angeles, and had all the modern stainless steel appliances.

The third bedroom and bath were tucked behind the kitchen, a perfect setup for a live-in housekeeper. Jack would have been comfortable in there, but Covyeau insisted he take the master suite, and a few days to get over the jet lag and explore the neighborhood.

At the end of Jack's first week, Covyeau arrived at the apartment with his attractive assistant, Joëlle Pierrot, who would also double as Jack's interpreter. Covyeau made himself at home in the alcove, and Jack and Joëlle set up their laptops at opposite ends of the large farmhouse table in the dining room. The three spent the first few days creating e-mail accounts and electronic files, and discussing strategy. The first order of business would be a trip to Hamburg to interview Horst Wolpert's widow, and research his movements before his untimely demise in Hollywood.

Covyeau and Joëlle had other responsibilities in the morning, so they settled into a routine where they would start with a working lunch at the dining room table, then continue through until early evening. Jack took advantage of the lingering evening light and, along with the first crush of summer tourists, wandered endlessly through the streets of Paris.

He adjusted to the sound of the small and noisy cars. There were also a plethora of motorcycles and scooters, which sounded like the noise from a sewing machine Tim Allen had rewired, to a weed wacker on steroids, to the throaty, muscular roar of the big Yamahas and BMWs. The sound reverberated off the stone buildings and left him feeling like gnats had buzzed around his head all day.

The cars weren't the only things smaller. The people were, too. Sure, there were overweight men and women, but nothing approaching the obesity of Americans. In most cases, the grossly overweight were German or American; certainly not French.

The chairs and tables in the bistros Jack frequented weren't designed for his six-foot-four-inch frame either, and he had already banged his knees countless times.

Joëlle helped him with the Métro, getting him a "Carte Orange," which allowed him unlimited monthly access to the Paris subway system. He plunged through the pungent smell of urine in certain stations and suffered the cigarette smoke. Not everyone in Paris smoked, it just seemed like it, and they not only smoked everywhere, they smoked all the time. In restaurants, patrons didn't smoke only after their meal, but before and during. It was a huge adjustment, especially after living in California, where smoking in restaurants had been banned for well over a decade. He ate outside or asked for a nonsmoking section, at best a laughable concept in any Paris bistro.

Joëlle also played tour guide. She took Jack to the top of the Eiffel Tower on a stunningly clear night with a full moon, even climbed the steps to the Sacré-Coeur and the Arc de Triomphe with him. He spent his free morning hours alone, drinking coffee and eating *pain au chocolat* and croissants from the local pâtisserie. He wandered through the Musée d'Orsay, the Musée Rodin, the Louvre, and was overwhelmed by the dimension of Monet's water lily panels at the Musée de l'Orangerie. He bought and reread *The Sun Also Rises*. It was much thinner than he remembered, both in volume and content. The simple story didn't match the grand scale he imagined from his high school reading.

One of the first new habits he established was reading the *International Herald Tribune* every day. After so many years of local American newspapers, the perspective of the Paris-based publication was truly refreshing.

It also became quite clear the stereotype of the ugly American was alive and well. Many Americans he encountered were loud, spoiled, and treated non-Americans like they were the hired help. He had already seen several confrontations with local street vendors and shopkeepers.

One particularly glorious Sunday morning in late June near the Luxembourg Gardens he walked past a newspaper and magazine kiosk. A well-dressed American woman in her thirties was arguing with the old man hidden in his cubbyhole. She turned away disgustedly. "I can't believe he doesn't speak English! All I wanted was the latest edition of *Cosmo*."

ℭ

L'Avenue Bar & Grill was progressing nicely. Tim Schroeder designed the final setup of the bar plumbing and spent countless hours working with Greg Irvine in the wine cellar, "*la cave*," stocking and setting up the tracking system for the wine as it arrived from California and the various regions of France.

Nikki Dunn trained the waiters, numbered and placed the tables, set up the phone system, and implemented the emergency procedures. The international mix of waiters' names sounded so different she had to write them down to visualize and get them right. She now worked with people named Thorkil, Sharif, Gardie, Rasmus, Taki, Karsten, Rukman, and Saya. There wasn't a Bob or a John in the group.

In the few days prior to the grand opening on the Fourth of July, they staged several trial runs, with invited guests enjoying a free meal as Nikki worked with the waiters and Greg got back in the groove working behind the bar. At the final dress rehearsal, a small group of American male models living and working in Paris crashed the party. With their equally attractive girlfriends in tow, the crush at the bar was too much for Greg to handle alone. Tim jumped into the fray while Nikki played cocktail waitress. It was loud and boisterous, lasting into the early hours of the morning. There was so much laughter and camaraderie it was impossible not to get caught up in the moment. The evening left everyone with a warm glow and it wasn't just from the familiar cuisine, excellent wine, and spirits consumed. The new place would be a port in the storm, a familiar touch of home in a foreign land, and make them feel safer, a little less untethered.

ᔓ

On a beautiful summer evening, Jack was the last to enter the back room of L'Avenue Bar & Grill. A grateful Chief Inspector Covyeau had kept his promise: the task force was indeed a small group.

"Ah, Monsieur Oatmon, the final piece of the puzzle," Covyeau said.

Jack shook hands with Tim; Bill Seacrest, who had flown in from Washington, D. C.; Craig Lawrence, head of the United States Mission in Paris; Deputy Inspector Claude Bonnard; Inspector Hugo Leveque; and Joëlle.

Covyeau wasted no time.

"You have all been briefed separately, but now we are finally together to officially assign the duties of the task force," Covyeau began. "First, my good friend Inspector Leveque will direct the research and intelligence operation regarding smuggling routes. Our research shows these women are moved along the same routes as guns and drugs. They are simply another commodity to the smugglers. Inspector Leveque has extensive experience and will be an invaluable resource.

"Second, Deputy Inspector Bonnard will be in charge of tracking these women once they arrive in Paris. After many years working in Marseille and the Quartier Pigalle, he has a valuable network of informants we can utilize in gathering information.

"Third, Bill Seacrest will offer assistance through the State Department and the services of the FBI in America. There is ample anecdotal evidence to suggest some of these escort services specifically target diplomats in an effort to extort classified information. As a courtesy, we have asked Craig Lawrence to be a member of this task force. We will pass along any information about U.S. diplomatic personnel, as appropriate, and he might enlighten us as to which diplomatic staff levels are most vulnerable.

"Fourth, Tim Schroeder has been successful in recruiting an operative from Moscow. For that person's safety, and as per the conditions to help us, Tim will control all contact, fund the activities, and pass along information to us."

Jack thought it curious Covyeau kept Magda's name and gender a secret from the two French inspectors and Craig Lawrence.

"Last, but certainly not least," Covyeau continued, "Detective Oatmon will work directly with me to develop an overall strategy, acting as liaison between Interpol, the European Union, the French police, and the U.S. government as represented here by Bill Seacrest and Craig Lawrence."

Covyeau stopped and surveyed the room. "Any questions?"

There were none.

"Bon."

"We will meet here again at the same time a week from tonight, where we will deliver preliminary reports and compare notes. Tonight, however, my ever efficient assistant Joëlle will verify phone numbers, addresses, and e-mail. She has a portable printer, so you will all have an up-to-date contact sheet ready before you leave." The young woman smiled at the compliment.

"Please spend a few minutes getting to know one another. If you wish to smoke, please do so in the courtyard. Enjoy the fine wine Tim and his partners have graciously provided, even if it is from California." His remark brought a few chuckles, and a sigh of relief from the French inspectors, who immediately stepped outside and lit up.

Jack joined the two French inspectors. Both were polite, but aloof. Jack assessed Bonnard. A solidly built man slightly under six feet tall, with dark hair graying at the temples, he was clearly uncomfortable in the presence of the Americans. Leveque, on the other hand, was a smoother character. He wore an expensive dark blue suit that showed his taller, thinner frame to advantage. His thinning black hair was oiled and combed straight back, and he sported a neatly trimmed goatee. The overall look gave him an unctuous quality that Jack immediately disliked. Nothing of any consequence was discussed, and the two Frenchmen left as soon as the contact sheets were ready.

Craig Lawrence left soon after to get home before his kids went to bed. Tim excused himself to do paperwork in the office. That left Covyeau, Joëlle, Jack, and Bill to finish the wine.

"I have a present for both of you," Bill said to Jack and Covyeau. He withdrew two boxes from his briefcase and passed them over.

"The FBI has generously made a donation to the senior staff of Operation Mary Magdalene," Bill said. "They're state-of-the-art cell phones, can't be traced, tracked, or triangulated. I already have one," he said showing off a shiny black instrument a bit smaller than a typical iPhone. "Joëlle has programmed the speed-dial functions and is here to answer any questions."

The small group took a few minutes to familiarize themselves with the equipment. Like the others before them, they left by the back entrance one by one.

CHAPTER FIFTEEN

The spectacular sunset from his top floor apartment on the Île Saint-Louis distracted Frank DeMarchand as he sat at his computer and tried to work. Dante International's vast network of informants and bribed officials had forwarded information regarding an undercover operation designed to infiltrate their operation in Paris.

Jack Oatmon was in Paris and on the task force. DeMarchand had no illusions about that bit of news.

Oatmon was here to get him.

DeMarchand wasn't overly concerned; his cover as an investment banker who traveled extensively was thorough and sophisticated. His neighbors and the French authorities knew him by a completely different name, and he had friends in high places. It had cost him a fortune, but it was worth it.

In addition to the information regarding the task force, there was a trail that led back to Moscow and the questionable disappearance of a high-class call girl, rumored to be hiding in Paris. There were scores of Russian girls rotating through the local *Femmes Invitée* operation. Trying to ascertain if any of the girls had been compromised would be difficult enough, but adding in the hundreds, if not thousands, of mostly anonymous customers would complicate the situation enormously. Plus, he had to do it without arousing suspicion or disrupting business. He sent several encrypted e-mails to order the physical surveillance of several individuals and pull together an electronics team to bug and videotape certain rendezvous at the various *Femmes Invitée* locations. They would set up programs to filter the data and red-flag any information containing certain phrases, locations, or names deemed suspicious. Frank DeMarchand would review them personally.

ಌ

Henri Toulon, Dante International's director of security in Paris, could have delegated the job, but he loved these kinds of assignments, exposing the hypocrisy of the high and mighty, both in the corporate world and in politics. It gave him immense pleasure to compromise them and then use them for his own purposes. It was pure sport for him now.

The instances of corporate greed and public official malfeasance were so widespread it was barely a step above shooting fish in a barrel.

The current target was Craig Lawrence, the director of the U.S. Mission in Paris. Henri was on his second night of surveillance, the previous night having been spent watching Lawrence help his wife and children pack and putting them in a taxi to the airport for their summer trip to Maryland. It was a matter of time before weakness overwhelmed Lawrence. Two months of freedom from the traditional façade of a happy family life was too much of a temptation, especially in Paris where all manner of sexual fantasy could be fulfilled.

Henri saw movement behind the sheer curtains of the window and lights being turned off. Lawrence emerged and went to the rear of the two black Mercedes sedans parked tandem in the driveway. He backed out and drove away.

Lawrence was easy to follow as he made his way to the Arc de Triomphe, veered right and crossed the Seine at Pont de l'Alma. They were in the shadow of the Eiffel Tower now, an area mixed with old apartment buildings, government offices, and ugly, nondescript postwar concrete apartment blocks whose only saving grace was underground parking garages.

Henri watched as Lawrence stopped in front of a garage on Rue Saint-Dominique, punched the keypad, and disappeared into the dark passageway. If Lawrence was going to visit someone in the building, Henri's job would be harder. He would have to research every tenant in the building, which took time and a lot of legwork. He got lucky and squeezed his tiny Renault into a parking spot down the street. He opened a shoulder bag on the passenger seat, retrieved a small digital camera, and got out. There were plenty of tourists out on the warm evening, making it easy to get lost in the crowd.

He stood by a sidewalk vendor and bought a ridiculously expensive bottle of water. Serves me right for hanging out with the tourists, he thought. He kept his eye on the building, but still almost missed him. Lawrence emerged from a door to the left of the garage opening and walked up the ramp to the street. He had disguised himself with a wig, golfing cap, and a fake mustache, but Henri was not fooled. Lawrence, in no hurry, walked past Henri toward Les Invalides.

Henri followed a safe distance behind, stopping occasionally to take pictures. Lawrence finally turned right down one of the many side streets between Rue Saint-Dominique and Rue de Grenelle. Henri got to the corner in time to see Lawrence enter the lone restaurant halfway down the long dark street. He quickened his pace and stole a glance inside the restaurant to see Lawrence sitting alone at a table, looking at a menu.

He continued to the end of the street and waited, pretending to read the map he pulled from his pocket. There were a few people going both ways on the narrow side street, including a group of half a dozen drunken American college boys arguing where to have dinner. One of them, a large bottle of Heineken in his hand, noticed the light of the restaurant.

"Hey, man, that looks like a quaint little out-of-the-way Parisian bistro; let's check it out."

There was the usual argumentative, testosterone-laden banter at the suggestion, but in the end the group moved toward the restaurant. Henri followed, using them as cover as they approached. They quieted as they surrounded the menu stand.

Henri looked inside again. Lawrence had shed the disguise and was joined by a boy even younger than the college students. They were holding hands across the small table. Henri brought the camera to his eye and began snapping photos, pretending to take pictures of the college students.

"This place is too expensive," complained one of the more sober young men.

There was more banter, but the cheapskate won out and the group started back up the street. Henri zoomed in as far as possible as he moved with them, but not before he got a shot of Lawrence leaning over and kissing the boy full on the lips.

CHAPTER SIXTEEN

Jack and Joëlle disembarked from the train at Hauptbahnhof Süd in Hamburg late in the afternoon. They had a meeting in the morning with Horst Wolpert's wife and son, but their evening was free to enjoy a leisurely dinner. They took advantage of the warm weather, walked down the Adenauerallee to the Hotel St. Raphael, and checked in.

"What time do you want to meet?" Jack asked as they stood outside their adjoining rooms.

"Let's go early, shall we say, eight-thirty?" Joëlle said.

Jack had adjusted to the European habit of eating late dinners. "See you in the lobby then."

On the train ride from Paris, their conversation was work-related as they reviewed reports and proposed plans for Operation Mary Magdalene. Now, at a decent restaurant near the hotel, over fresh seafood and a tasty and refreshing local brew, the conversation eased into more personal territory.

"Are you enjoying your stay with us, even considering the circumstances?" Joëlle asked.

"Actually, I am," Jack said. "In the moments I can get my mind off why I'm here, I find it fascinating and different. I haven't been away from the United States in a while."

"So, your girlfriend doesn't mind you being gone for so long?"

"She broke up with me a few weeks before I left," Jack said. "She wanted to settle down and start a family, and I'm not ready for that now. I might not ever be ready for that."

"Some people are not meant to be parents," Joëlle said. "Maybe you are one of them."

Jack looked at the simple gold band she wore. "What do you and your husband think about children?" he asked.

Joëlle was silent for a moment, nervously twisting the ring with the fingers of her right hand.

"My husband is dead," she said. "Claude was killed by a roadside bomb in Afghanistan last year."

"I'm sorry, I didn't know."

"There would be no reason for you to know. We French are not as forthcoming as you Americans about our personal lives."

"Do you want to talk about it now?"

"Only to tell you that I might not want to be a parent either; I haven't decided. Claude volunteered for military service because he knew it would take him away from me for a while. He wanted to start a family right away, but I refused to get pregnant until my career was more established. It caused many arguments and bad feelings between us."

Jack could imagine those confrontations, considering he'd had the exact same ones with Maria.

"I really enjoy helping Inspector Covyeau," Joëlle continued. "He treats me well, and with his guidance and support I will always be in line for promotions, and do more interesting things. I refuse to give up that opportunity, but Claude could not understand. Now that he is gone, my maternal instinct has gone dormant."

"You are still a young woman; maybe you'll change your mind later," Jack said.

"Perhaps," Joëlle said.

They finished off the dinner with brandy, apple strudel, and talk of art, culture, and life in Paris. Joëlle linked her arm in Jack's on their after-dinner promenade along the waterfront. They walked in silence, enjoying the late light and summer air. It was after midnight when they got back to the hotel, again standing in the hallway outside their rooms. Joëlle took Jack's arm and pulled his face down for a peck on the cheek.

"Good night, Jack, see you for breakfast at 7:30?"

"Sounds good. Good night."

Neither hesitated.

They both swiped their keys and entered the separate rooms.

ꕥ

Two hours later, Jack was still awake, sprawled on the bed in the dark. The television was tuned to a commercial-free classical music station, the sound from the inadequate speakers low enough not to bother any of the neighboring guests. His thoughts wandered all over the map: memories of Eric, Maria, and other girlfriends over the years, ideas on how to track down DeMarchand and Ischenko, and the beautiful and vulnerable Joëlle next door.

A light knock on the door adjoining their two rooms roused him.

Jack was only wearing boxer shorts and an LAPD tee shirt, so he put on the hotel robe he found on a hook in the closet, and unlocked the door from his side. Joëlle did the same from her side.

Jack almost moaned out loud at the sight. Joëlle stood in the semidarkness, her thin, black silk robe only covering her to mid-thigh. Her tanned skin seemed to glow in the filtered light, her long brown hair loose to her shoulders.

She was stunning.

"I don't want to sleep alone tonight," was all she said.

Jack opened his door wider and allowed her in.

She made her way to the unruffled side of the bed, pulled back the covers, dropped her robe, and got in.

Jack went to his side of the bed, picked up the remote, and turned off the television. In the darkness, he took off his robe and shirt, then went searching for Joëlle.

They found each other right away.

She kissed him softly on the lips, her right hand lightly tracing the contours of his face.

"Tonight we sleep, okay?" she said.

Jack managed a consenting grunt.

Joëlle turned her back to him, pulled his right arm over her, guided his hand to cup her left breast, and snuggled her butt comfortably into his abdomen. They fit together well.

"*La position de cuillère A*," she giggled. "*Bonne nuit.*"

Yeah right, thought Jack. How the fuck am I supposed to sleep now?

But he was wrong.

In what seemed like seconds, calm enveloped him. The tension in his shoulders noticeably eased, and the warmth and intoxicating scent of Joëlle's body soothed his soul.

He was lulled to sleep in minutes by the rhythmic purr of her breathing.

❧

Jack woke up to the sound of running water. It took a few seconds to realize where he was. The adjoining doors were open, steam from the shower in Joëlle's room wafting into the space. Memories of falling asleep with Joëlle wrapped in his arms brought a smile to his face, and what Richard Pryor would call a hard-on that could cut diamonds. He rolled to Joëlle's side of the bed and drank in the smell of her, closed his eyes, and imagined the possibilities. He was lost in a half sleep, drifting with thoughts of future pleasures, when he felt Joëlle sit on the edge of the bed.

"*Bonjour, Monsieur,*" she said. "You were sleeping so soundly I didn't want to wake you."

She wore the black silk robe again, her dark hair still wet from the shower. As she leaned down to kiss him, two things happened accidentally, commencing the inevitable chain of events leading to the consummation of their physical relationship. The delicate fabric of her robe fell open to reveal Joëlle's slightly damp breasts, and her forearm and elbow rubbed against his impossible-to-hide diamond cutter.

The sensation Joëlle would remember was like an electric shock, followed by the whoosh of a furnace catching fire. Warmth spread through her body, confirming how much she wanted to be in Jack's bed.

They proceeded slowly, enjoying the kisses, and the initial realization that something wonderful was about to happen. Joëlle loved the feeling of his big hands through the silk robe. She pulled off his boxer shorts. She had imagined what his naked body would look like many times, and she was not disappointed. It was obvious he took very good care of himself.

"You seem awake now," she said.

"Uh huh," was all Jack could get out before he buried his face in her chest. The scent of her freshly showered, warm, and slightly damp body was overpowering. He forced himself to take his time, following her lead when he could, taking the lead when he could stand it no more. He pulled her on top of him. She positioned herself, tantalized him, slowly swayed, and brushed her now fully erect nipples through his chest hair. As she straddled him, Jack allowed his hands to roam freely on her back and thighs, amazed by the softness of her skin and the firmness of her athletic body.

She stopped swaying and sat up, the robe open now to frame her and draw Jack's eyes. She slid herself along the length of him, moaning with pleasure. Jack savored the view and went along for the ride, positioning himself to maximize her arousal.

It didn't take long.

Joëlle leaned back down, kissed him hard, and maneuvered to allow Jack to ease inside her.

The adrenaline/hormone cocktail coursed through their bloodstreams for a half hour. Both tried to sense what the other wanted or needed, sometimes slow, sometimes fast and furious, but always headed toward the natural conclusion, out of breath, hearts pounding, and minds floating lazily in the postcoital haze.

They spent the next hour enjoying the intimacies of new lovers, looking unashamedly at each other's nakedness, dozing contentedly with their bodies entangled in all the usual ways.

☙

"Oh, no!" Joëlle gasped.

They had drifted off again.

"It's after nine already and our meeting is at ten."

"So we'll be fashionably late," Jack said without conviction. He rolled on top of her and kissed her.

"Are you crazy?! This is *Germany*. It is very bad form to be late."

Jack knew she was right.

"Meet me in the lobby in twenty minutes," he said.

He was up, showered, and ready to go in fifteen minutes. It was nice to know he didn't have to pack or clean up the room. The maid would repair the damage, and he could look forward to another night with Joëlle before heading back to Paris.

CHAPTER SEVENTEEN

The Wolpert house was in the Alsterpark section of Hamburg, about a ten minute cab ride from the hotel. They were met by a local detective named Dieter Schmidt. He spoke little English, but the ever efficient Joëlle spoke fluent German and translated for Jack.

"It seems Frau Wolpert is in the early stages of Alzheimer's and her behavior is quite erratic. The son, Franz, will be here to help us," she said.

Schmidt led them up the narrow walkway, and knocked on the door.

Franz Wolpert was in his mid-twenties, elegantly dressed in dark wool slacks, black loafers, and an open-collared dress shirt. He shook hands with everyone and invited them into the small but tidy living room.

Frau Wolpert was sitting in a side chair sipping a cup of tea. She noticed the visitors and brightened noticeably.

"*Guten Morgen*," she said cheerfully.

Franz spoke to her in German, Joëlle translating again.

"Mother, these people are here to ask you some questions about Dad," he said.

"He should be home today from America," she replied.

Franz turned to Joëlle and Jack and spoke in English. "I'm sorry, she seems to not be very lucid this morning. She goes in and out more frequently now. Is there any way I can help you?"

Jack and Joëlle had discussed their strategy on the train yesterday, deciding she should take the lead because of her language skills, hopefully making the interviews more comfortable.

"Your father traveled a great deal, both in Europe and the United States, is that correct?" she asked Franz in English.

"Yes, he was gone all the time, leaving his family for long periods," Franz replied. "My mother did not handle his absences well." There was a hint of disdain in his tone.

"Do you know if he kept any records here at the house? Is there a home office?"

"Perhaps. There is a locked room on the top floor. My father never allowed anyone in there, and he had the only key. He would hide in there sometimes for days at a time."

"Was the key in the personal belongings we sent back from Los Angeles?" Jack asked.

"I don't know," Franz said. "There is a box that my mother hasn't opened yet. I'll go get it."

Franz got up, went to the dining area and brought the small packing box the LAPD had sent, along with the cremated remains of Horst Wolpert. He handed the box to Jack.

"Do we have your permission to open it?" Joëlle asked.

"Yes," he replied.

Joëlle turned and asked Schmidt in German if they were on solid legal ground with only verbal permission. It wasn't until she was satisfied with his answer that she nodded to Jack. He sliced the clear plastic tape with his Swiss Army knife and opened the box. There was a key chain with five keys of various size attached to a metal ring, along with Wolpert's wallet, shaving kit, and a few manila envelopes filled with paperwork. It was all in German, so Jack gave them to Joëlle.

"Do you recognize any of these?" Jack asked Franz, handing him the keys.

Franz identified the ones to the house, the car, and the family post office box. "This is the only key I don't recognize," he said. "It might be to the room upstairs."

He handed them back to Jack, holding the suspect key between thumb and forefinger.

"May we go see if it works?" Jack asked.

"Certainly," Franz replied. "If my father was involved in anything illegal, I want no part in hindering your investigation. He can't embarrass or hurt my mother any more now."

Joëlle again looked to Schmidt for confirmation they were on solid legal footing.

"Could you lead us to this room now?" Joëlle asked.

Franz rose and led them to a narrow, winding staircase at the back of the house. "It's two flights up, and the only door on that floor. Please let me know if you need anything." He retreated to the front of the house to keep his mother company.

The key did in fact work. The door opened out into the hallway, revealing a very steep set of stairs that led to a loft-style room. A small window let in the bright morning light. A mattress with rumpled bedding lay along the right wall, and a cardboard box functioned as a nightstand, with an alarm clock and a reading lamp.

A makeshift table designed like a workbench took up the entire left wall; a computer setup was in the middle, and a two-drawer metal filing cabinet underneath. The far wall was a built-in floor-to-ceiling bookcase overflowing with books, magazines, and newspapers.

All three donned surgical gloves and began their search. Dieter Schmidt booted up the computer, Jack started with the filing cabinet, and Joëlle the bookcase.

What they all found was an astonishing array of pornography. There were hundreds of American issues of *Playboy*, *Penthouse*, and *Hustler*, plus every imaginable European imitation, from the cheap newsprint variety to the glossy, upscale versions. The computer was not password protected, and contained thousands of images and movies.

The filing cabinet contained detailed records of Herr Wolpert's travels, the brothels he frequented, and the names and ratings of the prostitutes he hired. They revealed a pattern of behavior that was less than exemplary, and certainly not confined to the recent past or only when he was out of the country. There were receipts from every major city in Germany, too.

Dieter said something in German to Joëlle.

"He says the problem of trafficked women is much worse here in Germany than in France," Joëlle told Jack. "His department is interested in participating and coordinating with our efforts if it's feasible."

"First things first," Jack said. "Ask him to request some help to catalogue the contents of this room, copy the paper files, and see what else might be on the computer. We'll figure out how to coordinate once we digest what we have here."

Jack and Joëlle spent the entire day in the sweltering garret, the now open window doing nothing to promote air flow. Dieter Schmidt's team showed up with the necessary equipment and authorizations, and after Franz signed off on everything, the files and computer were boxed and loaded into a black police van.

The team had brought a portable copy machine so Jack could have copies of all the Paris-related information. He sat on the floor of the upstairs hallway and read the files. One referred to a service called "*Femmes Invitée*," with a cell phone number attached. He would start with that as soon as he got back to Paris.

The return trip could wait another twelve hours though; he wasn't going to give up a free night with Joëlle.

They politely declined Schmidt's invitation to dinner, promised to meet him in the morning at his precinct house, and returned to their rooms. The European-style showers were too small to accommodate two people, so they retreated to their respective rooms and showered quickly. Jack turned on his air-conditioning unit full blast; the cold air felt refreshing against his newly showered skin. He threw the thick bedspread off, sprawled naked on the freshly laundered sheets, and closed his eyes.

"*Mon Dieu*," Joëlle said from the doorway. "You are quite sure of yourself, Detective Oatmon."

This time she wasn't wearing the black robe, just a towel. It wasn't on her by the time she reached the bed.

CHAPTER EIGHTEEN

The second meeting of the Operation Mary Magdalene task force started right on time, the same night Jack and Joëlle returned from Hamburg. After Covyeau's brief introduction, Inspectors Bonnard and Leveque gave their preliminary reports, each taking less than five minutes. Jack realized right away they were both masters of departmental doublespeak. Neither presented anything new, but merely reformatted information; used impressive, but ultimately meaningless statistics; and complained about lack of staff and resources. They droned on about what they were doing to motivate not only their staffs but their stable of informants.

"It is going to take time," Covyeau said. "We must not get discouraged. If we stay diligent our break will come."

Jack couldn't believe he let them off the hook so easily. He would have to adjust to the French way of doing things.

"How about you, Tim, any word from your operative?"

"Yes," Tim said. "Contact has been made with a Russian prostitute. It has taken time to earn her trust because of the threats to her family back in Russia. Obviously, my operative is moving with extreme caution, fully aware of how dangerous these people are and the potential consequences. At their next rendezvous, the prostitute promised to divulge the exact route she took to get to Paris. I should be able to pass the information to Inspector Leveque in a few days."

"That is good news," Covyeau said. "Good work, Tim."

Jack briefed the group on his trip to Hamburg, conveniently leaving out the details of his extracurricular activities. He couldn't look at Joëlle while he spoke for fear of losing his concentration and sounding like a blithering idiot.

"I gave Tim the number for *Femmes Invitée* here in Paris," Jack said. "He can pass it on to his contact."

Bill Seacrest spoke last. "We know Ischenko was in Russia recently, but has fled the country again. Indications are he doesn't plan to return, and might be hiding here in Paris. The trail to DeMarchand also leads here. There is no evidence he moved on after fleeing the United States. We might get lucky and be in the right place at the right time for both of them. Jack also has an idea about tracking DeMarchand, and we will have more on that next time."

The meeting broke up a little after ten. Tim asked Jack to hang around for a few minutes; he needed some help.

“What’s up, Tim?” Jack asked. They were in the back alone, finishing a bottle of Kenwood cabernet.

“I want a gun.”

“Why?”

“My conversations with Magda are disturbing,” Tim said. “She’s confirmed our suspicions about how ruthless and violent these people are. A little protection around here would make me feel more comfortable.”

“Do you even know how to use a gun?”

“I’m the brother of a cop, Jack. Eric insisted I know how to handle a gun, and he took the time to teach me. I’ll be fine.”

“What about Greg Irvine?”

“Greg grew up on a ranch in Texas with five older brothers; he’ll be fine.”

“And Nikki?”

“She took self-defense classes before moving here from California. She can take care of herself, too.”

CHAPTER NINETEEN

Frank DeMarchand knew he had found her. After countless hours listening to the digital recordings supplied by his team, he had narrowed his search to one girl. He bolted upright at his computer and listened to the live audio being streamed from the *Femmes Invitée* location in the 16th arrondissement. Despite the background music, his sophisticated filtering system software had distinctly isolated the phrase "task force" and the name Victor Ischenko. Under normal circumstances, there was no reason for the Russian girl, Svetlana, to know either of those names and certainly no reason to pass the names on to one of her lesbian customers.

He wasted no time getting the information to Henri Toulon, his head of Security.

"I want them both alive, if possible," he said. "It is imperative Svetlana's customer does not speak to anyone else; take her out immediately if you cannot apprehend her."

୧୨

Svetlana Dementiev watched from the upstairs window as Magda moved down the quiet street, turned the corner, and disappeared into the dark night. It was the last time she would ever see her. She would miss Magda's tenderness, her thoughtfulness, her kindness, and her kindred Russian spirit. Svetlana knew what she was about to do was very dangerous, but it was a risk she was willing to take for her freedom. Tonight she would escape or die trying.

The plan had been in place for days and was meticulously orchestrated. She was warned the room she and Magda used for their visits over the past few weeks was probably bugged. Even with the music on louder than usual and speaking in whispers, she couldn't be sure they hadn't been overheard. The information Svetlana received from her benefactor and passed on to Magda was sure to embarrass and discredit many powerful people on several continents. Tonight was the final installment. She divulged the names of American and French officials involved with the criminal activities of the Russian mafia and the fact Operation Mary Magdalene was deeply compromised.

She had to move quickly!

Her benefactor would be waiting in the back alley exactly five minutes after Magda left the front door.

Her instructions had been simple but emphatic. Svetlana was to leave with only the clothes on her back; everything else for her new life would be provided. Danielle Segova, the "madam," had been bribed and would be near the back stairs to the kitchen at the appointed time. Svetlana had heard stories of women in Danielle's position who were more vicious and cruel than the men. She mouthed a silent prayer Danielle would not be one of them and double-cross her.

Trembling like a frightened child behind the closed door, she hesitated one last time to catch her breath and steel her resolve. It was time to go.

Now!

She opened the door and, as casually and quietly as she could muster, started down the back stairs. She reached the bottom and looked into the large, empty kitchen, illuminated only by a light over the stove that cast a glow over the faded linoleum floor and the large dining table.

No time to waste.

She took two steps to the right and opened the back door. She turned around to make sure no one would see her leave. Danielle stood at the door leading to the formal dining room. They were both too shocked and scared to breathe.

"*Dasvidaniya*," Danielle whispered.

Svetlana gave her a look of gratitude, patted her heart with an open hand, turned, and fled. The car waited for her exactly as promised, the rear passenger-side door already open. She jumped in and slammed the door.

"Hey, beautiful!" the driver said.

"No talk, drive!"

The big embassy car roared away.

CHAPTER TWENTY

It had been a good night. Nikki Dunn leaned back with her head against the window at the short end of the L-shaped imported-Tuscan-stone bar, enjoying the one cigarette she allowed herself each day, a wonderful glass of Bordeaux, and listening to an Anita Baker CD on the restaurant's sound system. It was her first chance to sit down all evening, having ushered out the last of the bar patrons celebrating Bastille Day and locked the double glass doors a few minutes earlier. She was at peace with her new life here in Paris.

Greg Irvine was at the other end of the bar counting the night's receipts. A friend of his from Los Angeles, Rick Asher, was still seated at the bar enjoying an after-hours brandy and coffee. Tim was in the back office reviewing the books. It was quiet, except for the occasional car going by outside on Avenue Franklin Roosevelt and Greg's intermittent tapping on a small calculator.

Nikki had almost dozed off when she was startled by someone rapidly knocking on the window. She turned and saw a woman in a hooded raincoat.

"Hurry, please let me in now!" the woman insisted. She opened the hood of her raincoat enough for Nikki to recognize Magda, a part-time hostess at the restaurant. Her eyes were wild with terror.

"What's up?" Greg asked from the other end of the bar.

"It's Magda, and she's very scared. Toss me the keys; I put them on the bar next to your calculator."

Greg flipped her the keys, and Nikki hurried to the front doors. She could see Magda constantly stealing glances down the street in the direction of the St. Philippe du Roule Métro station.

"Hurry, please hurry!" Magda pleaded. "Someone's following me."

Nikki fumbled the keys momentarily. As she opened the left-hand door the right side-door exploded into a thousand shards of glass. Nikki screamed and backed away toward the bar and the safety of the solid stone walls of the building. Magda tried to grab her arm but couldn't hold on, and slumped to the floor onto the broken glass. A split second later bullets ricocheted off the stone walls on the other side of the doors, then the left door exploded, raining more glass over Magda and the entryway.

Nikki knew she couldn't leave Magda exposed. She crouched and moved back toward the doorway, an instant before the window near where she had been sitting disintegrated in another loud explosion.

"Nikki!" Greg screamed from behind the bar.

"I'm okay!" She grabbed the hood of Magda's raincoat and pulled her to the relative safety around the corner of the entryway. Nikki hoped all the blood was from superficial wounds caused by the flying glass.

"Magda, where are you hurt?" Nikki asked as she cradled Magda's head in her lap.

In between agonized moans, Magda kept mumbling something. Nikki leaned closer to try and understand her. It sounded like "Magdalene."

"Yes, I know you're Magdalene," Nikki soothed.

"No, no. Mary Magdalene. They know. Tell Tim," she sputtered, and lost consciousness.

As soon as Nikki moved to get Magda, Greg reached behind the cash register and pulled out the Glock pistol Tim insisted be kept there at all times. Greg had argued against it, but now he was glad he had something to protect him and the two bloodied women in the entryway. He ducked under the bar, joined his friend Rick, and belly-crawled over to the leather banquette seats in the lounge area. They gave him cover from the front doors, in case anyone was planning a full out assault.

"Nikki!" Greg shouted again. "Are you sure you're all right?"

"Yes, but Magda's hurt. There's a lot of blood, but I can't tell if it's from glass or bullets. Can you see anything?"

"No. I'll cover you if you want to move."

"I don't want to move her right now, and I feel safe behind the wall."

At that moment, Tim scrambled over next to Greg. He had come from the back through the underground passageway that led to the cave and the toilets downstairs.

"What the hell happened?" Tim asked as he stole a look over the banquette at the damage.

"I have no idea," Greg said. "Nikki went to let Magda in and all hell broke loose. Magda is hurt."

"Magda? What the hell is she doing here this late?"

"I don't know," Greg said.

"Call the paramedics!" Tim ordered, but Greg had already punched in the numbers on his cell phone. Before Greg could stop him, Tim rushed over to Nikki and Magda.

"Has she been hit?" Tim asked.

"I don't know. She passed out and there's lots of blood. I'm trying to stop the bleeding." Nikki and Tim worked together to assess the damage.

Magda stirred.

Tim leaned down close to her face.

"Are we blown?" he asked.

Magda's eyes opened as a spasm of pain wracked her body. A faint smile crossed her lips despite the obvious pain. *"Bien sûr, mon cher. Désolée."* She closed her eyes for the last time and was still.

"What do you mean by 'are we blown'?" Nikki asked.

"I'll tell you later," Tim said in a tone that signaled the end of the conversation. Before Nikki could object, Tim dove to the other side of the bar and was gone.

ᔕ

Tim Schroeder was terrified, in full panic mode. He ran down the steps from the bar, through the underground passageway to the back of the restaurant and the office. He had to get away from the restaurant quickly, praying his previously established escape plan might give him a small advantage. The back stairs opened into a small, cobblestoned interior courtyard completely enclosed by the surrounding buildings. Access to the courtyard was by two narrow driveways: one led away from the restaurant to Rue La Boétie, the other to the front and Avenue Franklin Roosevelt.

He raced to the office and retrieved a hidden briefcase containing not only his passport and personal papers, but also a substantial amount of cash and an additional fake passport to use in an emergency.

He had a momentary flash of guilt about putting Greg and Nikki in danger. He opened the briefcase, grabbed most of the cash, and stuffed it in the top middle drawer of the desk. On a Post-it note he wrote, "Will explain later. Help is in the top drawer."

He stuck the note on the edge of the desk, ran back to the courtyard and his black BMW 325i. He jumped in, fired the ignition, punched the remote for the metal roll-up door, and slammed the accelerator to the floor. The car leapt down the narrow passageway toward the back as he heard someone shouting from the courtyard.

"Tim! Wait!"

Tim saw Greg in the rearview mirror. He hesitated again. Greg was alone, so Tim slammed on the brakes and leaned out the window.

"Help is in the office!" he yelled. He couldn't waste any more time. He took one last look at Greg, turned, and floored the gas pedal again, barely clearing the metal roll-up door. He jerked the wheel to the right, almost went around the corner on two wheels, and sped off into the darkness.

ഗ

Greg was dumbfounded. He had known Tim for a long time, knew he liked to live life on the edge, but this was way over the top, even for Tim. He noticed the open door to the small, cramped office and wondered what Tim meant. At first glance, nothing was amiss. He went to the desk, set the gun down, and sat facing the courtyard and the back of the restaurant, not knowing what to do. Through the back doors of the restaurant his line of sight went all the way to the front, where he could see his friend Rick huddled close to the fallen Magda.

Nikki burst into the office. "Was that Tim leaving?" she asked incredulously.

"Yes. He said help was in the office. Any idea what that meant?"

"Not a clue."

Greg looked at the desk with renewed interest, noticed the Post-it note, read it, and handed it to Nikki. He opened the drawer.

"Holy shit!"

Greg pulled the packets of 100-Euro notes, set them on the desktop, and started a rough count. "There must be 25,000 Euros here. Nikki, what the hell is going on?"

"I don't know, but let's not take any chances." She grabbed her backpack from her cubbyhole in one of the back shelves, crammed all the money into the bottom of the largest compartment, and covered it with her sweater, a paperback, and a Los Angeles Dodgers cap.

"Let's go back up front," Nikki said. "We'll figure the rest out later. And get rid of the gun. It's totally illegal and we already have enough trouble."

Greg found another sweater and wrapped up the gun. In the courtyard he decided on the large flowerbox next to the back door of the restaurant, quickly dug a hole with his hands, and buried the gun.

"Let's go."

They headed back into the restaurant as the police and paramedic vehicles screeched to a stop in front of the shattered front doors.

CHAPTER TWENTY-ONE

Alexei Persoff cared about no one except himself. He certainly didn't care about the whore he shot at the restaurant door. His instructions had been quite clear: if she couldn't be taken alive, kill the woman before she could talk to anyone. He had no idea who she was, or what she knew that might jeopardize the people he worked for, but that was not his concern. He did as he was told. He was certain she was dead, but uncertain if she died before saying anything to the people inside. Nobody needed to know but him.

In retrospect, he realized that she was smarter than he'd thought, and had sensed him following her as soon as she left the private club. She raced to the Métro and kept moving constantly, staying amidst the large crowds in town for the Bastille Day holiday. She exited the Métro at Charles de Gaulle-Étoile, ran up the stairs, and mingled with the tourists on the Champs Élysée. She walked down one side, crossed the wide boulevard, and walked back up the other side a few times. Alexei could tell she used the reflections in the shop windows, and even the side mirrors of the parked cars, to see if anyone was following her. It was easy to move with the stream of tourists, still out in force even though it was well after midnight. Alexei followed her from a distance and waited for the right opportunity. She never stopped to talk to anyone, so he didn't think he had missed her passing any information.

Her survival instinct was much more fine-tuned than that of the average person, and Alexei marveled at the way she always positioned herself with at least two, sometimes three, escape routes anytime she slowed down or stopped for a minute. She was no match for him, but still he was impressed. It was only a matter of time before she made a mistake or got tired.

She finally made the mistake as she neared the restaurant on Avenue Franklin Roosevelt. In her haste, she knocked on the restaurant window without looking around. It was not his ideal kill zone, but he had no choice. From across the street and twenty yards behind Magda, he had drawn a silenced Beretta from his light windbreaker and emptied the clip at the figures at the glass doors. His instructions were only to kill Magda, but if others died in the process, he felt no remorse. He saw Magda and the other figure go down, and closed the distance between them. His angle of sight gave him a clear view into the bar area where he saw someone pointing a gun at the now shattered entryway. He stayed long enough to make sure Magda wasn't moving anymore.

The few tourists on Avenue Franklin Roosevelt had run for cover, so in the noise and confusion, Alexei returned to the Champs Élysée and disappeared in the crowd.

A few blocks from L'Avenue Bar & Grill on the Rue du Colisée, Alexei entered a small bar called La Cervoise. A pure coincidence it was so close to the kill zone. He had picked the place for several reasons. It was a small establishment with only four or five cocktail tables and six seats at the bar along the right wall. It was open all night, dimly lit by red shaded lamps, and the cigarette smoke hanging in the air made it almost impossible to see from one end of the room to the other. Around a curved wall there was a small room in the back, unseen from the street and the front of the restaurant. He approached the bar, ordered "*un demi*," and found his way to the last table in the back. There were only a few other patrons at this hour and, as his eyes adjusted to the dimness, he waited.

He was on his third beer when his contact arrived. Alexei knew him only as Henri, and didn't want to know any more. He always paid well, on time, and with a minimum of questions. He was a large man, well over two hundred pounds, slightly over six feet tall with longish hair more gray than its original black. His dark eyes were malevolent, and his face was marked with several scars that could only have been caused by knife wounds. One started above his right eyebrow and curved down toward his temple and then back underneath the eye socket; the scar tissue sagged over the corner of his eye, hooding the opening. Henri never mentioned the history of these scars, and Alexei never asked.

"*Ça va?*" Henri asked as he sat down with his beer and a fresh one for Alexei.

"*Oui, ça va.*" Alexei's French was only passable, so after realizing no one was paying any attention to them, they switched to English.

"You have succeeded in closing our loophole?" Henri asked.

"Yes," Alexei said without hesitation.

Henri withdrew a large envelope from the inside breast pocket of his sport coat and slid it across the table. Alexei quickly secured it in a zippered pocket of his windbreaker, next to the still warm Beretta.

"I like that you never count the money, Alexei. It shows class and that we trust each other, up to a point, of course." He roared with laughter. "To success!" he said as he guzzled the rest of his beer.

Henri's cell phone buzzed as he slammed down his empty beer glass.

"Oui?"

He listened for a few minutes and his mood darkened.

"D'accord." He ended the call and glared at Alexei. "That was my man from the Prefecture. Our target survived long enough to say something to the hostess and the restaurant owner. The hostess is on her way to the American Hospital

for a cut on her arm. Her name is Nikki Dunn. Get the information from her, and I will find out why the owner found it necessary to disappear."

Alexei didn't know what to say or do. He could agree, take the money, and disappear too, but he had no doubt that Henri or one of his associates would find him and the result would be extremely painful. He removed the envelope from his windbreaker and gave it back to Henri. "I only accept payment for a completed job."

"I knew you had class." Henri re-pocketed the envelope. "We meet back here in two days. Do we understand each other?"

"Absolument."

Henri got up and left the bar.

A few minutes later Alexei made his way to the queue of taxis on the *Champs Élysée*. There was no line this early in the morning, so he jumped in the first taxi.

"Hôpital Américain. Rapidement, s'il vous plaît."

CHAPTER TWENTY-TWO

Nikki rode to the Hôpital Américain in the back of the ambulance with Rick Asher, the backpack of cash clutched to her chest. She was horrified by the amount of blood on her clothes, but most of it turned out to be Magda's. The paramedics had done everything they could to revive Magda, but it was too late. One bullet had destroyed the back of her skull and another had ripped through from the back and damaged her aorta. Nikki's wounds were merely superficial cuts from the shattered glass, and only a gash near her left elbow needed a few stitches. She was reassured there would only be a small scar, little consolation considering the loss of Magda.

The police had questioned them before leaving the restaurant, but they were unable to offer any help in identifying who might want to kill Magda. She had only worked a few days as a hostess, usually on Nikki's day off. The police were understandably upset and suspicious of Tim Schroeder's fleeing the scene, but Nikki or Greg could offer no reasonable explanation.

The eastern sky was a deep pink when Rick and Nikki exited the hospital via the lower level emergency doors. The available taxis were back up the hill at the center of the building.

"We could have stayed inside and taken the elevator," said Rick.

"This is fine," Nikki assured him. "I want to get home. I'm exhausted."

Rick shouldered Nikki's backpack and they went up the hill and got into one of the waiting taxis.

"Where are you staying?" she asked Rick.

"I'm at a small hotel near Rue Cler," he said. "I promised Greg I would make sure you got home safely, so let's go there first."

"60 Rue de Bellechasse," Nikki said to the dozing driver.

In the gray and pink light of the early dawn, neither one saw the small, compact man emerge from a taxi at the bottom of the hill. Their taxi left the grounds down the opposite side of the hill before the man noticed them.

ഗ

Alexei instructed the taxi driver to stop in front of the Boulevard de la Saussaye entrance to the Hôpital Américain. The hospital was L-shaped, sloping up to the south and then down again to the east. There were more taxis at the top of the short incline leading to the front doors, so he dismissed his taxi and made his way up the narrow sidewalk.

Inside the doors at the reception desk sat a pleasant looking older woman. Alexei approached and asked in English, "Where is your emergency room, please?"

"Through the door on your left and follow the hallway to the elevator," she said pleasantly, with the hint of a British accent. "Go down one floor and follow the signs. It is very easy, actually." She smiled.

"Thank you."

At 5:30 a.m. it was quiet, the halls and elevator empty. After exiting the elevator, he followed the signs down another long hallway. There were offices on the right side facing an interior courtyard, and examining rooms on the left side. The hallway finally opened up into a small waiting area with a wall mounted television tuned to CNN International, and beyond that another reception desk with a weary night nurse working at a computer terminal.

"Excuse me, do you speak English?" he asked.

"Of course," the nurse replied. "Can I help you?"

"I am looking for my friend, a woman. Her name is Nikki Dunn. I was told she was brought here tonight."

"We discharged her a few minutes ago, and she left with another man through that door over there." She pointed to the emergency room doors that led out to the lower level and the east gate. "If you hurry you might be able to catch them."

"Thank you," Alexei said as he moved quickly to the doors.

Rick and Nikki's taxi had cleared the east gate and was long gone.

Alexei ran up to the waiting taxis. There were only two left, both loading patients leaving the hospital in wheelchairs. Commandeering one would only draw unwanted attention, so he decided against it. He looked for more taxis down the hill at the north entrance, but was out of luck.

Alexei acted quickly. He hurried back down the hill and reentered the hospital, figuring his best chance was to plead his case to the nurse.

"I missed them," he said, trying to make her feel sorry for him. "I forgot to ask if she is okay."

"She'll be fine, a nasty laceration above her left elbow. It took a few stitches."

"I am glad to hear that," Alexei said with fake sincerity. "However, I have a problem. I fly back to Vienna this morning and I do not know their hotel. Could you help? I want to send flowers."

"We're not allowed to give out personal information," the nurse apologized. "I'm sorry."

"Could you make an exception this one time?" he pleaded. "Maybe ask your supervisor?"

The nurse hesitated. She had pulled a double shift and was dead tired. The last thing she wanted to do was chase down a supervisor for what seemed like a harmless request. "Oh, all right." She moved a few papers around and found the admittance form she was looking for.

"The address she left was 60 Rue de Bellechasse, Apartment 7. That's in the 7th. Near the Musée d'Orsay, I think."

"I think you are right … Alexandria," he replied, eyeing her name tag. "What a coincidence, my name is Alexei. Do you have a card? To show my gratitude, I will send you flowers, too."

"Oh, you don't have to do that," Alexandria blushed.

"I insist," Alexei said.

She wrote her name on a standard hospital information card and handed it to him. What a nice man, Alexandria thought.

She had no idea how wrong she was.

∽

The taxi pulled to a stop at 60 Rue de Bellechasse and Rick and Nikki were greeted by a local Paris policeman, a *flic*.

"Monsieur Asher and Mademoiselle Dunn."

"*Oui*," Nikki said. "Is there a problem?"

"*Non*, Mademoiselle, I am here to guard you today."

"Is that really necessary?" Rick asked.

The *flic* shrugged. "Who knows? Rather safe than sorry, no? I will be here in the lobby. I have instructions to let no one see you."

Rick took the keys from Nikki and unlocked the building's entry door, and they stepped inside.

"Has Monsieur Irvine returned?" Nikki asked.

"*Non*. He is still at the restaurant."

"*Merci beaucoup*," Nikki said as she and Rick got in the small elevator. Rick made sure Nikki's apartment was secure, then stood in the hallway and listened as she bolted the door behind him. He'd done all he could for now; it was time to head back to his hotel for some much needed sleep, and maybe a beer, too.

☙

A hundred yards down the street another taxi unloaded its fare in front of L'Ambassadeurs café on the corner of Rue de Grenelle and Rue de Bellechasse. The extra twenty Euros Alexei promised the driver to make up for lost time was money well spent. He arrived in time to see the *flic* escort Rick and Nikki into the apartment building. The information they have must be important if the French police were already protecting them, Alexei thought. All the more reason to be careful and come up with a workable plan, one that wouldn't get him killed or arrested. Alexei had no desire to spend the rest of his life in prison, a fait accompli if the authorities from several countries ever caught up with him.

Alexei was experienced enough to know when to regroup. Rick and Nikki weren't going anywhere for the next few hours, and making decisions when one was tired was never a good idea. He would think more clearly after a few hours of sleep. He walked back toward the river, found another taxi in front of the Musée d'Orsay, and retreated to his apartment across the river.

CHAPTER TWENTY-THREE

Greg Irvine was still at the restaurant, calling employees with a brief explanation of the tragedy. The police secured the restaurant as a crime scene, so it would be closed for at least the next couple of days. Thierry, the contractor Tim and Greg used to remodel L'Avenue Bar & Grill, had arrived at nine, saw the damage, and immediately was on the phone to his supplier for new doors. He and one of his workers used plywood to board up the opening, using the existing hinge supports from the shattered glass doors.

"*Bon.* That will be sufficient for a few days until the new doors arrive," Thierry said as Greg joined them.

"I'm grateful to you for coming on a holiday weekend. I'll make sure you get overtime pay," Greg said.

"Now is not the time to worry about finances. Right now the important thing is for you to sleep and make sure Nikki and your friend Rick are safe."

"Thanks, Thierry, I'll call you tomorrow."

"A bientôt, mon ami."

With the front sealed off, Greg let them out the door that opened to the alley, locked the office, and left through the same door. The alley was really a driveway; to the left led to the courtyard, but Greg went right and exited through the typical large, black, double wooden doors to Avenue Franklin Roosevelt. As he dragged his exhausted body toward the taxi stand on the *Champs Élysée*, he didn't notice the small Mercedes as it pulled out and followed him.

ઌ

Nikki slept until early Sunday evening. Greg called at seven, and they agreed to meet Rick for a drink at a small brasserie up the street from the apartment building. Nikki was so disoriented from having her routine altered, she completely forgot to notice that the *flic* sent to guard them was no longer in the lobby.

"Have you heard from Tim yet?" Nikki asked Greg as they settled in with their wine. She noticed that Rick's hand shook a little bit as he raised his glass.

"No. I've called his cell phone a dozen times, but he doesn't pick up. I have no idea where he is or why he ran away."

"He had a strange exchange with Magda right before she died," Nikki said. "She muttered 'Mary Magdalene' and 'They know' over and over again. When Tim was next to her he asked, 'Are we blown?' and she said 'Yes.' What that means I have no idea."

"It means there was something else going on between the two of them," Rick said. "Any suggestions?"

"Maybe she had an old jealous boyfriend from Moscow," Nikki said.

"Perhaps, but that seems like a lot of effort and expense to come all the way from Moscow and then kill her from a distance. I would imagine an ex-boyfriend would want to make it more personal," Greg said. "This doesn't appear to me to be a crime of passion, but more of an execution."

Further speculation was interrupted by the police. Deputy Inspector Bonnard, the detective who had briefly questioned them at L'Avenue Bar & Grill appeared at their table.

"*Bonsoir.* I need to ask you a few more questions."

"Sure, pull up a chair. We're sitting here trying to sort it all out ourselves," Rick said politely. "And thanks for sending the *flic* to guard us here today."

Bonnard looked at him quizzically, followed by a moment of awkward silence. "You are welcome," he finally stammered. "I prefer our discussion take place in private. Let us use your apartments, no? Monsieur Irvine, I will question Monsieur Asher and Mademoiselle Dunn first. I shall meet you in your apartment in a few minutes."

The group exited the small brasserie and walked back to the apartment building. A large man got out of a police car double parked on the narrow street and approached them. "This is my assistant, Gorky. He will stay with you, Monsieur Irvine, until I finish with the others."

Gorky merely grunted as they moved inside and made their way to the respective apartments. All five did not notice Jack, dressed in a dark windbreaker and jeans, arrive at the front door right before it closed. He slipped into the foyer behind them.

"Would you like some coffee, Inspector?" Nikki asked as they entered her apartment.

"No, *merci*, this will not take long."

Nikki led them to the living room, offered the Inspector the wing chair while she and Rick sat on the couch.

"What can you tell us about the investigation so far?" Rick asked.

"I will ask the questions, Monsieur," Bonnard said.

"There is no need to be rude, Inspector, we're only trying to help," Nikki said. "We have done nothing wrong and answered all your questions regarding the incident already. Unless you have something new to add, please leave us alone."

"You are a visitor to this country, Mademoiselle Dunn. I would suggest you do as I say, or I will personally make sure your work visa is revoked and you and your friends are asked to leave our country."

"On what grounds?" Rick asked.

The inspector shocked Rick and Nikki into silence. He removed a small plastic sandwich bag filled with what looked like baking powder. "I am sure you realize that cocaine is illegal in this country, Monsieur Asher. We don't appreciate arrogant Americans smuggling it into our country for your depraved habits. I am sure my superiors will be most interested in why these drugs were found in Mlle. Dunn's apartment."

He placed the bag on the small end table next to his chair.

"That's enough," Nikki said. "Come on, Rick, let's get Greg and go to the American Embassy. He can't do this to us."

"Both of you sit down, or you will regret it."

Nikki gasped.

Rick turned to see Inspector Bonnard pointing a silenced pistol directly at Nikki's forehead.

"Sit down," he repeated quietly, "or this lovely young woman will die right here. Don't worry, your friend Greg is in good hands. Gorky can be very persuasive and I am rarely disappointed with his results."

Suddenly, Nikki understood. Bonnard was somehow involved with Magda's killers and was going to make it look like a drug deal gone bad. Considering how cruelly Magda had died, she had no doubt Inspector Bonnard would not hesitate to kill them, too.

"*Bon*," he said once they were seated again on the couch. "You will tell me everything I need to know. If you don't, I will most definitely kill you."

"You are going to kill us anyway," Nikki said.

"Perhaps, *ma chérie*. Now tell me *exactly* what the woman said before she died."

"Her name was Magda. She said nothing," Nikki replied. She didn't want to divulge anything to the Inspector.

There was a quick flash and spitting sound from the gun and the sofa pillow to Nikki's right exploded. Nikki screamed, moved to her left, and grabbed Rick's arm.

"Do not lie to me again, or the next one goes into Monsieur Asher's kneecap," he said. "Let us try again. What exactly did Magda say before she died?" He pointed the gun at Rick's knee.

"She said 'Mary Magdalene' and 'they know.' That's all."

"Do you know what she meant?"

"None of us have any idea what she was talking about. You have to believe us!" Nikki said.

"And what of Monsieur Schroeder?"

"We can't reach him, and that's the truth," Rick said.

"A pity, he could answer so many of my questions," the Inspector said.

Nikki and Rick flinched as they heard the front door open.

"Gorky?" Bonnard called around the corner.

"*Oui*," came the grunt from the front of the apartment.

Bonnard's back was to the wall off the hallway and he could not see around the corner. Coming down the short hallway was Gorky, his hands tied behind his back. Jack was behind him, holding a gun to his right temple. He mouthed the word "Where?" to Rick.

Rick would later recall he had no conscious thought of why he moved his eyes to the right to indicate Inspector Bonnard's location. He was confused, terrified, severely jet-lagged, and supremely hungover. He had to focus; the next few minutes would determine whether he and Nikki lived or died.

Jack mouthed the words "On three, okay?"

Rick blinked once, hoping that was the universal sign of yes. He had no idea what he was going to do "on three," but knew instinctively he would have to do something.

Jack's left hand was on Gorky's left shoulder. He maintained eye contact with Rick, as one finger, then two were raised. On three, Jack stuck his left foot in front of Gorky and gave a forceful push to his shoulder blades. The huge Russian stumbled into the small living room, unable to break his fall with his hands tied behind his back.

Bonnard was momentarily distracted, taking a split second too long to realize it was Gorky on the floor, not Greg. He swung the gun in Jack's direction, but it was too late. Rick leapt off the couch, putting his body between Bonnard's gun and Nikki, and barreled into the Inspector. The momentum of his head crashing into Bonnard's shoulder forced the gun toward the ceiling as he got off a shot. The bullet missed Jack by inches and plugged in the far wall, sending shards of plaster raining down on the prostrate Gorky.

Rick was in a fight for his life. He focused on the gun. As long as it was neutralized, he and Nikki would stay alive. The wing chair toppled in the collision and the two men were flung toward the wall. Rick was taking blows to his head and face from Bonnard's left fist, but he didn't care. He was holding Bonnard's right wrist with both hands when Bonnard shifted, and using Rick's own momentum, smashed him into the wall. Rick let out a big "oooff" and lost the grip on Bonnard's wrist. Bonnard, realizing his advantage, swung the gun at Rick's chest.

"I don't think so, Inspector." Before Bonnard could get his gun in position to fire, Jack's gun was pressed below the policeman's left eye socket. "Drop the gun. Now!"

"You!" Bonnard said, but did as instructed.

Rick immediately grabbed the gun and stood up. In his peripheral vision he saw Gorky maneuver to his feet, preparing to charge. As Gorky took his first step, Nikki came flying in from his right and attempted to tackle him. With her arms around his neck and the rest of her body on his back, they fell toward the small glass-and-metal entertainment center against the wall between the living room and the bedroom. Gorky was a large man, but with his hands behind his back he could not maintain his balance. As if in slow motion, the two bodies fell, their heads perilously close to the sharp corner of the entertainment center. At the last second Nikki released her grip, separated herself as Gorky's forehead squarely caught the corner, making a sickening sound. Gorky collapsed and did not move, as blood poured onto the cheap carpet. Nikki recoiled in horror and covered her eyes with her hands.

Bonnard made a desperate attempt to wrestle away Jack's gun. It discharged once and blood splattered the wall. Rick and Nikki couldn't tell who had been hit.

"Ah, shit."

Jack moved away and revealed a gaping wound to Bonnard's shoulder, an ugly mass of flesh and bone. Bonnard's eyes glassed over and closed.

"Is he dead?" Rick asked.

"No. Get something to stop the bleeding."

Nikki ran into the bedroom, grabbed a t-shirt, and gave it to Jack. "Who are you?"

Jack ignored her as he expertly covered the wound. "I'll tell you later. We need to leave immediately. I think there's one more goon outside. We have no time to spare. Grab a few things, throw them in a bag and be ready to go in sixty seconds."

They had just saved each other's lives, so Rick and Nikki weren't going to argue. Nikki did her best to avoid the sight of Gorky's damaged head and Bonnard's destroyed shoulder. She grabbed a shoulder bag, stuffed it with jeans, blouses, and toiletries, then returned to the living room.

Jack was holding the small bag of cocaine. "I hope this isn't yours."

"Of course not," Nikki said. "He was going to use it to frame us for something."

"I wouldn't put it past him." Jack stuffed the bag in the pocket of his windbreaker. "Let's go."

Nikki held back, stepped into the bedroom, and retrieved the backpack stuffed with Tim's money, added her laptop, passport, and an unused Eurail pass. She didn't know where they were going, but she knew they wouldn't be back here for a while.

They reached the bottom of the stairs in a few seconds. Jack opened the door to Greg's studio and led them in. "He's unconscious, but alive. Gorky gave him a nasty blow to the head."

They found Greg on the bed, a big knot on his forehead starting to turn blue and yellow. "What the hell is going on here?" Nikki asked. She leaned down to assess Greg's condition.

"Nikki, there is no time to explain, but you have to believe I'm a friend. If we don't get out of here in the next few seconds, we could all be dead."

Nikki stopped cold. "How do you know my name?" Now she was really scared.

"I'll explain everything when we're safe. Rick, help her with Greg, and I'll get us out of here." He picked up Nikki's shoulder bag and the backpack to allow Rick and Nikki to carefully lift Greg to his feet, each having an arm over a shoulder.

Greg's limp body was awkward, but they managed to get him out the door and down the hall toward the front door of the building.

"Here," Jack said.

There was a short hallway Nikki had never noticed off one side of the foyer with a door at the end. Jack pulled out a set of keys, knew exactly which one to use, and opened the door. There was darkness on the other side, but Rick and Nikki followed blindly, trying desperately not to jostle Greg too much. Jack closed the door behind them.

"Where are we?" Nikki asked. She smelled the remnants of strong coffee, wine, and baked bread.

"In the brasserie next door. This is the hallway leading to the bathrooms in the back. There's a storage room toward the front with table cloths and napkins. Try to make Greg comfortable. I'll go to the bar and find ice for that bump on his head. Be quiet and don't turn on any lights."

Jack moved ahead of them, stopped after a few yards, and pointed to a storeroom on the right, the only light coming from the streetlamps in front of the restaurant. Rick and Nikki moved Greg inside the storeroom, and eased him to the floor. Nikki held his head in her lap while Rick fumbled in the dark for something soft.

Jack was back in a few minutes, his windbreaker used to haul several handfuls of ice. He found table linens, and made a small ice pack and a pillow to rest Greg's head. Nikki eased his head off her lap and made him as comfortable as possible.

"Let's go take a look out front," Jack said to Rick.

They scurried their way to the front of the brasserie and the slightly open shutters covering the windows. Jack peeked out.

"Ah, shit," he whispered.

"You keep saying that," Rick whispered back. "What is it now?"

"Exactly what I was afraid of. There's another one out there."

"Ah, shit."

Jack chuckled quietly. "Welcome to my world, Rick."

Before they could continue the whispered banter, Jack put his finger to his lips and pointed to the front door of the apartment building, a few yards away. They snuck a look and saw a small, solidly built man approach the door to the apartment building, stealing glances in every direction. His movements were compact and efficient, reminding Jack of a gymnast. The man turned to look down Rue de Bellechasse toward the river, exposing the right side of his neck. It was decorated with a tattoo of what looked like a snarling black leopard, stretching from below his right ear to the nape. With amazing speed he moved to the front door, expertly broke the cheap lock, and disappeared into the apartment building.

Jack and Rick retreated to the storeroom to check on Nikki and Greg. They heard the man move up the stairs to Nikki's apartment, and then a momentary silence. Jack thought he heard the spit of a silenced gun, but couldn't be sure. It was only a minute or two before the man came back down and moved to the door of Greg's studio. This time, the spit of his silenced gun was easy to recognize, as a bullet crashed into the door jamb and shattered the lock.

There was nothing to find in Greg's small studio so the man returned and stood silently in the foyer, like an animal attempting to sense his prey or imminent danger. "Where could they have gone?" he thought.

The question would not be answered because he heard sirens in the distance. *"Merde!"*

He rushed out of the building, down the street toward the river, and the crowd gathered on the steps of the Musée d'Orsay. He wouldn't find out until later the sirens had nothing to do with the events at the apartment building.

❧

The sound of the sirens neared, but then drifted into the distance. Jack went to the door leading back toward the apartments.

"Stay here, I'll be right back." He opened the door and left before either Nikki or Rick could protest. Greg was starting to regain consciousness, so they had their hands full anyway.

"How do you feel?" Nikki asked. She lifted the ice pack away from Greg's forehead.

"Like someone hit me with a hammer."

"You might have a concussion, so lie still until we can figure out what we're going to do."

Jack returned.

"It's nice to see you are back with us, Greg. How's the head?"

"It hurts like hell."

"I'd imagine so. Sorry I didn't get there until after the big ape hit you."

"It happened so fast. As soon as we were in the apartment, he asked me what I knew about Magda and Tim. When I told him I didn't know anything he hauled off and hit me with his gun. He got me good because I wasn't expecting to get assaulted by a French police officer."

"He definitely was not a French police officer."

"Was?"

"He's dead and so is Inspector Bonnard. The third guy must have thought Bonnard would be a loose end, so he killed him. The shoulder wound was bad, but not fatal. The bullet to his left temple certainly was."

"What the hell is going on here? And who are you?" Rick asked. "And quit being so mysterious and vague."

"I'm trying to protect you. The less you know the better."

"Listen, I know you just saved our lives, but you've got to tell us something," Nikki said.

"All right, that's fair. I'm Jack Oatmon, an American agent on special assignment. I'm working with an elite task force investigating the Russian mafia's trafficking of Eastern European women. They discovered Magda was working for us, but they don't know how much she passed on before they killed her at the restaurant. That's why they're after you."

"But we don't know anything," Nikki said.

"I know that, and you know that, but they don't. Believe me, these people are cold-blooded killers. They'll stop at nothing to protect themselves. We have to get out of here and avoid them at all costs."

"Do you have a plan?" Greg asked. He cautiously rose to a sitting position.

"Yes, but we have to move fast. The police will be here any minute, and they're going to have a lot of questions about the two dead bodies in that apartment upstairs."

"Why don't we stay here and help them sort it all out?" Rick asked.

"Look how well that worked for you the first time. Besides, Inspector Bonnard was on the task force with me. I never trusted him, so I've been following him. When I saw him introduce Gorky as a police officer, I knew you were in danger. I haven't been able to find out how far up the chain of command it goes. At least the *flic* here today was someone I trust."

"So that's why Bonnard looked so confused when I thanked him earlier," Rick said.

"Bonnard was not acting alone," Jack said. "Someone above him has to be involved and I'm not taking any chances until I know more. I'm sure someone will try to pin the two dead people upstairs on you. The longer I keep you away from them the more they might panic and make a mistake."

Jack looked each of them in the eye. "Okay?"

"Okay," they all said in unison.

"We'll split up. I'm in a safe place, so I'll take Greg there to make sure the bump on his head isn't more serious than we think. Nikki, it would be best if you and Rick disappear for a couple of days while I sort it all out. In fact, get out of France immediately. Do you have any cash?"

"Tim left us some," Nikki said evasively. She didn't want to tell him the extent of the cash.

"Good. The cash will be very helpful. Don't use *any* credit cards, and for God's sake don't try to fly home. They'll have the airports covered. Move as anonymously as possible. I know it's a lot to ask, but I really think it's necessary to save your lives. Plus, I have some pull with Interpol and the FBI, so I'll be able to protect you for a few days."

"I have an unused first-class Eurail pass I can use to get on any train anytime," Nikki said.

"I have one too," Rick said. "I only got here yesterday and haven't used it yet."

"Here." Jack handed Rick a cell phone. "This can't be traced or triangulated by the authorities to determine your location. I want the two of you as far away from here as you can get in twenty-four hours; your best bet is Switzerland or Germany. You can reach me on my other cell phone by hitting speed dial #1. Call me Tuesday afternoon."

"How long will we need to be gone?" Nikki asked.

"Could be a few days, could be a few weeks. It all depends on things out of our control for now," Jack said. "Now we really need to move. Are you ready, Greg?"

"I guess so, not that I have much choice."

Rick and Nikki helped Greg to his feet and passed him over to Jack. They picked up the shoulder bag and the backpack, and the four made their way through the apartment building foyer and out to Rue de Bellechasse.

"Your best bet is to head up to Boulevard St. Germain and get a cab," Jack said. "We'll go the other way."

Greg noticed Rick and Nikki's hesitation. "He's right, you have to go now. Don't worry about me, I'll be fine. Rick, take care of Nikki for me. And be careful."

"Greg …" Nikki didn't know what to say.

"It's okay. Go before it's too late."

Jack watched Rick and Nikki run toward the river. He readjusted his support of Greg Irvine, then moved off in the opposite direction.

The shrill sound of more sirens echoed in the distance.

CHAPTER TWENTY-FOUR

Rick and Nikki were lucky. They found a cab right away and were on the concourse at Gare de l'Est in twenty-five minutes. They scanned the list of departing trains.

"Where do we go?" Rick asked.

"My instinct is to get the first train out of here and hope for the best," Nikki said. "Nobody in the world knows where we are, so as long as we keep moving randomly, we'll be very hard to track. Our first-class Eurail passes allow us to get on any train, anywhere, anytime throughout most of Europe."

"The possibilities are endless," Rick said.

"When I was a little girl my dad was stationed at the Air Force base in Birkenfeld, a small town outside Munich, so that way is as good as any," Nikki said. "There's a night train to Munich at 10:45. Let's get on it and go."

They found the office and waited for the next available clerk to initiate their Eurail passes. Nikki watched carefully to see if the clerk scanned the bar codes on the passes or did anything she thought could trace them. The clerk simply checked their passports against the names on the passes, put in the start date, and handed back all the paperwork.

"Bon voyage."

"I need a beer," Rick said as they exited the office.

"Now?"

"A little hair of the dog, if you don't mind."

They stopped at a kiosk, where Rick bought two large beers and a bottle of water for Nikki. He opened the first beer immediately and took a long swallow.

"Feel better?" Nikki asked.

"I'm getting there. Now let's go find our train."

There were no couchettes or sleeper cars available, so they were left to fend for themselves in a first-class car. They found an empty compartment and quickly stowed the shoulder bags in the overhead rack. Nikki kept a firm grip on the backpack. She had taken several vacations using first-class Eurail passes and remembered the efficiency of the train schedules in Northern Europe. She hoped tonight would be no exception.

They both watched the final preparations of the people on the platform, keeping a keen eye to notice anything or anyone suspicious. The next few minutes seemed to drag on for hours, but both noticeably relaxed as the train began to leave the station. The train picked up speed, and in twenty minutes they were on the outskirts of Paris on a steady pace east.

A young man entered the compartment. He stowed his large backpack in the rack after extracting a handful of deli-wrapped items and a bottle of wine. He settled comfortably in the window seat opposite Rick and Nikki and began to open the cheeses, meats, and sweets. He pulled out a Swiss Army knife and, using the corkscrew, opened a vintage bottle of red wine.

Rick and Nikki realized that in all the excitement they had not eaten a real meal in over twenty-four hours and were famished. "They usually have a food cart on these night trains; I'll go find it and get us something," Nikki said.

"I don't mean to eavesdrop, but that won't do you any good tonight," the young man said. "This particular train doesn't offer food service. I found out in enough time to stock up."

"How long before we get to Munich?" Rick asked.

"Eight a.m. tomorrow morning." The young man noticed the forlorn looks that this information caused his fellow travelers. "Listen, I've been backpacking through Europe for two months and this is my last night. I fly back to San Francisco from Munich tomorrow. I've taken dozens of night trains to save money and eaten alone too many times. I would be honored if you would share the last meal of my trip with me. I hate to drink alone."

"That's very generous of you," Nikki said. "At least let us chip in; that looks like a very expensive bottle of wine."

"It is, but it'll taste better if I share it. I only ask a small favor in return, that you do something nice for a fellow traveler someday. A wonderful Swedish girl named Mia did something nice for me at the beginning of my trip, and that was all she asked in return, too. You are actually giving me the opportunity to fulfill her wish and keep the tradition going. It's a small-scale attempt to keep civility and random acts of kindness alive in this increasingly rude world."

"Well, if we are going to eat together, we should at least introduce ourselves. I'm Nikki and this is Rick."

"Nate Becker, pleased to meet you both," he said as they shook hands. He pulled out a large baguette, extra napkins, and an extra plastic cup. Nikki and Rick shared what turned out to be excellent pinot noir, even if it was from a plastic cup. They savored the varieties of ham, cheese, and sausage, topped off with chocolate mousse tarts.

During the meal, the conductor entered the compartment, checked everyone's Eurail pass, and asked for their passports.

"They will be returned to you in the morning, after we cross the border into Germany," Nate said. "Not to worry."

Nikki held her breath as the conductor verified the passport photos matched the people in front of him. She looked for any signs of recognition, but saw none.

Rick and Nikki excused themselves after thanking Nate one more time, moved into the hallway, and closed the door.

"I'm worried," Nikki said. "If there are people after us, and they have contacts with the police, we could be in danger if they can track our passports."

"I know," Rick said. "But we have to assume that first, they don't know where we are; second, they probably can't mobilize in the few short hours we've been gone; and third, it's the middle of the night for Christ's sake. That should buy us enough time to get into Germany and disappear."

"I hope you're right."

It was after 2 a.m. before they made their last trips to the toilet, used the remaining bottled water to brush their teeth, turned out the lights, and tried to get into a comfortable position to sleep.

Nikki rested against the backpack filled with cash, her mind spinning around the impossible and surreal events of the past twenty-four hours. Three people had died violently, she was running for her life in a foreign country with a man she hardly knew, and she had shared a wonderful meal with a total stranger on a night train to Munich. She was sure of one reality though: she was very scared.

She was a long way from Grass Valley, California, where she grew up in a military family with four older brothers, an alcoholic father, and a long-suffering but moody and selfish mother.

She looked out the window, mesmerized by the train's rhythmic movement, and the flashes of moonlight glistening off the shining steel of the parallel set of tracks.

⁂

A new conductor, this one German, returned their passports at seven-thirty the next morning. He was pleasant and professional, and showed no sign of suspicion. Rick and Nikki were simply two more of the thousands of summer tourists.

Stiff and tired when they disembarked in Munich, they said goodbye to Nate. "Good luck and a safe trip home. And thanks again for your hospitality," Nikki said. "We promise to pass the tradition along."

"I'm sure you will," Nate said. He hoisted the big backpack to his shoulders, turned away, and was soon lost in the crowd.

It didn't take Rick and Nikki long to get oriented. At the end of the platform, the first thing they saw was a Starbucks! Shrugging off their disbelief, they went inside and settled down with some real American coffee and muffins.

"I need clothes and toiletries," Rick said. "I still have about five hundred Euros in my wallet, so why don't I go find something while you figure out our next step. Will you be all right here by yourself for a little while?"

"Of course."

Rick finished his chocolate chip muffin, grabbed his coffee, and left.

In the forty-five minutes he was gone, Nikki mulled over their options with the timetable booklet from the Eurail packet. She decided their best bet was a train leaving at 10:30 a.m. for Mannheim, from there they could transfer to Kaiserslautern, then catch a bus arriving in the small town of Birkenfeld late in the afternoon.

Rick returned wearing new sunglasses and carrying a new backpack, shoulder bag, and shopping bags with new jeans and tee shirts. "Have you figured out the logistics yet?"

Nikki leaned closer to show him the recommended itinerary, and smelled fresh beer on his breath. Just what she needed. In a foreign country, on the run from homicidal maniacs, and burdened with an alcoholic stranger.

Rick agreed with her recommendation, and suggested a few more purchases before boarding the train. They picked up an *International Herald Tribune* and a couple of cheap thriller novels at a news kiosk on the concourse, and headed to the platform.

The train left Munich precisely on time and the German conductor barely glanced at their passes, which Rick took as a positive development. They shared the *Tribune*, read their books, and watched the beautiful German countryside go by.

They took some time to get to know each other. Their immediate futures were inescapably thrust together and they had to make it work, or they could both end up like the other three who had lost their lives in the past forty-eight hours.

Rick was from Los Angeles, and admitted he was in Europe to get over a nasty breakup with his girlfriend of five years. "I travel all the time on business, so we spent a lot of time apart," he said. "She left me for another man, one of my teammates from a recreational league softball team."

"Ouch," Nikki said.

"I don't remember much of the last few months. I've been feeling sorry for myself, and drowning my sorrows in single malt Scotch and beer. It started affecting my work, mostly little stuff like filling out my expense reports wrong. I hated doing them, the boring details of matching the right receipts to the right clients, so I got sloppy sometimes. My boss and the bean counters were not amused."

"How do you know Greg?" Nikki asked.

"The softball team would hang out at his bar in Marina del Rey after the games. He told me he was leaving for Paris, and I invited myself over. I only arrived on Saturday morning, so I'm still adjusting to the time change."

"Let me give you a hint," Nikki said. "Drink lots of water for a couple of days and minimize the beer and wine. It will help more than you think."

"I'll try," Rick said. He sounded sincere.

"I hope Greg is okay," Nikki said, changing the subject.

"Are you two together?" Rick asked. "We didn't get too far in our conversation the other night before the shit hit the fan."

Nikki hesitated. "It's complicated," she said.

Rick laughed. "It always is."

"We haven't figured out what we are yet, especially because we work together, and he's technically my boss."

"He's a nice guy," Rick said. "And smart. You two will figure it out."

"I hope you're right."

∽

There were no hitches in Mannheim or Kaiserslautern, and they arrived in Birkenfeld in time for happy hour on Monday afternoon. As they wandered around town, they saw several American servicemen going into a bar called "The Office."

"The base must still be here, so there should be somebody who speaks English," Nikki said.

"Sounds good to me. I think there's a cold local brew in there with my name on it."

"That even sounds good to me," Nikki said.

It turned out to be a typical tavern, with more of an American than German feel. The four-sided bar was in the middle of the large room, a huge but empty stone fireplace along the left wall, and the Rolling Stones were playing on the stereo. The place was about half full with mostly American soldiers, but some locals were there sharing big baskets of French fries and pitchers of beer. Rick and Nikki found two seats at the bar and ordered glasses of dark draft beer from the young, English-speaking bartender. Her name tag read: JENNY.

"That's eight Euros. If you want to start a tab, I'll need a credit card."

"We'll pay as we go, thanks," Rick said. He handed her a ten Euro note. "Keep the change, Jenny."

"Thanks. So where are you from in the States?"

"How did you know we were from the States?" Nikki asked.

"It's easy to tell Americans from locals and other Europeans. Your clothes, your accents, your haircuts."

"We're from California," Rick said.

"I'd love to live in California again someday," Jenny said.

"Again?"

"My dad was stationed there when I was a kid, but my mother is German and wanted to come back home. I've been stuck here for the past decade trying to save enough to go back on my own. I have dual citizenship so it won't be a problem."

"What a coincidence!" Nikki said. "My father was stationed *here* when I was a kid. We had a German housekeeper named Frau Fruener, and we lived in an apartment building near Premier Mart."

"You're kidding! That's only six blocks from where you are sitting right now."

"I'd love to go see if I can remember it. Can you give us directions?"

"It's real simple: turn right as you go out the door, go up four blocks, and turn left. The apartment building is two more blocks down on the left side. You might even be able to find Frau Fruener. There are several families of Frueners in that area. Maybe you'll get lucky."

"Thanks a lot, Jenny," Nikki said. She drained the last of her beer and looked at Rick. "Want to go down memory lane with me for a few minutes?"

"Sure, it'll be fun," he said.

Nikki was blinded by the bright sun as they exited into the hot late afternoon. In the thirty second rush to get out of her apartment, sunglasses weren't high on her priority list. Several shops along the way displayed racks of them, along with sunscreen and other summer related items, so they made a short detour and found her some reasonably stylish Bolles.

Following Jenny's directions, they found the apartment building right where she said it would be. "My God, it's so small," Nikki said. "My memory is of a huge building complex with hundreds of units and a big grass lawn out front. There are only twelve units here."

"You were a little girl."

"I know. It's a strange, interesting feeling, though." Nikki stood in the driveway and let the memories flood over her. She was six when her brothers dared her to throw a rock at a teeming hive of wasps. She didn't get away fast enough and suffered dozens of painful stings. Her mother was unsympathetic, telling her she got what she deserved, while her complicit older brothers got away without punishment. She remembered getting yelled at by the old German man in the neighboring yard for climbing the fence and stealing small sour apples from his tree. She had stood in this exact spot as a seven-year-old waiting for her parents to return from a week in Rome, and was a few feet away from the spot where she slipped on the ice while running toward a still moving school bus and came dangerously close to being crushed under the rear wheel. She lost her favorite gray winter jacket with the shiny silver buckle somewhere on these grounds and got in trouble for that, too.

"I remember we lived in apartment number six. Let's go take a look inside."

They entered the small lobby. Nikki was not conscious of any particular memory of the stairs, but they seemed oddly familiar as she was drawn like a magnet to the third floor.

"I must have run up these stairs a thousand times in the three years we lived here. It's giving me goose bumps."

As they arrived on the landing, Rick and Nikki were startled when the door opened.

"Oh!" Nikki jumped back into Rick's arms.

"I didn't mean to scare you." The middle-aged man was slight, no more than five-foot-eight, with rapidly thinning, sandy blond hair, fair skin, black horn-rimmed glasses, and the nondescript look of a career bureaucrat. He wore a yellow, short sleeved bowling shirt with CHUCK stenciled on the breast pocket.

"It's okay. I was so caught up in reminiscing I didn't even think someone would actually live here," Nikki said. "You see, I lived in this apartment for three years when I was a little girl."

"That must have been when it was an Air Force base; it's an Army base now. Would you like to see the apartment?"

"Oh, I couldn't impose," Nikki said, but really wanting to with all her heart.

"Nonsense, I would be delighted to show you around. You've come so far. Take a few minutes to reminisce, besides, it might be fun to watch your reactions."

"Are you sure?"

"Positive. Please come in."

The memories were overpowering once Nikki stepped into the small foyer. She remembered sliding on the wood floors in her booted pajamas, and her father almost taking a tumble on his crutches after hurting his knee at the base picnic softball game.

The kitchen off to the right overlooked the driveway and lawn. She remembered her mother standing at the window and cheering as a particularly nasty family, with several rambunctious boys sure to be future felons, was leaving after finally being transferred. She saw her old bedroom where she lay in agony after the wasp attack, and the living room, where her father would let her lie on the floor in front of his prized German hi-fi cabinet and listen to classical music.

Rick and Chuck followed politely as Nikki moved around the apartment, amused by the looks of wonder on Nikki's face as she enjoyed her private memories.

"You have been very kind, Chuck, thank you very much."

"The pleasure was all mine, believe me. Where are you off to now?"

"She wants to find the woman who was their housekeeper back then. It's possible she's still living here," Rick said.

"I've been here for more than two years now; I might be able to help. What's her name?"

"Frau Fruener."

"I think I know who you mean. She lost her husband a few months ago. If she's the same woman, she lives very near here. Come on, I'll walk you down and point you in the right direction. I'm afraid if I dawdle any longer I'll be late for bowling."

Chuck locked his door and led them back out into the bright sunshine. "She stays with her daughter now, one of those little houses over there," he said, pointing to a small residential neighborhood a little further down the street. Rick and Nikki shook Chuck's hand and thanked him again. He merely smiled, said he was glad to help and headed off to the carports in the rear of the building.

"I wonder if she'll remember me?" Nikki said.

They approached the well-kept neighborhood. An elderly German lady with a broad-brimmed hat was tending rose bushes in front of a small bungalow.

"Excuse me, do you speak English?" Nikki asked.

"Leetle beet," the old woman said.

“We’re looking for Frau Fruener,” Nikki said.

The old woman smiled in recognition and pointed to a house three doors down on the other side of the street. “With daughter now, number 19.”

“Thank you very much.”

“Bitte.” The old lady returned her attention to the roses.

Rick and Nikki walked down the street and knocked on the door of number 19. The door was opened by a short, older German woman who could have been the sister of the one tending the roses. There was only a moment of slight hesitation in the old woman’s face.

“Nikki! Nikki! Nikki!” She took Nikki’s face in both hands and kissed her on both cheeks several times.

“I guess we don’t have to worry about whether she recognizes you,” Rick said.

Nikki was pleasantly surprised by the reaction and returned the hugs and kisses. It took a few seconds for her own sense of recognition to stir up fond childhood memories of this German woman. Frau Fruener and Nikki’s mother had exchanged cards several times a year for at least a decade after their departure, but Nikki had not seen or spoken to Frau Fruener in over twenty years since her family transferred back to the States.

“Bitte, bitte!” Frau Fruener said. She motioned them into the cool darkness of the living room. Standing next to the couch was a tall, slightly overweight German woman of about thirty-five.

“Hi, you probably don’t remember me, Nikki, I am Isolde, Frau Fruener’s daughter.”

"I'm sorry, I don't. It's very nice to meet you now," Nikki laughed as she shook hands and introduced them both to Rick.

Isolde invited them to sit on the couch, followed by a rapid-fire exchange in German neither Nikki nor Rick understood. "My mother still does not speak English," Isolde said. "I will stay and translate before I go back to work. Make yourselves comfortable while my mother gets coffee. She really would like to find out what has happened to your brothers."

While Frau Fruener could be heard rattling dishes in the small kitchen at the back of the house, Rick, Nikki and Isolde chatted amiably.

"I'm so glad you're here to help, Isolde," Nikki said. "I guess I really didn't think through how I was going to communicate once I found your mother. I'm still in shock that she recognized me."

"It is not as unexpected as you might think," Isolde said. "This is a very small town and gossip travels quickly. After your stop at the bar, my mother received several phone calls from nosy neighbors telling her there was a tall, attractive American woman looking for her. Of all the American families my mother worked for over the years, yours was the only one with a daughter about your age now. So she had a little time to narrow it down before you arrived."

There was another exchange in German between the mother and daughter. "Okay, okay!" Isolde called back toward the kitchen.

"She wants me to show you the picture albums." Isolde moved to the built-in bookshelf to the left of the simple stone fireplace and began rummaging through the dozens of large albums.

"Here we are," she said.

Frau Fruener returned with the tray of coffee and pastries. They settled on the couch with Frau Freuner seated between Rick and Nikki. Isolde hovered over her mother's shoulder and translated as her mother guided Nikki through the albums. As they laughed and reminisced over the next hour, Nikki was moved by Frau Fruener's genuine reactions to the photographs neither had seen for years. Many of the pictures were duplicates of those in her own mother's albums, but there were many others Nikki had never seen before, offering her a view of that time in her life from Frau Fruener's perspective.

Nikki brought Frau Fruener and Isolde up to date on the lives of her brothers and parents. A sense of sadness showed in Frau Fruener's eyes when Nikki told her of her youngest brother's death in a motorcycle accident. Nikki realized this old German woman, whom she barely remembered, probably spent more time with the Dunn children than her own parents had during their time here. Frau Fruener remembered her own experiences, and despite the language barrier and cultural differences, strong emotional attachments had been established with the Dunn children that were still evident today.

They finished with the last album and sat in a comfortable silence, and it occurred to Nikki that Frau Fruener had been a part of her family. In some strange and wonderful way, they had stolen a few moments to recapture that sense of family, so strong it refused to go away even after two decades.

Isolde broke the silence and asked where they were staying.

"We arrived today, and don't have any set plans yet," Rick said evasively. "Can you recommend a decent hotel?"

There was another discussion between mother and daughter.

"My mother won't hear of you staying in a hotel. We own the house next door. It has been empty since my father passed away and my mother moved in here with me. My mother would be pleased if you would stay."

Rick and Nikki looked at each other and quickly agreed. Frau Fruener retrieved the key from a drawer in the kitchen and led them next door. The house was identical to the one they just left, and it had the musty smell of being closed up in the summer heat. Isolde went around the lower floor, opened all the windows, turned on the floor fan in the living room, and found some clean linens in one of the closets.

"There are plenty of towels in the bathroom, so please make yourselves at home," Isolde said.

"Thank you," Rick said. "Right now a shower and some clean clothes sounds pretty good."

Rick helped Nikki make the bed upstairs, then took some linens and made up the couch in the living room.

"Why don't you shower first," Rick suggested. "I'll give you some privacy and run into town to get fixings for dinner. Maybe something light, like a big salad with fresh bread, and a bottle of white wine."

Nikki didn't argue.

She undressed and stood in the steaming shower for a long time. It felt good to have some privacy and a few minutes alone. Refreshed and dressed in running shorts and a tee shirt, she went downstairs. Rick was in the kitchen chopping vegetables and washing the lettuce for the salad.

"Did you leave me enough hot water?" he asked.

"I have no clue, I wasn't even thinking about that, sorry."

"It's okay, I'll shower after dinner," Rick said. He poured her a glass of wine. "Sit, relax, and have a glass of this local chardonnay. It's really quite good."

She accepted the wine, sat at the plain wood table next to a window overlooking a small garden in the back yard, and took a sip.

"Oh, it is good."

"I take no credit," Rick said. "The lady at the market suggested it."

They ate dinner mostly in silence, winding down after twenty-four hours on the run. The wine hit Nikki quickly, so she said goodnight and went back upstairs.

As tired as she was, she didn't fall asleep right away. Rick asking her about Greg had touched a nerve. Greg had made his feelings quite clear: he was madly in love with her and wanted to spend the rest of his life with her. While Nikki didn't doubt his sincerity, she had only known him a few months, and she worried the depth of her feelings toward him weren't as strong. Maybe in time she would know, but for now she preferred to take it slow. It had caused tension in their working relationship, something that would have to be worked out sooner rather than later once she returned.

If she returned.

CHAPTER TWENTY-FIVE

While Rick and Nikki slept in Birkenfeld, Alexei Persoff was a worried man in Paris. The accidental death of Gorky and his murder of Inspector Bonnard had complicated the situation enormously, and he had nothing to report at this meeting at La Cervoise. Henri arrived with a large manila envelope, and dropped it on the small table where Alexei was nursing his second beer.

"This is what we have so far," Henri said. "It was the holiday weekend and it took longer than expected."

Alexei was impressed with the detailed information in the dossiers. There was complete biographical information on all four subjects, including employment histories, education, and family information. He noted Nikki's family had spent time in Paris when she was a child, that she spent a semester at the Sorbonne and spoke French reasonably well. He briefly scanned files for Tim Schroeder, Greg Irvine, and Rick Asher. They revealed nothing that led him to believe any of them were with the police or an intelligence agency. Henri's cell phone buzzed as Alexei put the files down.

"Oui." Thirty seconds later, he ended the call.

"A small break perhaps," he said. "My contact at border patrol has learned Rick Asher and Nikki Dunn crossed the border into Germany yesterday morning on the night train to Munich, using their own passports. The Germans log all Eurail passes on their initiation date."

"Typical German efficiency," Alexei said. "Wait a minute." He picked up the dossiers again and rifled through them again until he found what he wanted.

"That's very interesting. Twenty years ago, Nikki's father was stationed at the Air Force base in Birkenfeld. That's only a couple of hours from Munich. Maybe they are running there to hide."

"They could have stayed in Munich, gone on to Berlin or a dozen other places," Henri said.

"Can your contacts at Interpol put out a bulletin to look for them specifically?"

"Not yet," Henri said. "We must be careful until we see how the authorities react to the deaths on Rue de Bellechasse, especially with regard to Deputy Inspector Bonnard. I have seen only a brief mention of it in the papers, which makes me very suspicious."

"We have to do something though," Alexei said.

"I agree. Considering the circumstances, it does seem a coincidence. Rent a car and drive directly to Birkenfeld. If these people are amateurs, we should catch up with them quickly."

"Any luck with the owner of the restaurant?" Alexei asked.

"Yes, he is at a safe house here in Paris. We will deal with him when the time comes. You concentrate on finding the other two. Don't worry about deadlines, our orders are to find them and eliminate them. Quickly."

ᔕ

Henri walked off, head down deep in thought. As he made his way through the narrow, dark streets east of the *Champs Élysée*, Henri Toulon assessed the latest developments, and frowned. He had done many unscrupulous and despicable things in his life, and passing on orders to eliminate two potentially uninvolved young people was a line he thought he would never cross. Whoring, drinking, and manipulating the financial markets by using insider information was one thing, but the murder of innocents, even by association, was something else entirely. He knew the time had come for him to disassociate himself from his dangerous cohorts.

Besides, his carefully created tough guy image was all an act. In his youth, Henri dreamed of becoming the next Gerard Depardieu. He took acting classes, but was only successful in landing minor roles in stage productions in Paris and London. The scars on his face were indeed knife wounds, inflicted by a stoned, overzealous actor in a fight scene from a production of *Henry IV*, not a street fight. Henri Toulon wasn't even his real name, but a pathetic homage to Henri de Toulouse-Lautrec.

As a young man, Henri realized he had an inherent understanding of complex calculations and how the financial world worked. As he was always at the top of his classes throughout his education, everyone saw a bright future for him in the business world.

Henri would have no part of it. He was so naturally intelligent he was easily bored, which led to experimenting with drugs and associating with a decidedly unsavory crowd. His parents and professors were horrified by his lack of concern regarding his future and were constantly reminding him what a waste he was making of his life. In his early twenties he abandoned their conventions and began life on his own. The idea of taking his talent and intelligence and working to make others money was not going to be his path. He would succeed, keep his earnings for himself, and live life his way, not the way others wanted.

Taking the proceeds from a particularly profitable drug deal, he invested in several thoroughly researched companies. He continued to educate himself with his profits, becoming a self-taught expert in international exchange rates and commerce. He traveled extensively, kept himself informed on international politics and upcoming technologies. He was a multimillionaire by the time he was thirty, and was now in his early forties.

He met Victor Ischenko and Frank DeMarchand while acting as financial advisor for a quasi-legitimate agricultural trade deal between a European Union company and a former Soviet bloc country. Their mutual love of breaking the rules, making easy money, expensive booze, and cheap women had blossomed into a tacit business arrangement benefiting both sides. He ingratiated himself into Ischenko's inner circle and had provided assistance to them for several years now, acting as a conduit for the transfer of orders, brokering information, and as their security chief in Paris. He smoothed the way for the slave-trade smuggling operations by using his high-level contacts at the Prefecture and the local embassies, and was quite adept at eliciting insider information on upcoming transactions. He shared the obscene profits generated by his timely investments with both Dante International and his informants.

His main contact at the Prefecture considered it gauche to accept a bribe. He traded information with Henri, allocated resources away from any serious investigation of smuggled women, and, in exchange, they both enjoyed the delights provided by *Femmes Invitée,* at Victor Ischenko's expense.

The arrangement had run smoothly for years, but like all other business cycles, the current arrangement had run its course. Henri prided himself on his ability to read situations, and believed it was time for him to sit on the sidelines for a while. Like many astute investors, he realized it was better to leave a little on the table and not get greedy.

CHAPTER TWENTY-SIX

Greg Irvine woke up in a cold sweat. It took a minute to get his bearings and realize he was not at home. Jack had taken him to the huge top floor, three-bedroom apartment on Rue de la Tour in the 16th, near the Bois de Boulogne, tended the bump on his head, and made him comfortable in the bedroom behind the kitchen.

Greg had slept most of the day on Monday. Late in the afternoon, Jack brought him soup, bread, and tea, and checked his wound again. Both decided there was probably no concussion, and Greg quickly tired and drifted off to sleep again. The Tylenol with codeine helped the pain considerably.

Now, in the darkness and silence only the middle of the night can bring, Greg decided he felt a lot better. He slowly moved to a sitting position on the bed, rested for a moment, and tried to stand. He wobbled at first, but gradually regained his sense of balance. He went through the kitchen and found the door leading into the living room ajar, a dim shaft of light making a diagonal pattern on the floor. He moved cautiously, stepping into a room three times the size of his small studio. The light emanated from a lamp near the front window.

Jack sat on an ottoman watching the traffic on Rue de la Tour. "How do you feel?" he asked.

"Better. I'm thirsty, hungry, and I really need a shower."

"Good idea. Meet me in the kitchen after; I'll rustle up scrambled eggs and toast. You want coffee, too?"

"That would be great."

"Call me if you need any help," Jack said.

Ten minutes later, Greg entered the gourmet kitchen in an undersized terrycloth robe and watched Jack work efficiently at the stove. A large mug of steaming coffee was already on the granite-topped island.

"So, are you going to tell me where we are, and what the fuck is going on?" Greg asked. He sat down and sipped his coffee.

Jack turned and smiled. "I guess I owe you that, since I sent your friends running for their lives."

"Rick's smart and resourceful, and Nikki is no dummy. That improves their chances until we figure out what to do. Now, please start at the beginning and tell me how we got here?"

"Well, since you asked so nicely," Jack said. He expertly whisked the eggs in a large bowl and poured the mixture into the skillet.

"Tim Schroeder's brother, Eric, was my partner in LA. I didn't get there in time to save him, but I'm doing everything I can to make sure those responsible don't get away with it. I'm on special assignment with a top-secret, joint French and American task force, code-named Operation Mary Magdalene. We're trying to stop the smuggling of women as sex slaves by the Russian mafia and find Eric's murderer. I report to Bill Seacrest of the FBI in Washington and work directly with Chief Inspector Covyeau at Interpol here in Paris. The task force set up your apartments so we could keep an eye on you and protect you in case of an emergency. I'm sorry I didn't get there in time last night to save you that bump on your head."

"So Tim's known about it all along?" Greg asked, dumbfounded.

"A few days after the funeral, Bill Seacrest approached Tim and me for help with the task force. After recruiting Magda in Moscow, Tim's job was peripheral. We use the restaurant as a safe place to meet and exchange information away from the watchful eyes of the rank-and-file. None of us thought you would be in any real danger, especially with the task force keeping a constant eye on the restaurant and your apartments. It doesn't help when a task force member is one of the bad guys."

"You're playing with people's lives here, Jack. We could have all been killed and none of us knew anything. That's really chickenshit, man."

"You're right, and I'm sorry. We briefed Tim extensively, plus gave him a complete set of false documents and a protocol to follow in case he needed to leave in a hurry. I've already heard from him; he's in a safe house here in Paris waiting further instructions. I know he never meant for any of you to be in any danger. We're going to make it right, I promise. We were getting close to a breakthrough, and that's why they killed Magda."

"What was Magda's role in all of this? Who was she really?"

"Magda was a high-class call girl in Moscow, somehow escaping the fate of the other girls. She knew Katarina, the girl left for dead in Los Angeles who got this whole thing started. After debriefing Katarina, Bill Seacrest got Tim to contact and recruit Magda. She volunteered to infiltrate an exclusive private escort service called *Femmes Invitée*. She posed as a customer who preferred women, and got one of the girls, Svetlana, to open up and trust her. We were finally putting together some big pieces of the puzzle when it all went south. At her last Saturday night tryst with Svetlana, Magda was going to get the name of a high-ranking official who controls the whole operation here in Paris and possibly Lyon, too. Magda must have learned their cover was blown and tried to get to L'Avenue Bar & Grill to warn Tim. We didn't have the brothel's address until earlier tonight. By the time we raided the place, there was nobody there. We have no idea where Svetlana is."

"Considering what happened last night, do you think Inspector Bonnard was the high-ranking official?" Greg asked.

"He was certainly a major player, but he wasn't high enough in the chain of command to control everything. He reports to someone else, and we think that's the name Magda got before she was shot. That person is very high up, wields enormous influence, and has a lot of resources at his disposal."

Jack served up the eggs, toast, and more coffee. The two sat in silence and ate. They both jumped at the sound of Jack's cell phone buzzing on the counter.

Greg listened to Jack's side of the conversation while he finished the surprisingly good breakfast.

When Jack hung up the phone he looked worried.

"What?" Greg asked.

"These folks we're after have some serious juice. We have a couple of people stashed with the Paris police and Interpol monitoring all special requests for data. In an effort to protect Rick and Nikki, I told them to watch for any unusual requests regarding Eurail passes. Not only was there an unauthorized query on Eurail pass initiations, but someone accessed and downloaded complete dossiers on you, Tim, Nikki, and Rick."

"Jesus Christ, this is out of control," Greg said. "Were Rick and Nikki's names on the Eurail list?"

"Yes. They initiated their passes and entered Germany early yesterday morning."

"We've got to warn them," Greg said.

Jack was already dialing. He put the phone on speaker and they waited for the connection.

"If we don't know exactly where they are, neither do the bad guys," Jack said.

The call went to voicemail.

"Rick probably turned it off when they went to bed. It's the middle of the night, you know, even in Germany." Jack handed the phone to Greg. "Leave a message for Rick. He'll recognize your voice. Tell them to keep moving and to call us immediately. Maybe they'll figure out how to pick up the message. If not, he's supposed to call in later today anyway. We'll be okay."

Greg left a quick message and handed the phone back. "This is insane, Jack. Rick is a good friend, and Nikki is the love of my life. You've put them out there all alone, in terrible danger through no fault of their own. We have to help them."

"As long as they stay on the move and keep in touch with the untraceable phone, they're probably safer than if they were here in Paris."

"I feel helpless," Greg said.

"It helps to keep busy. Since I cooked, why don't you clean the dishes? Take it easy; you don't want to overdo it with that bump on your head."

CHAPTER TWENTY-SEVEN

Nikki came downstairs on Tuesday morning and found Rick still asleep on the couch. More like passed out. There was a second bottle of wine on the coffee table.

Empty.

So far, Rick didn't seem to be taking her advice.

She went to the kitchen, found the coffee, and set it to brew. The aroma wafted out to the living room and roused Rick. He stumbled to the kitchen in his boxers and a three-day beard growth.

"Is the coffee ready yet?" he asked.

Nikki was worried. Rick obviously never made it to the shower last night, opting to dive into the second bottle of chardonnay.

"In a minute," Nikki said. "Why don't you go shower? It'll be ready by the time you're finished."

Rick grumbled something inaudible, picked up his backpack, and headed upstairs.

I guess he's not a morning person, Nikki thought.

Frau Fruener insisted Nikki and Rick come for breakfast and meet her entire family: Isolde's two teenaged sons, her husband Peter, and the old lady they met the day before tending roses, who turned out to be Frau Fruener's widowed cousin. Isolde and her teenaged sons patiently acted as translators, while the older German women and Peter were fascinated by stories of life in the United States and Paris. Nikki and Rick pretended they were starting an extended vacation with no set destinations. There were many suggestions as to where to go next, and Rick suggested they might visit an old friend of his in Florence. The gathering finally broke up when Isolde and her husband returned to work.

"So, what's our next move?" Rick asked.

"Jack said to keep moving, so I guess we should follow that advice, pack, say our goodbyes, and get the hell out of here."

"Where do you want to go?" Rick looked over Nikki's shoulder as she pored over a map of Western Europe.

"Let's let fate decide, the unpredictability will increase our chances. There's a number of trains heading in all directions from Saarbrüken; we'll pick one and go."

They repacked their small bags. "I should check the phone battery," Rick said as he rummaged through his back-pack. "We'll need to pick up a charger and an adapter soon."

The phone beeped when he turned it on and checked the display. "Seems to be fine; all the bars are full." He was about to turn it off when it beeped again.

"There's a message in the voice mail, but we don't know how to access it or the password," he said.

"Try *86."

"It worked. Now it's asking for the password."

"Try 1234#," Nikki said. "Maybe we'll get lucky."

Rick punched the numbers. "Nope."

"Try MAGDA#."

"Unbelievable, it worked. You're a genius."

Nikki didn't like the look on Rick's face as he lowered the phone. "What is it?"

"Greg wants us to call him back ASAP. He insisted we keep moving, too."

"That settles it, let's go!"

They were out of the house and next door saying good-bye to Frau Fruener in less than two minutes. They promised to come back and visit, and not wanting to use their numbers in Paris, Rick gave her the cell phone number. Without Isol-de, Frau Fruener didn't understand everything, but she had tears in her eyes as Rick and Nikki left, trying not to look like they were in too much of a hurry.

As soon as they were out of sight and headed to the bus station, Rick hit speed dial #1, and waited.

"Hi, Rick, are you okay?" Jack asked.

"We're fine, so far. We are on our way …"

"Don't tell me where you are, just in case. I see you figured out the password. Good work."

"Nikki figured it out, I followed instructions," Rick said. "What can you tell us about what's going on?"

Jack spent the next few minutes coming clean with Rick, and bringing him up to date.

"They know we entered Germany, but that's all they know for sure at this point, right?" Rick asked.

"Yes, but with the dossiers they can make some educated guesses, so we'll have to assume they have people on the way to find you."

"Wait a minute," Rick said. "Now that we're out of France, why don't we find the nearest American Embassy and get help there?"

"I considered that. Unfortunately, we have concerns that some of our embassy people are involved. The Russians have targeted our diplomatic and military personnel with these women; you know the cliché, spilling state secrets over pillow talk. I can't take the chance someone would sell you down the river to save their own hide. We're starting to sense the power and reach of these unnamed officials, including a highly placed American. Maybe we can change plans in a few days after we learn more on this end. For now, keep moving! There should be plenty of opportunities this time of year to find crowded tourist areas. If you cross a border into another country, do it on a packed bus or train or in the middle of the night."

"When should we check in again?"

"You have the password for messages; check in sometime every day and I'll keep you up to date. If anything happens here, I'll call you. If I miss you, I'll leave a message. "

"How's Greg?"

"Better. Talk to him," Jack handed the phone over.

"Hey, Rick," Greg said.

"How's that nasty bump on your head?"

"Getting better by the minute, especially now that I know you're both safe. Please watch out for Nikki; I don't know what I'd do if something happened to her. Be careful." He said goodbye and handed the phone back to Jack.

"Remember now, stay with the tourists and keep moving!" Jack cautioned once more.

Rick and Nikki raced to the bus station, catching the first available bus to Saarbrüken, arriving in midafternoon. They made the short walk to the train station and found a train leaving in twenty minutes, heading south to Zurich. From there they could connect with a night train to Florence.

"Fate has led the way," Nikki said.

"What do you mean?"

"You said we might visit your friend in Florence."

"That was idle conversation; I didn't mean it."

"Even better. Let's go."

"Geez, you figure out one password, and all of a sudden you're the boss?" Rick teased.

Nikki ignored him and walked toward the train.

CHAPTER TWENTY-EIGHT

Alexei got out of his rented car and stretched his legs after the long drive. Like Rick and Nikki, he gravitated to The Office. He went in, sat at the bar, and ordered a local brew. As the bartender set down the large cold stein, Alexei took some postcards and the dossier photographs of Greg, Rick, and Nikki from his shirt pocket and set them on the bar. He pretended to be oblivious to everyone, reading some of the postcards and writing others; however, he strategically placed the snapshots so those around him could see them.

As luck would have it, Jenny was on duty again. It took about ten minutes before her curiosity piqued. "Friends of yours?" she asked.

"Yes, college friends from many years ago," Alexei said pleasantly. "I haven't seen them for a long time."

"You're kidding! She was in here yesterday." Jenny pointed to Nikki's picture. "She was looking for her family's housekeeper from years ago, Frau Fruener."

"An amazing coincidence," Alexei agreed. "Are they still in town?"

"I don't know. I gave them directions to Premier Mart and off they went. I assume they found Frau Fruener because they haven't been back."

"Would you be so kind to give me directions too?" Alexei asked. "Maybe I can catch them."

For the second day in a row, Jenny gave the same directions.

Psychopaths can be very charming at times, and it was certainly true when Alexei got lucky again. Isolde was leaving her house as Alexei approached.

"Excuse me, do you speak English?" he asked Isolde politely.

"Yes, can I help you?"

"I have just had an amazing coincidence. My name is Tim Schroeder," he lied. "I am on vacation and found out some old college friends of mine arrived yesterday, looking for a Frau Fruener. Do you know where I might find her?"

"You are not the only one with an amazing coincidence," Isolde said. "Frau Fruener is my mother. You must be looking for Rick and Nikki."

"Are they still here?"

"You've just missed them; they left a few hours ago, but didn't say where they were going."

Alexei's shoulders sagged in disappointment. "That's a shame. I haven't seen them for years and would love to catch up with them. Are you sure they didn't say where they were going?"

"Rick said they might visit a friend in Florence, but had no definite plans," she said. "I have an idea, wait here, please."

She rushed back into the house. There was a flurry of female German voices, and Isolde reemerged. "I almost forgot, they left their cell phone number with my mother." She handed him a small pink Post-it note with the hastily scrawled number.

"How can I ever thank you?"

"It is my pleasure. They are such nice people, and we had a wonderful visit. My mother was quite touched."

"I will be sure to tell them," Alexei said, gently putting his hand on her arm. "Now I must go; I have an appointment for dinner in Munich this evening. Thank you again."

"You are welcome. Travel safely."

Alexei walked back toward downtown. Before moving out of sight, he turned and waved to Isolde as she got in her car and drove in the other direction. As soon as he got back to his car, he called Henri.

"It is Alexei," he said without waiting for an answer. He was sure Henri would not be interested in pleasantries. "They were here, but I missed them. I have a cell phone number and the possibility they are going to Florence. I will fly there tonight and should arrive much earlier than them, if they are traveling by train. It will be a simple matter to monitor the train station and intercept them. Can you trace the cell phone?" He gave him the number.

"*Merci*," was all Henri said, and hung up.

CHAPTER TWENTY-NINE

The train from Mannheim had been crowded, with every seat in first class taken. The night train to Florence didn't leave until 10 p.m., which gave Rick time to reserve two couchettes. The English-speaking young woman at the ticket counter informed them they would have to share the compartment with four others, but at least they would be able to lie down. The train would arrive in Florence at six-forty-five the next morning, but additional charges of twenty-four Euros per bunk were necessary.

"Unfortunately, couchettes are not included with your passes," she said.

"That's fine," Rick said. He gladly paid the extra money. *"Danke."*

"Bitte."

The evening was still quite warm, so rather than carry their luggage, Rick and Nikki stored the extra bags in one of the train station lockers. Zurich is geographically almost the exact center of Western Europe, so it made sense as a major center for train connections. There were three floors beneath the station with supermarkets, hair salons, luggage stores, newsstands, waiting rooms, showers, bathrooms, bars, and restaurants. They found an electronics store and bought a charger and adapter for the phone.

With several hours to kill, they wandered into town with no particular destination, and ended up in a restaurant tucked away on a side street. Through the windows they could see the candlelit tables, white tablecloths, and a sign that said AIR CONDITIONED in three languages

"This place looks fine," Nikki said.

A welcome blast of cold air hit them as they entered. They were greeted immediately by a well-dressed host. "A table for two?" he asked.

"Yes, please."

He led them to a small table near the window, holding the chair for Nikki.

"Danke."

"You're welcome," he said. "I speak English." He handed them menus and the wine list. "I recommend the Wiener schnitzel, the specialty of the house. May I get you something to drink? We have a wonderful house red wine; a carafe perhaps?"

"Not for me," Rick said. "Pellegrino, if you have it." If their enemies already knew they had been to Germany, Rick knew it was time for him to clean up his act.

"Of course," the host said.

"We'll have a large bottle, chilled please," Rick said.

"And you, madam?" the waiter asked Nikki.

"I'll share the Pellegrino," she said.

"Right away." He left them alone at the table.

"It won't bother me if you have wine," Rick said.

"Thanks, but I think it's best if we keep our wits about us," Nikki said.

A waiter who didn't speak English returned with water and bread, accompanied by the host, who quickly translated their order for the house specialty. Rick and Nikki relaxed in their little nook, enjoyed the ice cold mineral water in silence, and watched the flow of people through the window. The air conditioning did its job, a respite from the summer heat.

"We've been lucky so far finding others who speak English," Nikki said. "We are at a disadvantage in really being fluent in only French and English."

"I know," Rick said. "But it's the tourist season; we should do okay with French, English, and a good pair of hands."

"We can only hope. If homicidal maniacs weren't chasing us, this would be a lot more fun," Nikki said.

"It does put a slight damper on things," Rick said, "I hate being on the defensive. I'd like to turn the tables on those killers."

"So, let's assess the situation. Between the two of us we should be able to come up with something," Nikki said. "Let's start with the basics. First, we don't know for sure they're after us, but I suggest we assume they are. That's bad. Second, we don't know where we're going, so neither do they. That's good. Third, they know what we look like, but we have no clue about them, and that's a real big problem. It could be anyone, and we wouldn't know until it's too late."

"All good points," Rick agreed. "Any suggestions?"

"As a matter of fact, yes," Nikki said. "We're supposed to be tourists, so let's play the part. We go back to the electronics store and buy a good digital camera. We can take pictures of those around us and see if we notice anything. If we do find something, we get the pictures to Jack and Greg by setting up an online e-mail account at a cyber café somewhere. We can run the idea by them the next time we call."

"That's a great idea, Nikki."

Buying the camera was straightforward. Rick opted for a moderately priced digital SLR with an extra zoom lens, a USB connection, and a handsome black leather carrying case. They wandered back upstairs to the platform level and retrieved their bags from the locker. They had learned their lesson on the night train to Munich, so they took the time to stock up on bottled water, bread, cheese, and chocolate bars.

They arrived at the platform in plenty of time and, while waiting to board the train, repacked the bags. They decided to keep the passports, passes, cash, some of the food, the laptop, and the new camera in Rick's backpack, in case they needed to move fast and only carry one bag.

The receipt from the ticket vendor, listing the car and compartment numbers, made it easy to get settled. They were still vigilant though, watching the platform for any suspicious behavior. Their traveling companions in the compartment were an Indian computer programmer named Krishnan going home to Florence; a Zurich housewife, Gabi, taking time away from a husband and kids; her friend Evelyn, avoiding a jealous boyfriend; and a young woman so painfully shy she never said a word. The quarters were extremely cramped; the six of them would be spending the next nine hours sharing a space the size of the average walk-in closet in America.

The train pulled out of the station right on time and they all started to relax. Twenty minutes later, the Swiss conductor arrived and took their passports and passes.

"The Italian conductor will return them in the morning before arriving to Florence," he said.

This caused Rick and Nikki some consternation, but unless there was an Internet connection on the train, there was little danger before they disappeared into the swarms of tourists in Florence.

Gabi and Evelyn turned out to be fun. They wanted to practice their English, so they shared their wine with everyone to encourage the conversation. Rick declined the wine and sipped bottled water. Gabi had been an au pair in Florence as a teenager, caring for two rambunctious little boys, ages one and three. She was on her way to see them for the first time in two decades.

"I can't wait to see them, even though they probably won't remember me," she said.

"You never know," Nikki said. She proceeded to tell the story of her visit with Frau Fruener. The coincidence of the two stories spurred on the conversation.

Gabi and Evelyn were full of questions about America, India, and Krishnan's life in Florence. They spoke of art, Italian food and wine, and other travel experiences. Evelyn had only seen pictures of Michelangelo's *David* and couldn't wait to see it in person. Gabi fondly remembered a torrid affair with a waiter on the Greek island of Santorini. Rick kept everyone laughing with his story of a four-day conference in New Orleans. He got a total of three hours' sleep in the four days, praying every morning he wouldn't see his boss in the elevator as he dragged his drunk, bedraggled ass back to his room to change before meeting the boss for breakfast.

The impromptu party finished with the news of an impending Italian rail strike.

"The rail mechanics union is not happy with the negotiations for a new labor contract, so in sympathy, all rail workers might go on strike tomorrow at 6 a.m. in an act of solidarity," Gabi explained.

"But we are due in Florence at six-forty-five, surely they'll take us all the way," Rick said.

"Perhaps not," Evelyn said. "Two years ago I was between Rome and Brindisi when a strike began at midnight. I spent a hot night in a second-class compartment without air conditioning, food, or water, and hassled by obnoxious teenaged boys. It was terrible."

"How long was the strike?" Rick asked.

"I don't remember," she laughed. "The train moved to an abandoned station sometime around 3 a.m. At dawn we were loaded on buses to Naples, switched buses, and went on to Brindisi. I immediately took the ferry to Corfu and Piraeus.

By the time I got back three weeks later, the trains were running again."

"Maybe we'll get lucky this time," Rick said.

For the second time in three nights, Rick and Nikki prepared to spend the night in close quarters with perfect strangers. There were three numbered bunks on each wall, the seats becoming the lowest bunks and the upper two pulled down and hanging on chains. Rick and Nikki ended up on the top two with Gabi and Evelyn on the bottom two. It was impossible for all six to prepare the space at one time, so they took turns making last trips to the toilet and pulling down blankets and sheets from the cubbyhole above the door.

After everyone was settled, Rick climbed down the small ladder and eased into the corridor. He powered up the phone and punched speed dial #1 again. Jack picked up on the second ring.

"Hey, Rick, are you guys okay?"

"We're fine, on the move as instructed. Any news?"

"The French authorities are obviously interested in talking to you and Nikki. Covyeau and I stalled them as planned, truthfully saying we don't know where you are. We're lying to them about you leaving early Sunday afternoon, long before the murders in your apartment took place. When I went back up to the apartment from the brasserie and found Inspector Bonnard dead, I put the cocaine back in his pocket. It's buying us enough time to keep the heat off you for a least a couple more days. We're still trying to find Svetlana, but so far no luck."

"How's Greg?"

"The swelling is down dramatically and, except for a slight discoloration, he looks almost normal. He was at the restaurant most of the afternoon supervising the installation of the new front doors. He's been cleared by the doctors, so we sent him back to his apartment. I've got a man keeping an eye on the area. I spoke to him about an hour ago and he said he was going to get some sleep."

"Don't you ever sleep?"

"I'll sleep after I get you and Nikki back here safely."

"Don't get too macho; we need you to help us stay alive."

"Thanks for the vote of confidence," Jack said.

"We should all try and get some sleep; talk to you tomorrow," Rick said.

"Take good care of Nikki," Jack said.

Rick turned the phone off, quietly reentered the compartment and climbed up to the cramped bunk. He drifted into a fitful sleep as the train headed south through the dark Italian countryside.

CHAPTER THIRTY

"You know, we have other things in common other than not wanting children," Joëlle said.

They were in the massive bed in the master bedroom, lying naked in *la position de cuillère B,* this time with Joëlle snuggled to Jack's back. This left Joëlle's right hand free to roam about his body, lightly tracing the contour of his muscled thighs, fingering his chest hair, and then wandering lower.

Jack had figured out Joëlle's pattern. *La position de cuillère A*, with her back to him, was a precursor for sleep, while *la position B* was a prelude to sex. Her hand was reaching even lower when Jack gently grabbed it and held it still.

"Like what?" Jack asked.

"We both have lost a loved one to violent death," Joëlle said. "That alone is enough to cause a similar grief, but it goes even deeper than that. We both feel responsible in some way for their deaths. If not for our actions, they might still be alive. That is a heavy burden to carry."

"I never should have let Eric go to that office building alone," Jack said. "It is my fault."

"If you had gone together, you might both be dead, did you ever think of that?" Joëlle asked.

"If we were together, DeMarchand would never have got the drop on us. This whole thing would have ended differently. For one thing, I probably wouldn't be here in Paris."

"Maybe it was meant to be," Joëlle said. "Maybe we were supposed to find each other, and help each other. In a way, we both need to redeem ourselves. I know Claude would have wanted me to be happy, and I think Eric would want you to move on with your life, too."

Jack said nothing.

"Jack," Joëlle said. "We need each other right now. That doesn't mean we'll need each other after we catch DeMarchand and Ischenko. I don't want anything from you other than your company and compassion. We'll figure everything else out later."

"All right, later," Jack said. He released her hand.

A few minutes later, he turned and rolled on top of her. He knew now, as he got lost in the warmth of her body, they would exorcise their mutual guilt, affirm their will to move on with their lives, and lift the black clouds hanging over them.

An hour later Joëlle was snoring lightly at Jack's side. He envied the ease of her slumber, because tonight he couldn't slow his mind down enough to sleep.

The open window allowed the cool summer breeze to blow across his still damp skin. It reminded him of summer nights as a child, lying awake in his parents' un-air-conditioned house in Torrance, California, listening to Vin Scully's radio call of the Dodgers baseball games from Chavez Ravine. Well, he wasn't in Torrance anymore, and no longer a child. He was a responsible adult, halfway around the world, and the reality was he had to find DeMarchand. He wouldn't stop until he did.

The task force investigation was proceeding slower than Jack would have liked. Covyeau worked at a deliberate pace, and too easily accepted the obvious unproductivity of Bonnard and Leveque. Jack wrote it off as a cultural difference, but not for much longer.

It was another hour before he nestled closer to Joëlle's warmth, and slept.

Finally.

❧

However, in Birkenfeld Isolde could not sleep. Thoughts of timing and coincidence kept making her mind run in circles. Something right outside those circles made her toss and turn, nagging her about the conversations over breakfast and the surprising arrival of Rick and Nikki's friend, Tim Schroeder. Every time she got close, it drifted away.

Rick and Nikki's visit had had an energizing effect on her mother. Since her father's death a few months ago, her mother was understandably a little lost. The marriage, to a man she had grown up with and known all her life, had survived sixty-one years. Now he was gone, and, facing her own mortality, she had grown quiet and listless. Isolde was sure it was part of the natural grieving process, but it was very different from the fun-loving mother she had known. It was nice to see a spark back in her mother's eyes in the last twenty-four hours. The timing of the visit could not have come at a better time, she thought. Sometimes timing is everything.

She sat up, instantly wide awake. Now she knew what was bothering her, but she had to check with her mother to be sure. She put on her robe and went downstairs to her mother's room.

"What's the matter, Isolde?" She turned on the light and patted the bed for her daughter to sit.

"I am not sure. It is probably nothing, but I have a strange feeling the man I gave Rick and Nikki's number was not who he said he was."

"Why?"

"That's what I want to check with you. First of all, don't you think it is a strange coincidence he is here so soon after Rick and Nikki?"

"Not necessarily, Isolde. It is the summer tourist season. You have been very busy at the travel agency, so maybe it is not so strange."

"Perhaps, so let's go over our conversation at breakfast this morning. I remember translating to you that Rick and Nikki had only recently met in Paris and decided to travel together. They grew up in different parts of California and went to different colleges. Isn't that right?"

"Yes, that is what I remember you telling us. So?"

"The man calling himself Tim Schroeder told me they were old college friends and he hadn't seen them in years." Isolde said. "That doesn't make sense. Why did he lie to me?"

"Call them and put your mind to rest. Their number is next to the phone in the kitchen."

"But it is the middle of the night," Isolde said.

"I am old, but not feeble-minded. Just leave them a message."

"Of course, how stupid of me."

Frau Fruener encouraged her concerned daughter off the bed and followed her to the kitchen phone. She watched with interest as Isolde dialed the long number and waited.

"You were right mother, I am getting voicemail," she said.

Isolde left a message in English, none of which Frau Fruener understood. They wouldn't find out until much later the call saved Rick and Nikki's lives.

ᔕ

The train did indeed stop at precisely 6:00 a.m., on the outskirts of Florence. The passengers were restless, and roamed the corridors looking for an explanation. A few minutes later the engines shut down.

"It's déjà vu all over again," Evelyn said.

There was nothing any of them could do, so Rick took the opportunity to pull out the cell phone. "Might as well check messages," he said to Nikki.

"Typical sales guy, always an optimist." She saw her reflection in the train window: her hair was a mess and she felt self-conscious, but one look around proved everyone else had bed hair, too.

Rick waited patiently as the phone powered up. He was genuinely surprised when the phone buzzed in his hand, indicating a message. "Well, what do you know," he said showing Nikki the flashing icon. "I hope this is good news."

"Who was it?" she asked when he lowered the phone.

"Isolde," Rick said. "She said Tim Schroeder was looking for us in Birkenfeld yesterday, but missed us. She gave him this cell phone number and told him we might be on our way to Florence. She wants us to call her back right away."

"How would Tim Schroeder know we were in Birkenfeld?" Nikki asked. "*We* didn't even know we were going there."

"I'm sure it wasn't Tim," Rick said. "Jack already told us Tim is at a safe house in Paris."

"Let me call Isolde back and get a description of the guy."

"Good idea." He handed her the phone.

"Everything okay?" Gabi asked.

"Fine," Rick said. "There is some confusion about an old friend trying to find us. We won't bother you with the details."

Rick and Nikki moved out to the corridor, closing the compartment door. Nikki worked the buttons on the phone, pulled up Isolde's recent call, and hit redial. There was no one else in the corridor at the moment, so they hung close together facing away from the compartment. Nikki put the phone on speaker.

"Hello?"

"Hi, Isolde, it's Nikki and Rick. We got your message."

"Nikki, I am so glad you called back. I am sure it is nothing, but I wanted to make sure."

"Start from the beginning and tell us everything, please."

They waited patiently as Isolde explained her concerns about the stranger. When she finished, Nikki kept the concern from her voice.

"This can be solved easily, Isolde. My friend Tim Schroeder is easy to recognize, over six feet tall, mid-thirties, with reddish blond hair, and starting to go bald. He looks a little bit like the American actor William Hurt. Are you familiar with him?"

"Oh, yes, the actor from the movie *The Big Chill*," she said. "The man yesterday looked nothing like that, though. He was shorter, with dark hair and spoke with a slight accent. He moved like an athlete, a gymnast maybe, and he was self-conscious about a tattoo on his neck, trying to hide it with his shirt collar."

Nikki thought quickly. "I know who you are talking about, Isolde. It's a college friend of mine, a foreign exchange student from Bulgaria who likes to play practical jokes on me. I'm sure he will be in touch with us now that you have given him our number." Nikki laughed, hoping to sell the bullshit story.

"That makes me feel much better. I was worried I gave your number to somebody I shouldn't have."

"It's fine, Isolde, we really appreciate your concern," Rick said. "We'll come back and visit later this summer on our way back to Paris."

"My mother would love to see you again. She is starting to be her old self again. Thanks again for looking for her, Nikki," Isolde said, her voice catching a bit.

"Believe me, it was my pleasure," Nikki said. "See you later this summer. Bye."

"Goodbye, travel safely."

Rick got in a goodbye too before she closed the phone. "A foreign exchange student from Bulgaria? Where did that come from?"

"I have no idea; it was a total shot in the dark so she wouldn't worry anymore. Where do we go from here, though?"

"From Isolde's description, it's got to be the guy who killed Bonnard at our apartment. As soon as we figure out what's going on with this train, we'll check in with Jack. Don't worry, we'll think of something," Rick said.

"I hope so."

ം

The Italian conductor made his way down the corridor, his name tag read A. PAVONE. "*Firenze*, Campo di Marte twenty minutes," he announced. "Final stop due to strike."

"That's the station on the outskirts of Florence, not the Statione Principale," Gabi said. "At least they're getting us close."

"But how will we get to our hotel?" Evelyn asked. "It is more than a kilometer to the city center."

"Don't worry, we'll figure it out as we go," Nikki said.

During her years living and traveling abroad, improvising and changing plans on a moment's notice became a necessary skill, so she wasn't worried. "I think better when I'm moving," she said to Rick. "Let's take a walk." She grabbed her backpack and moved down the corridor to the next car. She didn't say anything until they were two cars away.

"I didn't want to talk in front of them, because I have a plan. We're going to use the rail strike to our advantage and become the hunters rather than the prey," she said.

"What did you have in mind?"

"We need to leverage our anonymity, and the cash, to our best advantage. We'll share a taxi with Gabi, Evelyn, and Krishnan into the city. There is no way on God's green earth someone could anticipate that and find us."

"I like it."

"Anybody chasing us will assume we'll arrive by train, so we turn the tables and stake out the train station, using the new camera. If we see anything suspicious, we get the pictures to Jack in Paris, and let him do his magic with the FBI, Interpol, and the French police."

"That's dangerous, Nikki. Especially if that man in Birkenfeld is the same guy who basically executed a French police inspector."

"I know, but what choice do we have?"

They were both silent as they pondered the alternatives.

"Your plan is doable, on two conditions," Rick said. "First, we change our appearances as much as we can, and second, we don't stay in Florence too long before we're on the move again."

"I'll go a step further," Nikki said. "We should hide in plain sight and sneak back to Paris. It's the last place they'll be looking for us. Plus, for some reason I trust Oatmon. We would be more effective working with him there."

"Let's go."

Gabi and Evelyn were booked into a small *pensione* near Piazza San Lorenzo. Using Gabi's confirmation receipt, Rick called and was able to book an additional room for one night only, Gabi's credit card guaranteeing the reservation. The *pensione* was completely booked for the rest of the week.

The train shuddered to a stop and the weary passengers disembarked onto the platform. "We should hurry," Nikki said. "This is an unplanned stop so the taxis will go fast."

Rick's offer to pay for a taxi to the *pensione* had been accepted, but they ran into a problem right away. Gabi and the taxi driver immediately began an animated discussion in Italian, which Rick and Nikki could not understand.

Krishnan translated.

"Unfortunately, the taxi is legally allowed only four passengers. Gabi is arguing there are three small women, surely he can make an exception and take five this one time," he said in Indian-accented English. "She will lose the argument."

Krishnan joined Gabi. Rick could tell his Italian skills were not as refined as his English. A few moments later, the argument was over.

"It is decided; I will take the next taxi," he said. "It makes sense for the four of you to go to the *pensione* together. Let's exchange phone numbers; maybe we could meet for a drink later?"

It seemed such a silly rule, but everyone agreed Krishnan's solution made sense. There was a flurry of bags hoisted into the taxi's trunk, while numbers and e-mail addresses were scribbled on slips of paper. Polite hugs and kisses were exchanged and they were finally on their way.

The streets of Florence were virtually empty at this time of the morning. The ancient buildings looked dingy and dirty in the misty gray fog as they skirted the back side of the Duomo. They reached the *pensione* in a few minutes and hauled the bags from the trunk.

Gabi and Evelyn checked in first and headed upstairs, promising to get together later in the day. Rick paid cash for the room, ending up paying for two nights due to the early check-in. Their second floor room was in the back, away from the street noise; the covered balcony overlooked a well-tended flower garden and faced northeast to the hills above the city.

The stress of the last seventy-two hours and two nights trying to sleep on trains caught up with them. It was a treat to brush their teeth in a real sink with potable water instead of the bottled water and paper cups they were forced to use on the trains. Neither thought it unnatural as they collapsed on the bed fully clothed, and fell asleep.

CHAPTER THIRTY-ONE

They woke to the sound of thunder.

"How far off, they sat and wondered," Nikki said.

"A Bob Seger fan, I see," Rick said.

"We should get up."

"Yeah, we should. We have a lot to do."

"You want the shower first?"

"You go ahead," Rick said. "I want to read the manual for the camera, so I know what I'm doing."

While Nikki showered, Rick gathered the new equipment and settled into a metal chair at the small table on the balcony. The air was heavy and humid. In what seemed like an instant, the sky darkened. Huge drops of rain began to splatter on the railing and the narrow stone walkways in the flower garden below. Another clap of thunder exploded overhead as Nikki arrived on the balcony, making them both jump.

"Wow," she said, as she cinched her robe. They watched the rain in silence and enjoyed the momentary feeling of safety. The rain forced them back into the small room, so Rick opened the drapes and the windows while Nikki stacked pillows against the headboard. The foot of the bed was near the balcony, so sitting on the bed offered a substantial view of the dark skies and the hills beyond.

"My turn in the shower," Rick said.

Five minutes later, Rick emerged from the tiny bathroom to see a fully dressed Nikki, lost in thought.

"What are you thinking?" he asked.

"There's so much history and art here in Florence, it's easy to see how these same dramatic skies inspired the work of artists for centuries. It's humbling in a way, I guess."

The storm passed through quickly and, refreshed from the rest and showers, they made their way onto the cobblestoned streets of Florence. They blended with the hordes of tourists, and shopped in the trendy stores where Nikki bought a summer hat, blouses, and hiking shorts. Along with the sunglasses she bought in Germany, the new purchases would go a long way in making her more invisible.

Rick took a lot of pictures, an easy thing to do in the beautiful city right after a rainstorm, especially from the Ponte Vecchio and the other bridges. The practice made him familiar with the camera and the different lenses. He didn't want to miss a picture because he couldn't use the equipment.

They found a little café east of the river on Borgo San Iacopo, enjoyed the beautiful sunset and a pleasant dinner. It was after eleven by the time they paid the bill and found themselves walking back across the Ponte Vecchio. They ran into Gabi, Evelyn, and two good-looking young men.

"Ciao!" Gabi said. She looked happy and full of wine. She introduced the two companions as Roberto and Marco. "My charges," she giggled.

Everyone laughed and shook hands politely.

"I feel like dancing," Gabi said. "The night is still young."

"That's a great idea," Evelyn said. "Do you want to join us?" she asked Rick and Nikki.

"Why don't you go ahead? We have some things we need to do tonight," Nikki replied. "See you in the morning for breakfast."

If Gabi and Evelyn were offended, neither showed it. They said goodbye and were soon lost in the crowds.

"That reminds me," Nikki said. "Florence is actually a real small town. We need to be extra careful here."

They walked back to the hotel and dropped off the shopping bags. The young woman behind the desk directed them to a café around the corner called Antica Drogheria, which had free wi-fi, (she pronounced it "wee-fee").

Rick stuck to Pellegrino while Nikki ordered wine, hooked up her laptop, and got to work. She went to Yahoo and set up a new e-mail account, then went to Google and set up another one. Rick assisted by writing down the usernames and passwords for each account. Nikki inserted the camera's installation disk and downloaded the software to her hard drive, connected the camera with the USB connection, and downloaded Rick's pictures into the My Pictures folder. Using the Yahoo account she composed an e-mail to the Google account, attached several of the photographs and hit Send. She switched to the Google account and in seconds the message arrived in the Inbox. She opened the message, including the attached photos, and everything worked perfectly.

"Let's check in with Jack in Paris," Rick said.

Jack picked up on the first ring. "Hi, Rick, are you safe?"

"Yes, we're fine. We have an idea, too."

"Yeah?"

Rick started to explain their plan, but Jack interrupted.

"I don't like it at all, it's too dangerous," Jack said.

"But you haven't heard the whole plan yet."

"Listen, Rick," Jack's voice went up a few decibels. "It's my job to keep you alive, and you're not helping. Keep moving and don't engage these people. Do you understand me?" He was talking so loud Nikki could hear him without the speakerphone.

"I do," Rick said. "However, there are mitigating circumstances we might be able to use to our advantage. If you'll give me a chance to explain, you might change your mind."

"You have two minutes," Jack said.

Rick took five. The unexpected rail strike was a critical factor in the opportunity, so Rick couldn't hide the fact they were in Italy. He explained using Gabi's credit card to guarantee the room, the plan for them to change their appearances and then sneak back into Paris. When he finished, there was silence on the other end.

He waited. It was almost a full minute before Jack answered.

"I will agree to your plan on two conditions. First, you only stay in Florence for one day, then you start moving toward Paris. Second, make sure you have an escape plan and be ready to move on a moment's notice. As soon as you are on the road again, call me. Understood?"

"Yes," Rick replied. "Any luck finding Svetlana?"

"Not yet. We continued to canvass the brothel area; turns out it was right around the corner from where I'm staying, and some neighbors across the street gave us a partial license plate number. We're checking. It's not much, but it's all we have right now."

"Good luck, we'll talk to you tomorrow. Say hi to Greg and get some sleep."

"I'll try. Say hi to Nikki, and be careful!"

"You keep saying that. Good night." Rick ended the call and leaned back in his chair.

"You're very persuasive," Nikki said. "I can't believe you convinced him, especially after all the yelling."

"Remember, in another life I was a salesman."

CHAPTER THIRTY-TWO

The next morning at breakfast Gabi and Evelyn were in desperate need of coffee. After leaving Rick and Nikki, they had found an all-night club and danced until the wee hours. The plan was to meet up with Roberto and Marco again at L'Accademia to see Michelangelo's statue of David and have lunch.

"Why don't you come with us this time?" Gabi asked.

"That's a great idea," Rick said. "Unfortunately, I have some business to take care of this morning."

"I would love to come with you," Nikki said.

They had already decided to split up for a few hours, convinced whoever was following them would expect them to be together. Playing tourist with Gabi and Evelyn would be good cover for Nikki. She would find a way to change her appearance, while Rick would check the area around the main train station entrance/exit. He hoped to find a safe vantage point for surveillance with his wide-angle and telephoto lenses.

"Any word on the rail strike?" Nikki asked.

"Roberto said the trains are supposed to start running this afternoon," Gabi said. "His uncle works for the railroad, so he should know."

As if on cue, a waiter turned up the volume on the small television in the dining room. They didn't understand the words, but they did get the message. The strike was over, the trains would start running again at 3 p.m.

ᔓ

When the three women arrived at L'Accademia, the wait was already two hours. They spent the time in the sun, sharing an *International Herald Tribune* and waiting for Roberto and Marco. Although there were many Americans in line, Nikki was amazed at the international representation, hearing at least seven languages. There was a wonderful camaraderie among those in line, taking each other's pictures, helping with directions, other sights to see, and any new information regarding the rail strike. Too bad this type of cooperation and civility doesn't extend to global politics, she thought. Any further deep thoughts on solving the problems of the world were cut short by the arrival of Roberto and Marco.

"*Ciao!*" they both said. There were double kisses all around.

Once inside the museum the young men turned out to be quite knowledgeable and were excellent tour guides. They offered a lot of information, especially regarding the unfinished pietàs, but in the presence of Michelangelo's classic statue, they had the good sense to allow the women to appreciate the artwork with a minimum of chatter.

Nikki was overwhelmed. She got goose bumps. She turned into the hallway leading to the atrium, and saw the huge sky-lighted marble form. The moment was unforgettable. She was unmistakably in the presence of art. She had seen pictures of *David* before, but being here was a perfect example of a picture's inability to do justice to the actual piece.

They stayed for over half an hour before reluctantly leaving to find lunch. The experience left Gabi and Evelyn in a quiet mood, too. Roberto and Marco again impressed Nikki by not trying too hard, leading them across the river to a small, off-the-beaten-path restaurant. The conversation was light and pleasant, the food wonderful again. It was obvious to Nikki she was soon to become a fifth wheel, so leaving more than enough Euros to cover her meal, she said thank you and goodbye. As she started to move away, Marco leaned close, nuzzled Evelyn's neck, and said something in Italian. Evelyn smiled and kissed him gently. The scene put Nikki in a good mood as she began her search for a salon.

ဖ

Rick spent the day playing tourist, wandering along the side streets east of the train station, taking pictures and shopping. He bought a maroon baseball cap with a picture of the Ponte Vecchio embroidered on the front. Tucked down low with sunglasses, and his beard filling in, he felt reasonably anonymous. He ended up on the lawn in front of the Statione Principale, where hundreds of people were milling about, waiting for the trains to run again.

He thought like a hunter, and imagined how someone would try to spot him. The midafternoon sun was intense, offering bright views of the surroundings, but nothing looked remotely suspicious. Suddenly, he had another idea. He used the cell phone to catch Nikki at their hotel.

"Hello?"

"Nikki, I'm glad I caught you."

"Are you okay?" Nikki asked.

"I'm fine. I have an idea."

ᔓ

The Statione Principale was mobbed; the first trains had arrived and disgorged thousands of tourists from all over the world. Rick scanned the crowds for Nikki, but couldn't find her. The main lobby of the Statione was particularly crowded as people watched the overhead board noting arrivals and departures.

"Signore?"

Rick turned to the woman's voice. She wore sunglasses, had long blonde hair, and wore a large brimmed hat.

"Si?"

The woman lowered her sunglasses.

Nikki! The transformation was unbelievable. From a few feet away, even he couldn't recognize her.

"So what do you think?" she asked, flipping the wig in a mock flirt.

"You couldn't have done better. Now let's get to work."

It wasn't long before they found what they needed. An American group was making their way to the exit. The tour guide, a tiny woman with a big voice, encouraged everyone to quiet down and gather around so they could proceed to the bus waiting outside.

"Let's count heads and then stow the luggage," she barked. "The sooner we get done, the sooner we can get going." They were typical Americans, loud enough to be heard throughout the lobby.

Rick and Nikki moved closer and pretended to be part of the group as they slowly made their way outdoors. There was a delay in getting the group on their way, so a few couples sprawled on the lawn to rest and enjoy the sunshine. The pair used it to their advantage and plopped down near them. Rick pretended to take pictures of Nikki from several angles, but in reality he was scanning the crowds and the hotel windows with a view of the station entrance. He started with the large hotel to the right.

Nothing.

He repositioned himself and scanned to the left.

Again, nothing.

Across the lawns and the main intersection in front of the Statione was the Hotel Baglioni. Rick hadn't noticed it due to the construction scaffolding that covered the front of the building. He couldn't tell if it was open for business, so he decided to check it out anyway. Starting on the lower floors he methodically checked each window with the powerful telephoto lens. He took his time, maneuvering slightly whenever the scaffolding obscured his view. Nikki was a good actress, striking a new pose any time Rick was forced to move.

Rick froze.

The sun reflected off something in a top floor window. He zoomed in to get a closer look, just as a pair of binoculars was lowered. A chill ran through him. The high-powered lens brought the man into sharp focus. There was no mistaking the black snow-leopard tattoo on his neck. Rick was so stunned he almost forgot to take the pictures. The afternoon light was helpful through the open window and he got several clear shots. Hopefully, they would be enough.

"What is it?" Nikki asked.

"We got him," Rick said. He lowered the camera and scrolled the digital display to make sure he really had the shots.

Nikki started to turn. "Are you sure?"

"Don't turn! He has binoculars."

"Sorry."

"I didn't mean to snap at you," Rick apologized. "It's definitely the guy who killed Inspector Bonnard. We've done our job, so we get out of here. We can't take any chances. You leave first and get back to the hotel and pack. I'll be a few minutes behind you. Now!"

Nikki was momentarily shaken, but regained her composure. She wasted no time. She walked back into the station and exited through a side door.

Rick waited a couple of agonizing minutes, made sure the man in the window was still there, turned, and followed Nikki. He made it to the hotel in less than five minutes, hoping Nikki was already upstairs packing. He approached the young woman at the front desk and asked her to call a cab.

"Your wife has already ordered a taxi. Where will you be going?" she asked.

"The airport," Rick said.

He moved toward the stairwell, but Nikki was already wrestling their luggage down the marble stairs. She didn't wait for Rick to help, but walked straight to the taxi pulling up in front of the *pensione*.

The driver jumped out, opened the trunk, and helped Nikki stow the bags.

"Did you get everything?" Rick asked.

"Yes, besides, you have all the important stuff in your backpack anyway," Nikki said. "Which reminds me, give me 200 Euros from the stash, please."

Rick dug into the backpack and gave her the money. Nikki rushed back to the front desk. "Do you have an envelope and a piece of paper, please?"

Nikki stuffed the two 100 Euro notes into the envelope and hastily scrawled a note on the house stationery.

Dear Gabi & Evelyn:

Sorry, we had to leave on such short notice and won't get a chance to say a proper goodbye. Please use this money to take yourselves and those two young men out to a nice dinner, with our compliments. It's the least we can do for your kindness in letting us use your credit card.

Also, we are passing along a tradition of doing something nice for a fellow traveler. All we ask in return is that you do something nice for someone else on your trip, and then ask them to do the same.

Thanks again for your kindness and friendship. We were happy to meet you.

Nikki & Rick

Nikki ran back to the waiting taxi. "Let's get the hell out of here."

"What was that all about?" Rick asked. They squeezed into the cramped back seat of the tiny car.

"Remember Nate Becker?"

"Yeah, the guy on the train to Munich."

"I thought it would be good karma to repay his kindness while we had the chance. I passed along the tradition to Gabi and Evelyn and asked them to use the money to take the boys out to dinner."

"Another good idea; I'm glad you thought of it," Rick said.

"You are in hurry? Late for plane?" the driver asked as he pulled into the traffic.

"We're not going to the airport; we want to go to Lucca," Nikki said.

"Lucca! No, it is too far." The driver slowed down.

Rick leaned the short distance toward the front seat and showed the driver a wad of large Euro notes.

"We want to go to Lucca."

A huge grin spread across the driver's face. "Lucca is very pretty this time of year." He took the money and stuffed it in the pocket of his t-shirt.

CHAPTER THIRTY-THREE

It took them over an hour to clear rush hour traffic and start to move, arriving on the outskirts of the walled medieval city of Lucca with the sun sinking in the evening sky. Rick gave directions to the north side, where there was a large parking area he remembered from a previous trip. The driver still had a smile on his face as he drove away.

"Let's find a café and an Internet hookup and get these pictures to Jack and Greg right away," Nikki said. "We're safe for now. The bad guy is still in Florence and there is no way to track us here."

They found what they needed inside the north wall, a little jazz café called Betty Blue's. It took a few minutes to reconcile their 21st century need for the Internet, surrounded by buildings hundreds of years old. Nikki fired up the laptop, attached the newly downloaded pictures, and e-mailed them three at a time to Jack Oatmon's Yahoo account. If she tried to send more than three pictures, the message was kicked back for the attachments being too large.

Rick turned on the cell phone and called Paris.

"Jack, we did it," he said. "We got pictures of the guy that killed Bonnard. He's in Florence looking for us."

"I hope you had the good sense to get out of Florence," Jack said.

"Yes, we did. We're headed west. Nikki e-mailed the pictures to you. The guy has a very distinctive black snow-leopard tattoo on the right side of his neck; maybe it has some significance. Whoever he is, he'll be smart enough to figure out pretty quickly we aren't in Florence. We're going to stop using the Eurail passes now and use cash. There's no way to trace us any further, so maybe he'll head back to Paris. Can you stake out the airports and follow him?"

"Good idea. I'll download the pictures and run them through the system. At a minimum we'll distribute copies to airport security and the rest of the task force. Maybe we'll get lucky."

"Speaking of lucky, anything on the license on the car that took Svetlana?" Rick asked.

"Yeah, it's an embassy car, but we don't know which embassy. An educated guess would be Russian, but I'm not convinced. It could easily be American or French. There are many potential bad guys here, so I'm being extra careful. I've got someone I trust working on it, though. I should know more soon."

"Okay. How's Greg?"

"On the mend and back to work, which is good. Our meeting with the police cleared him of any wrongdoing, and I've assured them you and Nikki are innocent too. We'll only bring you back to Paris when we feel it's safe. L'Avenue Bar & Grill has been released as a crime scene, so Greg's getting ready to reopen. The task force will be providing security for the foreseeable future."

"Sounds good. We'll keep moving and talk to you tomorrow," Rick said.

"Be careful."

Rick lowered the phone.

"Should we keep moving, maybe go on to Pisa?" Nikki asked. She summoned the young woman from behind the counter for advice. Luckily, she spoke fluent English.

"You don't want Pisa: too many tourists, too much noise," the girl said. "The owner here sometimes rents an apartment that is quite nice. It belongs to an American writer who travels extensively. Let me ask if it's available."

Rick and Nikki couldn't believe their luck. An hour later they unloaded another taxi and settled into a cozy, well-decorated one-bedroom apartment outside the walls of the old city. It came with satellite television, Internet access, and a stereo system.

"All the comforts of home," Rick said.

"I take you to the finest places," Nikki said.

Rick dozed off on the couch, but Nikki couldn't sleep. She got a large bottle of San Pellegrino water from the well-stocked refrigerator, sat at the small desk in the bedroom, and turned on her laptop. If she was going to stay alive, and find out if she would have a real life with Greg, she knew to take it one step at a time. She needed a better plan other than run and keep running. She needed to know what would be the safest way to get back into Paris.

She had used a home-exchange website to find housing upon her arrival in Paris, and remembered there were as many rentals as home exchanges. Many times the landlords took cash, so that worked with their plan for anonymity. She logged on and found several listings. One near Gare Montparnasse in the 14th arrondissement fit the bill perfectly. It came with a free wi-fi connection and an existing phone number with unlimited international calls. She clicked on the link, inquired as to availability, and for an extra measure of protection said her name was Jack. She used the new Google e-mail account to communicate. She didn't expect a response until morning, so she spent the next hour surfing the net researching the Russian mafia and the sex slavery trade. She looked for a connection to the snow-leopard tattoo, but found nothing. Maybe Jack would have better luck with his resources in Paris.

It was well after midnight when she finally tired, shut down, and went back to bed.

CHAPTER THIRTY-FOUR

Jack was running on pure adrenaline. He hadn't slept more than three hours straight since Eric's death. Sooner or later it was going to catch up with him, but he hoped it would be after he nailed the bastards responsible. He was getting closer; he could feel it.

His contact came through on the license of the car that possibly had driven Svetlana away from the brothel. It was assigned to the French Embassy, confirming his suspicion someone high up was dirty.

He had forwarded Rick's pictures from Florence to Interpol as soon as he saw them last night, and already had a positive identification. He sipped coffee and read through the e-mailed file on Alexei Persoff. Suspected of at least five murders in Russia and dozens of other violent confrontations in both Moscow and Los Angeles, there was no doubt he was a very dangerous man. He had spent several years in a gulag in eastern Russia where one of his cellmates was Sergei Ischenko, the now-deceased younger brother of Victor Ischenko. They had been released together ten years ago, and immediately employed in Victor's ever-growing shady business dealings in the quasi-capitalistic free-for-all following the collapse of the Soviet Union.

After finishing the file, Jack went back and reread the LAPD file on Katarina. One of her assailants was definitely Alexei Persoff, and the description of the second man, Gorky, bore a striking resemblance to the still unidentified dead man in Nikki's apartment. Too many coincidences, thought Jack.

ഗ

In Lucca, Rick and Nikki took the opportunity to sleep in, finally getting around to coffee late in the morning. Nikki took her steaming cup to the small desk and logged in to find a message in her inbox from the home-exchange website. The apartment near Montparnasse was available for two weeks, starting Sunday, at three hundred Euros per week. The owner, Vincent, spoke English, would only take cash or a check drawn on a French bank, and didn't require a deposit. The money and timing posed no problems, so she e-mailed back they would take the apartment. They now had forty-eight hours to get to Paris.

Jack's return e-mail thanked Nikki for the pictures and filled her in on the developments. They had positively identified the assassin with the leopard tattoo, leaving Nikki with mixed emotions. While she hoped it would help get the tattooed man captured and brought to justice, the connection to others like Victor Ischenko, Frank DeMarchand, and corrupt French Embassy people was something else entirely. Plus, she felt helpless in Italy. It was time to get back to Paris.

Nikki went into the living room to find Rick packing. They were still traveling light even after Nikki's purchases.

"You need a new look, too," she said. "You should get a haircut and let your beard grow. With sunglasses and your new hat, it might be enough to make you look different."

"If I do half as good a job as you, I'll be fine."

Nikki smiled when she saw the blonde wig on the dresser. "Not bad, I must admit."

"It makes you look so different, it makes you safer, and that makes me feel better."

"I'm glad. Now let's get to work on you."

They spent the afternoon walking the narrow streets of the walled city, again feeling safe in the swarm of tourists. With the bags, camera, and Nikki dressed in her new Italian blouse and hiking shorts, they looked the typical tourist couple.

CHAPTER THIRTY-FIVE

Alexei was tired of Florence. The July heat was oppressive and the city was crawling with tourists. That made it easy for him to blend in, but nearly impossible to find the two people he needed to find. He took what seemed like his thousandth look through the powerful binoculars. His vantage point from the top floor of the Hotel Baglioni faced the entire expanse in front of the train station and down the side street leading into central Florence. Using a train schedule conveniently provided by the hotel, he carefully surveyed the crowds, concentrating on the trains arriving from Germany and Switzerland. So far he had seen nothing out of the ordinary. Either he had missed his prey, or they weren't coming to Florence anytime soon.

His last conversation with Henri made the necessity of finding Rick and Nikki even more imperative. Henri had traced the cell phone number Alexei got from Isolde in Birkenfeld, only to find out it was classified. Even Henri's powerful contacts were unable to help. Henri and Alexei were further frustrated and concerned when they learned the number was so secure it could not be triangulated or tracked. This led them to believe the United States government was involved, but the only people who would know this information worked directly for Chief Inspector Covyeau. In the meantime, Alexei was spinning his wheels waiting for Henri to call back.

His cell phone vibrated.

"Yes."

"Things here in Paris are getting interesting," Henri said without preamble. "You must be very careful, Alexei. My source tells me there was a special request for research on snow-leopard tattoos, and your file had been specifically requested from Interpol. There is even a picture of you holding binoculars in a hotel room window that is circulating in the research department."

Alexei was so stunned he sat down. Not only was he spinning his wheels in Florence, his prey had beat him to the punch and turned the tables on him. He not only missed them, he was now the hunted one, and he didn't like it one bit. "These people might be more competent than we gave them credit for," he said.

"I think you are right," Henri agreed. He hung up.

Alexei sat in silence for a moment. There was nothing more he could do in Florence. He packed his bags, checked out of the hotel, and left for Paris.

CHAPTER THIRTY-SIX

Rick and Nikki took the high speed train, the *TGV*, from Nice to Paris, arriving at Gare de Lyon. They joined the queue for a taxi rather than take the Métro, and fifteen minutes later arrived at a nondescript building on Rue Edouard Jacques. After paying the driver, Nikki retrieved the information from the e-mail and punched the code into the panel to the right of the outer double doors. The lock buzzed open and they entered the cool, dark entryway, found the button for the landlord, and made their way up the six flights of steep, narrow, winding, worn wooden stairs. The smell of mildew, age, boiled cabbage, and urine faded as they climbed higher, assisted by the breeze coming through the open top floor window.

Breathing heavily when they reached the landing for the two adjacent apartments, they were greeted amiably in English by an obviously pregnant woman. She introduced herself as Saskia, Vincent's wife.

"Welcome to Paris," she said. "I will show you around. Vincent will be back in a few minutes."

The apartment was a typical Paris studio. The living/sleeping area faced the street, the kitchen and bathroom toward the back. The front window was open, and even from seven floors above, the sound of the evening traffic of small cars, scooters, and motorcycles could be heard echoing off the stone façades.

"It is not as noisy with the window closed," Saskia said. "Please make yourselves at home. When Vincent gets here, he will collect the rent. If you need anything before that, I am right next door."

After saying thank you, they began to unpack.

"You know, I hate to sound negative, but after a week on the road, two night trains, and today's train ride, all I can think about is other people's stink," Rick said.

"Your last travel companion really got to you," Nikki laughed.

On the train to Paris, they had been specifically assigned two window seats across the aisle from each other. If no one filled the empty seats by the last stop in Marseille, they would be allowed to move and sit together. However, the last person to get on the train before the final four-hour nonstop ride to Paris was a shabbily dressed old lady dragging a suitcase and carrying a shopping bag. She looked confused, prompting the conductor to lead her to the seat next to Rick. She fussed for several minutes to get comfortable, pulled down the tray table, carefully covered it with a towel, and withdrew from the shopping bag what could only be described as a "rat dog." It was not only the ugliest dog Rick had ever seen, the small, bug-eyed creature smelled like it had been left in the rain for a week. Rick had to lean close to the window to gasp the miniscule trail of fresh air leaking from a vent. He looked helplessly at Nikki, but the seat next to her was filled too. The surrounding passengers noticed his discomfort, but could only smile in sympathy.

"It wasn't just the dog," Rick said. "What about the cigarettes, body odor, bad breath, the couple changing their infant's diaper two rows away, and that morbidly obese woman in the taxi queue?"

"Okay, I'll admit she had serious intestinal issues," Nikki said, amused by Rick's indignation. "Let's find a nice place for dinner tonight. You can replace the negative images, and now that we're safely back in Paris, you can treat yourself to the hearty bouquet of a rich cabernet."

Nikki was impressed by Rick's will power. He had stuck exclusively to Pellegrino water since leaving Florence, not even tempted when Nikki had an occasional glass of wine with her meal. In solidarity, she had even foregone her daily cigarette to support his effort to manage his alcohol intake.

Vincent arrived, helped Nikki log on with the wi-fi to make sure it worked properly, and showed both of them how to use the phone for international calls. Using a large detailed street map of Paris tacked on the wall over a low bookcase, Vincent oriented them to the landmarks, the neighborhood supermarket, and the nearest Métro stations. The bookcase was stocked with a variety of guide books for Paris and France, some of them quite out of date but possibly helpful for phone numbers and addresses.

"There is a complimentary bottle of champagne in the refrigerator," Vincent said.

Rick paid cash for a week's stay, with an option for another at a reduced rate, and ushered him out to the landing. "Thanks for your help, Vincent."

"My pleasure. If you need anything else, just knock next door, or call me. All my numbers are at the bottom of my e-mail messages. Welcome to Paris."

Nikki opened the bottle of champagne. Rick found glasses, rinsed and dried them by the time Nikki uncorked the bottle. They sipped champagne quietly, realizing once again that no one knew where they were, or what they were going to do. Then again, Rick and Nikki didn't know what they were going to do either.

They spent the evening exploring the neighborhood, finding most of what they needed on Rue Raymond-Losserand. They found a cozy pizza place near the Pernety Métro station, and discussed their options over the promised cabernet.

"How do we take advantage of everybody thinking we're still on the run somewhere else in Europe?" Rick asked.

"We need to check in with Jack, tell him we're safely tucked away where no one will find us, then get as much information as possible about those after us," Nikki replied. "Maybe Jack will let us follow the less dangerous ones until someone makes a mistake."

"We have no training for that," Rick said.

"I know, but we'll have to do the best we can. How much of the money do we have left?" Nikki asked.

"At least 20,000 Euros, more than enough, I'm sure."

"Good. The first things we need are two good scooters or small motorcycles, and helmets with dark visors. Vincent and Saskia might be able to help us find some used ones we can buy for cash."

"Why?" Rick asked.

"Lots of reasons. They're more maneuverable in traffic, and they're so prevalent now we can get lost in the crowd. With the right clothes and headgear, not only will nobody be able to recognize us, but they won't know if the rider is male or female."

"Do you know how to ride?"

"Are you kidding? I grew up in the country with four older brothers. I've ridden all kinds of ATVs and small motorcycles since I was old enough to reach the throttle."

"It's been a while for me. I'm going to need some practice before I tackle the streets of Paris," Rick said.

"Don't worry, I'll give you a crash course, you'll be a pro in no time."

They wandered back to the apartment, down the tiny Passage des Arts, past l'Arganier bistro, where a rowdy crowd of customers spilled into the narrow street below their building.

It was late by the time they called Jack. "We thought we'd let you know we're safely back in Paris," Rick said. "No one will be able to find us."

"That's good news."

"What's the plan now?" Nikki asked.

"I've been walking all over Paris today and I'm really beat," Jack said. "I'll be out all day tomorrow, too. Let's talk tomorrow night. Now that Greg is back in his studio, I've decided to bring Tim here from the safe house, where I'll be able to protect him better. I'll get Greg and we'll call you tomorrow night sometime and the five of us can come up with a plan. How's that sound?"

"That's fine," Rick said. "Talk to you tomorrow night. Sleep well."

Rick and Nikki settled into their new digs. The entire apartment was the size of her living room on Rue de Bellechasse, so it was a tight fit. They settled on the futon to watch television and found a rerun of *Sex and the City* dubbed in French. Rick was the perfect gentleman and settled on the floor with extra blankets he found stashed in the bathroom linen closet. They finally drifted off to sleep, despite the noise from the late night revelers at the party below.

CHAPTER THIRTY-SEVEN

The next morning, Nikki called Vincent about the motorcycles and got lucky. Vincent had recently upgraded to a bigger motorcycle and still hadn't sold his old, smaller Honda. Originally, he kept it for Saskia, but now that she was pregnant, she was terrified to ride it, preferring the Métro or walking. He led them down the six flights of stairs into the small interior courtyard shared by several buildings. Two sheds were off to the left, one housing the garbage and recycling bins and the other crammed with all sizes of bicycles and the small Honda.

"There is a little gas left in the Honda," he said. He rolled it to Nikki. "I also have a bicycle."

Rick helped extricate the bicycle from the tangle of other bikes. It was a decent ten-speed model, a little dusty but otherwise in pretty good shape. A bit of oil and a couple of adjustments to the brakes it would be as good as new. "Maybe I should start with this bike until we find something else that's motorized," he said.

Nikki didn't answer. She was familiarizing herself with the small motorcycle. "This will work," she said. "How much do you want for it?"

"I have no idea what it is worth," Vincent said. "Why don't you use it while you stay here? Consider it included in the rent. That will give me time to check the value in case you wish to buy it when you leave."

"That's very considerate of you, thanks."

Rick and Nikki wheeled their respective *deux-roues* down a dark cobblestoned passageway that opened into a narrow alley and eventually out to Rue Edouard Jacques. Nikki made sure there was enough gas in the tank, straddled the small motorcycle, adjusted the clutch, and with a swift motion kick-started the machine. It made an awful racket, and Nikki silently apologized to the neighbors for the annoying sound. Vincent came up to her, a little out of breath. He had run back up the six flights of stairs to retrieve the practically brand new helmet he had bought for Saskia.

"Try it on, it should fit," he said over the sound of the poorly muffled Honda.

Nikki slipped on the sleek black headgear, tightened the strap, and flipped the dark visor down. It fit perfectly. She gave a wave to the two men and started up the street on a test drive. She turned right on Rue Raymond-Losserand, and then right again on Boulevard Raspail. She shifted up and down through the gears to get the feel. Memories of long hot days riding with her brothers flooded back to her, and she was quickly comfortable with the physical motions of operating the motorcycle. The well-cushioned helmet blocked most of the surrounding sounds, and the streets of Paris were lightyears away from the foothills of California's gold country. There was something overtly sexual about controlling the noisy machine between her legs. She had to concentrate hard not to let her mind wander and envision Greg's athletic body. She was more than a mile down Boulevard Raspail before she turned around and wound her way back through the narrow side streets to Rick and Vincent.

"It's perfect," she said. "How's the bicycle?"

"We'll see." Rick handed a small oil can and rag to Vincent, jumped on the bike, and took off the same direction Nikki had gone. He turned around at the end of the street and rode back, doing a gear check similar to what Nikki had done with the Honda.

"This will work for me," Rick said.

"Good," Nikki said. "Now we shop for the appropriate clothing."

CHAPTER THIRTY-EIGHT

Victor Ischenko was now officially a fugitive from the Russian authorities. That didn't really bother him, considering he had numerous fake passports issued by several countries. Most of Dante International's assets, mainly cash, were safely tucked away in secret accounts in Switzerland, the Cayman Islands, and a few of the former Soviet republics. The Russian and American authorities would soon discover the worldwide offices of Dante International were just that, empty, nonstaffed offices. Victor had spent years creating the myth of a large international corporation, and it had paid off well.

He and Sasha had slipped out of Russia and back to Paris a few days ago using Bulgarian passports. They were now almost ready to disappear and split their time between a small villa in Tuscany and a dilapidated beach house in San Sebastián. Long ago he decided when the time came he would abandon the trappings of wealth and live quietly, anonymously. He was a firm believer in learning from the mistakes of others. Many like him were eventually caught because of the obvious, and ostentatious, use of their ill-gotten wealth.

But first, there were a few loose ends to take care of in Paris. A few officials, both American and French, had yet to be pumped for information regarding the task force investigation and bribed into silence. Then came the delicate handling of Frank DeMarchand. Victor knew DeMarchand had set up his own secret offshore accounts and was as prepared to disappear as Victor and Sasha. The trick would be to direct as much of the suspicion and guilt toward DeMarchand.

What he had told the police officers in Los Angeles was true. Over the past few years, Victor had delegated the day-to-day operations to DeMarchand, taking great pains to have any paper and electronic trails lead to him, not Victor. If Victor was apprehended, he would use the quintessential American defense of plausible deniability, and blame everything on his deranged, out-of-control, power-obsessed second-in-command. If DeMarchand was caught, the evidence would provide the authorities their scapegoat, leaving Victor and Sasha to bribe and/or plea bargain their way to freedom.

Victor's cell phone vibrated in his shirt pocket. "Yes?"

"They are moving the package," the voice on the other end said. "I will not be able to monitor the situation any longer without causing suspicion."

"What time?"

"Ten p.m. To the apartment in the 16th."

"Have you had a chance to interrogate our future guest?"

"He is under strict orders from both Oatmon and Covyeau to speak to no one, including me."

"Then we change the rules. I will call our mutual friend. Be prepared to act late this afternoon."

Ischenko ended the call and immediately called DeMarchand.

"We have a situation that needs immediate attention," he said. He hoped his manner would make DeMarchand forget he had been ignored for the last few days, and it was business as usual.

ೞ

Frank DeMarchand lowered his cell phone. It had been a bad morning, first the call from Ischenko, and now Henri. He was disappointed, but not surprised at Henri's "resignation"; he would get out, too, if their roles were reversed.

Unfortunately, DeMarchand's situation was much more complicated. Before this morning's call, he had not been able to reach Victor Ischenko for several days, and that worried him. Victor usually insisted on daily reports when the two were separated geographically, so with Victor ostensibly in Moscow and Frank in Paris, why didn't Victor return his calls?

Now, with Henri unavailable, he was forced to deal with the volatile and dangerous Alexei. Victor was leery of cell phones—one never knew who was listening—and maybe that was why Ischenko had avoided him. But he didn't think so.

Something was wrong.

Since Bonnard and Gorky's deaths, it had been almost impossible to get information from his contacts with the police. As in Los Angeles, he had scattered the girls from the mansion in the 16th throughout Europe. He still hadn't been able to track down Svetlana, which added to his worries. The trail was so cold Frank was convinced it had been planned well in advance, which could only mean one thing: Svetlana had a powerful friend. The fact she was picked up by an embassy car further proved that theory.

With Henri gone, he had no choice but to call Alexei.

CHAPTER THIRTY-NINE

Tim Schroeder was going stir crazy even though the apartment near the Bourse was deceptively large. He had been at the safe house for a week now, unable to venture out. The kitchen and living area were on one level, with a window overlooking a courtyard enclosed by the four wings of the building. The bedroom, up four wide steps from the center of the living area, was huge. There was a king-sized bed, nightstands, and a smaller window that offered a glimpse of the Sacré Coeur. As comfortable as it was, Tim didn't like being on the sidelines. Jack had kept him informed of the progress of the investigation, and convinced him it wouldn't be much longer.

Tim's bodyguard was Hugo Leveque, the surly Chief Inspector from the task force who lived in the apartment across the hall. Each evening about eight-thirty he would knock on the door and hand Tim his daily baguette, *Herald Tribune*, and other necessities, remind him to stay put, and retreat to his own solitude. Tim was sure the inspector thought the babysitting and grocery shopping were beneath him, women's work.

Tim passed the time reading everything he could find on the bookshelves, devouring every page of the *Tribune*, watching CNN International, and napping in the afternoons for the first time in his adult life. He used the heavier books as weights and worked out as best he could twice a day. He was sweating profusely from his evening work out when he heard a knock on the door. Immediately suspicious of the change in routine, he looked through the peephole and saw Leveque holding the usual supplies. Tim undid the deadbolts and opened the door.

"You're early."

"Detective Oatmon requested you be moved to his apartment this evening," Leveque said. He handed the bag to Tim.

"That's great. Let me take a quick shower and get my things," Tim said.

He turned to take the bag to the kitchen, wondering why Leveque would bring the usual supplies if he was leaving tonight. He turned back to question Leveque.

Too late.

Tim didn't have time to deflect the small sedative-laden syringe as Leveque plunged it into his upper right arm. He made a valiant effort to fight back. He dropped the bag and weakly tried to punch Leveque with his left fist. Leveque easily dodged the blow, caught him as he lost consciousness, and eased him to the floor.

"You should have let him take a shower first. Now we have to move him all sweaty and gross."

"Next time you do it then, Frank."

DeMarchand moved into the apartment and closed the door.

"It is too late now. Victor won't care as long as he is alive. Help me get him to the elevator and down to the car."

Leveque went to the bathroom, got a fresh towel, and wrapped it over Tim's sweat-soaked shoulders. They lifted him to a sitting position, then stood him up. Each man draped a limp arm over a shoulder and carried Tim down the stairs. They did not encounter any other residents or busybodies.

DeMarchand's car idled in the alley on the north side of the building. Alexei Persoff was at the wheel.

CHAPTER FORTY

Chief Inspector Daniel Covyeau looked at the top of his desk, and smiled. Three cell phones and his landline desk phone were all ringing simultaneously. The digital readout on the desk phone blinked, an internal call from someone he didn't want to talk to. His Department cell phone call was from the morgue, probably with the autopsy results on Bonnard and the Russian. His personal cell phone call was his wife, no doubt to remind him of some mundane errand. His task-force cell phone call was from Jack, so he let the others go to voice mail.

"*Bonjour*, Jack." He got up and moved toward the window, away from the buzzing phones.

"Any progress on finding Svetlana or the embassy car that picked her up?" Jack asked.

"Not yet," Covyeau replied. "There are seven cars fitting that description checked out on the night in question. All the drivers and embassy personnel have been questioned, with no results. Several of the drivers admit to leaving their cars unattended during dinner or while sneaking a drink against regulations, but nothing to indicate any of them were involved with Svetlana's disappearance."

"Is it possible someone knowledgeable about using these staff cars could take one out for an hour or two and return unnoticed?"

"It is always possible, but unlikely. We have been very firm with these drivers, and so far all of their stories check out."

"For the sake of argument, let's assume Svetlana's departure was planned in advance," Jack said. "If it was an embassy car, she had to know someone with access to those cars. Because we've also been covering the train stations and airports, let's further assume Svetlana is still somewhere here in Paris. She was taken away a little after midnight, right?"

"Correct."

"Let's start by identifying the cars signed out between eleven and one that night and left unattended during the same two hours. We'll concentrate only on those cars close enough to get to the house, pick up Svetlana, take her somewhere here in Paris, and get the car back without being missed. I would bet there are only a few. Maybe we'll get lucky."

"Good idea. I will call you later with the list. By then I should have the autopsy reports on Bonnard and the Russian."

"I don't think you'll find anything contradicting what I've already told you," Jack said.

"I am sure you are right. We also traced the cocaine found in the apartment. It came from the Prefecture's evidence room. Our search of Bonnard's apartment, bank, and phone records have convinced us he was paid handsomely every month by someone other than the Paris police department."

"We still need to find out who was working with Bonnard," Jack said. "I don't think he had the intelligence to run the whole operation."

"I agree. I have a few suspects, and will get back to you on that later, too."

Covyeau picked up the message from his Department cell phone, his instincts correct. The autopsy results for Bonnard and the Russian corroborated Oatmon's version, and he saw no reason to pursue it any further. At least they could use the results and attempt to identify the Russian.

He checked the other messages, including the predictable one from his nagging wife, who was still visiting her family in Montpellier. He hoped she'd stay there for the rest of the summer.

He felt no guilt for taking a mistress.

Lovely Chloé.

So different from his wife.

Chloé had recently returned from a short holiday to St. Tropez, and this evening would be spent exploring how successful she had been in eliminating her tan lines.

He finished up with the last of his paperwork a little after seven, plenty of time to go home, shower, select a nice bottle of wine, and stroll to Chloé's pied-à-terre for what he hoped would be a much needed evening of pure lust. The responsibilities of the task force provided the perfect alibi for the time spent away from his wife. He was actually humming as he fumbled with all the cell phones, turning off his Department one. He wouldn't realize until later he'd silenced his task force phone instead of his personal phone. He tossed all three into his leather satchel, and left.

CHAPTER FORTY-ONE

It was getting late. Where was Tim? He was supposed to be here half an hour ago.

Jack sat in the semidarkness of his apartment, watched the traffic on the street below, and sipped a beer.

And waited.

He had spent the last two days visiting upscale men's clothing shops throughout Paris. With Joëlle translating, and a picture of Frank DeMarchand, he hoped to get a lead as to DeMarchand's whereabouts. His rationale was driven by his belief in DeMarchand's vanity and expensive tastes. At their brief meeting in Los Angeles Jack noticed DeMarchand was very particular about his appearance, constantly fussing with his perfectly knotted silk tie, French-collared shirt, and gold cufflinks, and making sure the razor-sharp crease in his slacks fell over the center of his tasseled loafers.

They finally got a lead late that afternoon at a British owned shop called Savile Row de Paris on Boulevard Haussmann. The young clerk recognized the man in the picture, but did not know his name. The gentleman in question always dealt directly with the owner of the shop, who wouldn't be back until closing time at ten that evening. Jack left a copy of DeMarchand's picture and his cell phone number, and pleaded with the clerk to make sure the owner called him this evening if possible.

His phone vibrated in his shirt pocket.

"Oatmon."

"Detective Oatmon, this is Ian Blair from Savile Row de Paris. I have a message to call you immediately. My clerk said it was urgent. How can I help you?"

"Thank you very much for calling me back so promptly," Jack said. "I'm working with the French authorities. We are looking for a man who could be very helpful to our investigation. Do you have the picture I left with the clerk?"

"Yes," Blair answered.

"Do you recognize him?"

"Of course, he is one of my best customers. I haven't seen him in months though."

"We really need to speak with him. Would you by any chance have an address and phone number for him?"

"Detective Oatmon, I am very uncomfortable giving out the personal information of my customers, especially over the phone to someone I have never met. It is highly irregular."

"When we were there earlier today we showed our credentials to your clerk. I'm sure he can verify we are legitimate," Jack said. "Under normal circumstances I would wait until the morning and come back in person, but I assure you it is a matter of utmost importance. The sooner I can talk to Mr. DeMarchand the better."

"Well, that might solve our problem straight away," Blair said. "The man in the picture is a Mr. Marchand, François Marchand, not DeMarchand. He has been one of my best customers for several years. Obviously, there has been some mistake. What is your Mr. DeMarchand's first name?"

"Frank."

"That is curious. The names are very similar; perhaps you should do some more research and get back to me some other time."

"Wait, please," Jack said. He wasn't going to get this close and not get what he wanted.

"Mr. Blair, I'm a detective from the Los Angeles Police Department. A few weeks ago, the man in the picture shot and killed my partner in cold blood. He left the country using a Belgian passport with the name François Marchand. We are talking about the same man. The longer it takes to track him down, the less chance we have of catching him. I could come over there later this evening or in the morning, play the audio tapes, and show you the evidence, but every minute might count. If he slips through our fingers here in Paris we might not ever find him. Please help me."

There was a long silence on the other end. Jack had no idea if he had changed Blair's mind or not.

"Hold on." Jack heard a metal file drawer open and close, then a rustle of paperwork near the phone. "This is interesting, Detective. All of Mr. Marchand's orders were either delivered to a local hotel or he picked them up personally. As far as I can tell, there is no permanent address here in Paris. The cell phone number is consistent throughout, however." Blair read him the number.

"You're sure there is no local address?"

"In his file for his custom-made suits and shirts yes, I am sure. I keep another file for accessories. Hold on again."

Jack again heard one file drawer open and close, then another. The wait seemed interminable.

"Ah, here we are, as I suspected. I remember Mr. Marchand had a rush order for a very expensive silk tie; he simply had to have it for a special event. We delivered it to an address in the 2nd, 15 Rue de Mulhouse. It was several months ago. I don't know if that helps you, Detective."

"You have been more than helpful."

"Please let me know what happens. If Marchand really did what you said, he must be caught and punished. I certainly don't want a murderer as a client."

"I promise to let you know. In return, promise me if you see him don't do anything stupid. Call me at this same number if he makes any contact with you. He's a very dangerous man; I would hate to see you get hurt."

"I promise. Good luck."

"Thanks."

As soon as Jack finished the call, the phone buzzed again. "Detective Oatmon, this is Victor Ischenko."

CHAPTER FORTY-TWO

Jack almost dropped the phone. He recovered quickly and said, "Why don't you come to the Prefecture and make our conversations official?"

"I am afraid that will be impossible, for reasons I am about to explain to you. We have a mutual acquaintance, a Monsieur Tim Schroeder. He will not be arriving at your house as planned this evening. He is with me now, and for the time being, quite safe, I can assure you …"

"You bastard, you already killed his brother. If you harm him in any way, I will not rest until you pay for it."

"Please calm down, Detective Oatmon. I have no intention of harming Monsieur Schroeder as long as you do exactly as I say. For the record, I did not kill his brother, but I am willing to deliver you his killer, and Monsieur Schroeder, safely, in exchange for the promise to not pursue me and Sasha any further."

"You know I can't do that, Ischenko. You are responsible for at least three murders in the last few weeks, two defenseless women and my partner."

"I had nothing to do with any of those murders. They were all ordered and carried out by an out-of-control, power-hungry second-in-command and his hired assassin. Believe me, it is the last thing I wanted; it is really bad for business," Ischenko said. "I want this to be over as much as you. If we can come to a mutual agreement, you have my word I will retire from all my illegal pursuits."

"You expect me to take the word of a man who kidnaps innocent women and forces them into prostitution? Forgive me if I am not sympathetic."

"Many of these women are not as innocent as you might think," Ischenko replied. "They know exactly what they are getting into. It is a chance to escape desperate poverty. But that is a moral and sociological discussion for another time perhaps, and we do not have that luxury. I will return Monsieur Schroeder, and allow you to arrest Frank DeMarchand, in exchange for my freedom. We need to negotiate in person. You must come alone and must come now. Do not contact anyone else on the task force, or try to set a trap if you want to see Tim Schroeder alive again. Do I make myself clear?"

Jack did not respond right away. His mind was racing, exploring his options, none of which were good. "Okay," he said. "Where do you want me to go?"

"Good decision, Detective," Ischenko said, obviously pleased. "Take the Métro in the direction of La Défense, get off at Pont de Neuilly. Exit on the north side and wait on the median of Avenue Charles de Gaulle. Someone will meet you and bring you the rest of the way. It is now almost eleven. Be there by midnight. Again, don't try and involve anyone else; let's you and I get it done. Believe it or not, Detective Oatmon, I might be the only one you can trust right now."

"Then you and I have to agree on another thing before I put myself in harm's way, and trust you," Jack said. "Call your goons off Rick Asher and Nikki Dunn. You have *my* word they knew nothing about the task force. They are innocent bystanders in this whole thing. They were here to help with the restaurant. I want you to guarantee their safety from now on."

"Done. See how easy that was, Detective? Please do as I ask and no one else will get hurt. Now get moving. Time is running short."

Jack closed his cell phone in disbelief. Victor Ischenko had called his personal cell phone, which meant someone else on the task force besides Inspector Bonnard was on Ischenko's payroll.

He disregarded Ischenko's instructions and immediately called Covyeau's task force cell phone.

No answer.

He tried the land line to Covyeau's office. Same result. Where the hell was he? He left messages to call him immediately, and prepared for the coming confrontation.

Jack decided to take further precautions. Not knowing whom to trust, he felt he had no choice but to call Nikki and Rick and enlist their help.

CHAPTER FORTY-THREE

"Hi, Jack," Nikki answered. "What's up?"

"I need you and Rick to help me right away," Jack said.

"Rick had a case of cabin fever and went for a walk," Nikki said. "Can I help?"

Jack explained the situation quickly, trying to formulate a plan on the fly. "I need one of you to stake out the Mulhouse address in the 2nd and the other one to follow me, and go for help if all hell breaks loose."

Nikki sat at the small table in the kitchen and opened her Métro map. She found the Pont de Neuilly stop easily, but the map was not detailed enough to show Rue de Mulhouse.

She got up and walked into the other room where the large map hung on the wall.

"You said Rue de Mulhouse is in the 2nd?"

"Yes."

"Here it is," she said. "Above Les Halles between Rue Montmartre and Rue Poissonnière." Nikki was thinking on the fly, too. "Here's the plan," she said. "I'll follow you on the motorcycle and …"

"A motorcycle? That's way too dangerous, Nikki."

"Trust me, Jack. This will work. I've been riding these things since I was a kid. My helmet and clothes will make me look like thousands of other riders, male or female. I will actually be safer than if I was on foot, following you in the Métro. We can send Rick on his new bicycle to watch 15 Rue de Mulhouse. I'll leave him a note and the cell phone, and have him call you as soon as he gets back. I'll get going so I can beat you there."

Jack had to agree it was as good a plan as could be come up with on such short notice. "Remember, you're there as backup only. If the shit hits the fan, go find help, understand?"

"Yes, sir."

They spoke for a few more minutes about logistics. Nikki ended the call and wrote the note to Rick. The last thing she did was write down the secure phone's number on a scrap of paper and put it in her pocket, just in case.

ಌ

Rick opened the door and walked into an empty apartment. It was so small he could survey the whole place with a slight turn of his head.

"Nikki?" he called quietly.

No answer; maybe she decided to take a walk, too. He bent over to get a bottle of water from the floor refrigerator and noticed the note and the cell phone.

He called Jack, who had arrived at Trocadéro Plaza.

"I don't like it," Rick said right away. "It puts Nikki in too much danger. I promised Greg I would take care of her."

"Hold on, Rick, it was her idea. I made it clear she is only there as backup, and go for help at the first sign of trouble."

"I still don't like it."

"Neither do I, but at this point it might be our only chance to get Tim back alive. For some strange reason, I think Ischenko is telling the truth. We have an opportunity to get DeMarchand, too. We have to take that chance."

"Ah, shit," Rick said.

"My sentiments exactly. It's a nice warm night, Rick. Take a bike ride to the address on Rue de Mulhouse and keep your eyes and ears open. Like I told Nikki, just observe and call me with anything suspicious. If you can't reach me for some reason, call Inspector Covyeau. It's speed dial #2 on your phone."

"How long do you want me to stay there?"

"I'll check back with you in a couple of hours. We can regroup then. Be careful."

"You keep saying that," Rick said.

Jack gazed at the lit-up Eiffel Tower. The multilevel Trocadéro Plaza was crowded. On the lower level, someone beat a large drum, leading a group of Africans in spirited song; a young boy performed skillful moves with a soccer ball; and people from all over the world were taking pictures. A tangible feeling of anticipation and bonhomie enveloped the entire scene. It was exactly 11 p.m. as he turned away. A spontaneous round of applause erupted from the crowd when an additional set of white lights began twinkling on the Eiffel Tower. Against the inky black sky it was an amazing sight. Jack hoped it was a good omen, stayed a few moments, appealed to a higher authority for a quick and successful mission, then headed downstairs to the Métro.

CHAPTER FORTY-FOUR

Nikki was ahead of schedule as she negotiated the roundabout at the Place de la Concorde. She was only a minute away from L'Avenue Bar & Grill, closed at this hour on a Monday night. Her thoughts drifted to the gun hidden in the planter box as she waited at the traffic light on the Champs Élysée near the Hôtel Crillon. Nikki still had her keys, and, according to Greg, the new glass doors contained the salvaged locks from the wreckage of the original doors. The light changed. The closer she got to the *rond-point*, the more she tried to convince herself she should get the gun. It would take her less than five minutes to retrieve it, conceal it in her small backpack, and be on her way.

At Avenue Matignon she made her decision. She turned sharply to the right, cutting off a taxi. The driver was not pleased, and let her know about it by honking his horn, cursing her, and flipping her off. She didn't have time to wave an apology. She gunned the small motorcycle the two blocks to the restaurant.

To her relief, the keys worked, and she let herself into the dimly lit entryway and relocked the doors. Was it only a week ago Magda died on this very spot? Nikki couldn't think about that now. Her mission was to retrieve the gun and get to the Pont de Neuilly Métro station. She moved to the back of the restaurant, unlocked the French doors, and slipped into the courtyard. A wall sconce and faint glow from the windows of the surrounding buildings allowed enough light. She went to the large flowerbox, took off her backpack, knelt on the hard, uneven cobblestones, and dug with her hands. The soil was loose, and she made quick work of the task. She was a foot down before she realized something was wrong. Greg hadn't buried the gun that deep. Was she on the wrong side of the box? She switched to the other side of the big planter and frantically began digging again. Still nothing! Where was it?

"Are you looking for this, Mademoiselle Dunn?"

Nikki whirled at the sound of the voice and found herself looking directly into the barrel of a silenced Beretta. The face behind the gun was one she didn't recognize, but the voice was definitely French. The missing Glock rested in the palm of his left hand.

"Don't move."

Nikki had no intention of moving. She left both hands in the planter box with her fists full of the moist dirt. At this point it was the only weapon she had.

"I knew it was only a matter of time before one of you came back. You gun-crazy Americans are so predictable."

"Maybe so, but at least we are not using them to murder innocent women," Nikki said.

"The cost of doing business, *m'amie*."

"You prick."

"Please, Mademoiselle Dunn, you are in no position to be disagreeable. If you do not cooperate, my compatriots at the Prefecture will find your body and conclude your death was suicide by your own gun."

"It's not my gun."

"A technicality at this point."

"I have no idea how you found it," Nikki said. "Only a few people knew it existed, and only two other people knew it was in this planter box."

"You fool! I knew of the gun from the beginning. When it didn't surface after our initial investigation, I was convinced you had hidden it somewhere on the premises. It took me less than ten minutes to reconstruct the events of last week and find the gun. I knew one of you would come to retrieve it."

"So, here I am. Now what?"

"We will take a short ride. We need a quiet place to chat for a few minutes."

"I'm not going anywhere," Nikki said defiantly. "The only person taking a short ride will be you, going to jail." She was trying to provoke the man so she could find an opening.

It worked.

The man leaned closer and pointed the gun near her left temple. She vaulted from her crouch, lunged inside the arc of the man's outstretched arm, and hurled both fistfuls of dirt into his face. Caught by surprise and blinded by the dirt, the man fell back. Nikki grabbed him by the shoulders and pushed him to the ground. Both guns went flying, skittering to opposite sides of the courtyard.

The dirt in the man's eyes was uncomfortable, but certainly not fatal, and only temporary at best. Nikki retreated through the French doors and raced to the front of the restaurant.

"Shit!" She had relocked the doors, and the keys were still in her backpack in the courtyard. Her only options were to break the doors or go downstairs. There was no guarantee she would be able to break the glass in time, so she moved to the stairs and leapt down the narrow spiral staircase three or four steps at a time. She reached the level with the toilets and *la cave,* knowing the only other exit was through the dimly lit tunnel and out the door leading right back into the courtyard.

The enraged man was now in the restaurant above. Nikki heard him approach the locked front doors and stop.

She only had a few seconds.

She knew this part of the restaurant very well, having spent the better part of a week in the cave helping Greg store and catalogue the wine. A spare key was hidden in a tiny stone crevice near the ceiling above the door. Please, if there's a God in heaven, let it still be there! It might be her only chance. She gently moved her hands over the rough stone façade.

It was there.

As quietly as possible, she inserted the key and opened the padlock, doing her best to muffle any sound. There was a slightly audible click as the metal bar cleared the locking mechanism. She hoped the sound didn't carry to the floor of the restaurant.

She slipped inside and closed the door, enveloped now in total darkness, but she didn't dare turn on the light. She felt stupid holding the padlock, but couldn't replace it to make the door look locked from the outside, so she put it in her pocket. She would take her chances, maybe use it as a weapon as a last resort.

She felt her way to the center of the ten-by-twelve-foot room and found the long string used to turn on the bare light bulb hanging above. Using a case of wine as a step-stool, she slid her hand to the top of the string and unscrewed the bulb from the socket. As she felt around for an open case of wine to drop the bulb into one of the slots, her hands sensed the neck of a large magnum. Even with her mind going a mile a minute, her brain was alert enough to recognize a better potential weapon than the padlock. She lifted the magnum and replaced the space with the light bulb.

In the far upper right corner of the room away from the door, a niche large enough to hold about ten cases of wine was cut into the wall about six feet off the floor. She might be able to climb up, squeeze in, and hide. Moving completely by memory, she found the cases of wine leaning against the wall. She had set them up to use as steps to store wine in the niche. Holding the magnum in her right hand, she extended her left arm as far back into the niche as she could reach. There might be enough room for her to lie behind the first row of wine cases. She switched arms, reached in, placed the magnum on the rocky ledge, and carefully maneuvered her body over the cases of wine. She rolled on to her back, grabbed the magnum by the neck, and rested it along her right leg.

Lying in the darkness, Nikki's heart was beating so fast and hard she was sure it could be heard in the tunnel. She willed herself to breathe silently and concentrate, the darkness heightening her other senses. There was the undeniable scent of the cardboard wine cases, the stale smell of wine spilled long ago, and the musty smell of the ancient stone walls.

The soft scraping sound was surely the soles of the man's shoes; he was in the tunnel now, moving slowly but steadily toward the cave.

CHAPTER FORTY-FIVE

Nikki held her breath.

The man moved past the cave to the end of the tunnel and the locked door leading to the courtyard. His steps reversed and moved past the cave once more, to the doors to the bathrooms.

Nikki thought she had pulled it off.

Her hope was short-lived though. The man came back, worked the latch and opened the door to the cave. Moving only her eyes, she looked sideways through a tiny crack between two wine cases. She could see directly across the small space to the far opposite wall, but not toward the door. However, she could see the man's faint shadow cast by the tunnel lights, and smell the cigarette odor that permeated his clothing.

A hand scraped the stone searching the wall for a light switch. The pale light from the tunnel leaked in, illuminating the pull string and the missing bulb in the center of the room. The man took two steps into the cave, completely opening the door to allow in as much light as possible. He came further into the room, breathing rapidly. He slowly turned in a circle, checking the confined space.

The movement and breathing stopped suddenly.

Nikki held her breath again.

After what seemed like minutes, but in reality was only a few seconds, the man inched toward the niche. Nikki knew the height of the niche gave her an angle-of-sight protection, but only temporarily. Once the man stood on tiptoes, she was vulnerable. She kept her eyes locked on the tiny line of sight she had through the wine cases, paralyzed with fear and indecision, trapped like an animal in the tiny space.

The man stepped on a full case of wine and slowly pulled up for a look into the niche. His eyes found the same opening in the wine cases. The light from the tunnel leaked through to reflect Nikki's eyes on the other side. The split second it took his brain to decide if they were human eyes, or those of a cat or a rodent, gave Nikki her chance.

Acting purely on adrenaline and survival instinct, she summoned every ounce of her strength and courage, found leverage with her feet against the back wall of the niche, and pushed a case of wine off the ledge. The heavy box hit the off-balance man squarely in the chest, knocked him to the ground, and exploded on the stone floor. Wine spilled across the ground.

With a speed that amazed her, Nikki scrambled down from the niche right behind the wine, miraculously landing on her feet. Somehow the magnum had found a way to stay in her right hand.

This time, though, the man was able to scramble to his feet, still holding his gun. As he moved his arm into position to fire, Nikki didn't hesitate. She swung the wine bottle like a tennis racket forehand, and smashed the bottle as hard as she could against the left side of the man's head.

There was a sickening *thunk*.

The bottle survived the violent impact, but the man's head snapped to an unnatural angle as he crashed to the floor for the third, and last, time.

Nikki collapsed on a case of wine. The lifesaving bottle slipped from her hands and fell to the stone floor with a soft *plink*. She was overcome with relief, but also exhaustion, disgust, and sadness. She might have killed another man, and it was a horrible feeling.

The man on the floor moaned. She went to the prostrate form and knelt down to assess the damage. The whole left side of his head was already one big ugly bruise, his body lying at an odd angle, blood running down his cheek to the floor and mixing with the wine from the broken bottles.

She couldn't leave him here to die, even if he had tried to kill her. She didn't dare move him, so she pushed the destroyed case of wine into the tunnel to keep him dry. She rescued the gun from the oozing wine, did a quick search for the other gun, but only found his cell phone falling from his shirt pocket. She took it and ran to the tunnel and up the stairs.

At the reception desk, she called the paramedics. In French, she told the female dispatcher there was a severely injured man in the cave and gave her the address. She hung up immediately, hoping they didn't think it was a crank call. She ran back to the courtyard to retrieve her backpack, and take a quick look for the other gun. She found the Glock against the far wall underneath the sconce. The Glock was slightly smaller, so she put that in her backpack, and put the man's gun in the planter.

She ran to the front, pulling out her keys as she moved. She left the door unlocked for the emergency personnel, jumped on the motorcycle, and took off. The entire confrontation had taken less than twenty minutes. If she hurried she would still be there in time to help Jack.

CHAPTER FORTY-SIX

Sasha Medvedenko needed to be very careful. Mistakes would not be tolerated. As Victor Ischenko's girlfriend for the last five years, she had learned well not to upset him. He was unpredictable and mean when he didn't get what he wanted. Victor had told Jack to come alone, but Sasha was there to make sure, and so far her plan was working. Drinking espresso at a café with a view of the median of Avenue Charles de Gaulle, she would direct the players in the little drama. Alexei was positioned on the other side of Avenue Charles de Gaulle near the Paroisse Saint-Jean-Baptiste and would follow Jack on the round trip she would send him on

Avenue de Madrid. She wasn't happy using the volatile and violent Alexei, but if all went well tonight, she would never have to worry about him again.

She had a clear view of Jack when he exited the Métro and paced the median. She watched him and the surroundings closely before making the first call.

ꕥ

Jack rode the escalator up out of the Métro with all his senses on full alert. It did not escape his thoughts that when he sent Eric Schroeder to deal with DeMarchand and his crew alone, he ended up dead. Maybe we'll get lucky and resolve the whole thing tonight, Jack thought. He didn't think the chances were very good, but couldn't bear the thought of not helping Tim Schroeder. If all went well, Jack would be the only one in the line of fire.

He paced the north side of the median strip a little above street level. The traffic noise distracted his attempts to pick out Nikki. With all the motorcycles and scooters on the road, and if she was fully equipped with leathers, helmet, and tinted visor as promised, Jack wouldn't recognize her anyway. However, he wanted to make himself conspicuous enough so Nikki could spot *him*. He had no doubt Ischenko's people were already watching him.

Trying to look patient and in control as the minutes ticked away, he found a bench, sat, and waited. He kept his eyes moving over the crowd, not knowing how or when he would be approached. Any one of the dozens of people moving in and out the Métro station and along the street was a potential contact.

His cell phone vibrated in his shirt pocket. The lit display told him it was an unknown caller, so he knew it wasn't Covyeau, or anyone else from the task force. He answered the call.

"Yes?"

"Start walking south on Avenue de Madrid. It is directly across from where you are now. Keep walking until I call you back," the female voice said in barely accented English.

She hung up.

ઌ

Jack made his way past the eastbound traffic on Avenue Charles de Gaulle to Avenue de Madrid. He kept a steady pace as he passed local shops and apartment buildings. The further south he went, the more residential it became, with wider sidewalks, tree-lined streets and less traffic. It had a much different feel compared to the narrow, noisy streets in the center of Paris. It was also decidedly more upscale. Large, modern rectangular apartment buildings with gardens, lawns, and driveways were mixed in with the well-kept older buildings. It reminded him of the older sections of Los Angeles, like where he lived in Los Feliz and parts of Santa Monica and Brentwood.

He passed the Parc de la Folie St.-James on the right. Further down on his left began the vast expanse of the Bois de Boulogne. Warnings started flashing in his head. The Bois was not the best place for a rendezvous; too many dark and unfamiliar spots where he could be ambushed.

The hair on his neck prickled.

As he approached Boulevard Maurice Barrès, he noticed a motorcycle revving its engine at the intersection. He didn't acknowledge the noise and kept on walking. He hoped it was Nikki, but there was no way to tell for sure. The light changed; whoever it was took off north and away from him. He kept walking south.

CHAPTER FORTY-SEVEN

Nikki still shook from her close call at the restaurant, but made it in time. Not wanting to draw attention to herself, she mixed in with the traffic on Avenue Charles de Gaulle, first going a block west of the Métro station. She stopped at a small bistro in the middle of the block with a sight line to the median and pretended to get a quick coffee, then reversed course. She thought making the same loop was not a good idea, so she made several turns into some side streets, ending up traveling north on Avenue de Madrid. As she approached Avenue Charles de Gaulle again, she saw Jack. He had warned her of a probable tactic to see if he was being followed, so when he started walking south toward her, she continued north for several blocks.

The street name changed to Rue du Château. When she knew she was completely out of sight of any of the buildings surrounding the Métro station, she made two left turns and sped south on one of the streets parallel to Avenue de Madrid. She would get ahead of Jack and return north again on Avenue de Madrid. Hopefully, whoever was watching Jack wouldn't expect the move, and she would have a slight advantage. She was sure Jack would do whatever he could to make it easy to follow him, so she didn't do anything to attract attention except ride fast.

Practicing with the motorcycle had paid off, and exhilaration swept over her as she ripped through the gears. Several blocks on the other side of Avenue Charles de Gaulle she turned left again, convinced she would intersect Avenue de Madrid. Unfortunately, the street she chose ended in a roundabout with the Boulevard du Commandant Charcot. On the other side was the Bois de Boulogne. How could she have been so wrong? She had a good sense of direction and even though it was dark, she was sure she was in the right spot.

Then it came to her.

Streets changed names all the time in Paris, like it had when she crossed Avenue Charles de Gaulle a few minutes ago. She turned left on Boulevard du Commandant Charcot, and raced north.

She was right.

Within a hundred yards the street signs read AVENUE DE MADRID. Relieved, she slowed her pace and looked for Jack.

She finally saw him on the west side of the street walking steadily in her direction. He didn't have the cell phone to his ear, so Nikki assumed he was not being given up-to-the-minute directions. She stopped at the roundabout of Avenue de Madrid and Boulevard Maurice Barrès as their paths were about to cross. She revved the motor as a signal, not knowing if it would work. She saw no reaction from Jack as she stole a glance through the black visor of her helmet.

ꕤ

Jack's cell phone buzzed again.

"Turn around and go back to the bench," the female voice said. "It is a lovely night for a walk, don't you think?"

"Yes," Jack said, but she had already disconnected.

Jack knew they were trying to rattle him, put him on the defensive. He could sense someone watching him, but he had expected it, and tried to stay calm. He turned around, and with the same steady pace headed back to the bench, grateful to be moving away from the Bois de Boulogne.

ꕤ

Nikki continued north for a few hundred yards, turned into a small side street, and made a series of right turns to lead her back to the same intersection. She turned left, now back on Avenue de Madrid, hoping to come up behind Jack.

He wasn't there.

Nikki was frantic. Where was he? The series of turns she had made since she last saw him had taken no more than two minutes. He couldn't have gone far. She continued south on Avenue de Madrid sneaking looks down the side streets.

Still nothing.

She decided to go back to the point where she lost contact and start over. Maybe he had gone down an alley or into a neighborhood bistro she hadn't noticed.

For the next few minutes Nikki methodically searched the grid of streets surrounding the roundabout of Avenue de Madrid and Boulevard Maurice Barrès.

No sign of Jack.

Convinced she would have seen him if he was on the streets, she considered several logical explanations: someone had picked him up in a car and headed who knew where, he was inside one of the buildings, or he had reversed course and headed back toward the Métro station. The impracticality of searching for a phantom pickup car, or hanging around the nearby buildings waiting for him to reemerge, was obvious. Her only choice was to go back in the direction of Métro.

ና

Jack mounted the few steps to the median as nonchalantly as possible and walked back to the bench. One end was now occupied by someone reading a newspaper; the face was hidden, but Jack had no doubt it was his contact.

"Good evening, Detective Oatmon," said the voice behind the paper.

Jack recognized the voice as the woman on the phone.

"Good evening," he replied. "Nice night for a walk, isn't it?"

"I see you haven't lost your sense of humor," she said. "That is a good sign our business this evening might end successfully."

She lowered the paper.

It took Jack a moment to recognize the woman from the house on Coldwater Canyon. "Hello, Sasha. I almost didn't recognize you without the red bikini top."

If Sasha was surprised Jack knew her name, she didn't show it. In fact, she laughed. "I like your style, Detective. Keep it up and we will do fine tonight."

"Where do we go from here?"

"We stay right here until I get a call from my associate, and he convinces me you did as you were told and came alone."

"I did," Jack lied.

"We shall see. My man is very good, but he is also extremely dangerous. We would both do well to pay attention and watch our backs."

Sasha's phone buzzed in her hand.

"Da."

Jack tensed as Sasha listened. If he hadn't noticed Nikki, he was pretty sure they hadn't either.

Sasha lowered the phone and looked at Jack.

"So far, so good. Now, please give me your cell phone," she ordered. "I don't want to take a chance your colleagues can track you with a GPS system."

Jack pulled out his phone, turned it off, and handed it to her. She stood up, and to Jack's surprise, looped her arm in his. "Now we walk some more. It is not far."

They went north on Rue du Château, looking very much like any other couple out for a late night stroll.

CHAPTER FORTY-EIGHT

Nikki had guessed right again.

Jack was at the bench talking to a very attractive woman. They didn't seem to be in any hurry, so Nikki crossed Avenue Charles de Gaulle for the second time. She made a quick right turn into a narrow alley behind the buildings facing Avenue Charles de Gaulle, stopped, and idled the motorcycle. She quickly shed the lightweight black leather jacket and the leggings covering her jeans. From under the seat she pulled out and put on a light blue windbreaker, stuffing the leather jacket and leggings in its place. It had taken less than thirty seconds. She looked completely different as she sped down the alley, looped back on to Avenue Charles de Gaulle in time to see Jack and the woman head north on Rue du Château. She wanted to give them a little bit of a head start, so she pulled to the curb and pretended to look for something in her backpack.

She was about to set off again when something in her peripheral vision made her stop. Crossing Avenue Charles de Gaulle was a small, compact man wearing a heavy black turtleneck sweater. It struck Nikki as strange and incongruous on the still warm night. She waited to take a closer look as he passed twenty feet in front of her, and headed in the same direction as Jack and the woman. He looked toward her and Nikki's blood went cold. Thank God she had kept the visor on her helmet down.

The turtleneck couldn't cover it all.

Through the dark visor she saw the unmistakable markings of the top half of the black snow-leopard tattoo. The photographic images from the hotel window in Florence were etched in her consciousness.

Alexei.

Magda's murderer, the assassin sent to kill her and Rick.

Nikki was paralyzed with fear. She let Alexei walk out of sight around the corner while she contemplated her next move. She couldn't go to the police, and Rick was on his bicycle miles away. She had no choice. She carefully surveyed the crowd of pedestrians, nearby cars, and other motorcycle riders. She convinced herself there wasn't a third person covering Alexei. Slowly, she moved onto Rue du Château, and followed.

After a few short blocks the street widened and looked similar to the area south of Avenue Charles de Gaulle. Nikki could see for several blocks ahead and saw Jack and the blonde woman go through a gate into the yard of a large house. Suspecting Alexei to be on the alert for someone behind him, she turned right at the first opportunity, and then left again to parallel Rue du Château. She rode several blocks and parked the bike. She took off the light blue windbreaker, stuffed it into her helmet, and put them both in the fiberglass saddlebag. She rolled her hair up into a wrinkled baseball cap from her backpack, and cautiously worked her way back to Rue du Château.

ᔓ

Sasha ushered Jack past the two large Mercedes sedans in the driveway to a side entrance. They went through the kitchen to a large, dark library at the front of the house. The front windows were covered with heavy curtains, and the shutters covering the side windows facing the driveway were open to allow in a slight breeze. The solid oak, six-paneled door on the opposite wall, leading to what Jack assumed was the living area, was closed.

Victor Ischenko welcomed Jack from behind a large table, a green banker's lamp providing the only light other than the light through the open door to the kitchen.

Ischenko had traded in his expertly tailored suits and styled hair. He wore jeans, a plain gray sweatshirt, and sported a crew cut and a goatee. Even with the new look Jack couldn't deny the man had a presence, a demeanor of power.

"Please sit down. May I get you a drink?" He pointed to a nice leather reading chair to the left of the table.

"No, thank you," Jack said. "I prefer to conclude our business quickly and with my wits about me."

"All will go well as long as we trust each other," Victor said.

"I'm here, I'm alone, and have done everything you've asked for so far. In return, I need to know Tim Schroeder is alive and unharmed. That would be a good start."

"Certainly." He looked up at Sasha, nodded to the closed door.

"He is on the couch in the next room. He is still unconscious, but there will be no ill effects other than a headache. Please see for yourself."

Jack got up and followed Sasha to the door. They entered an even larger room, set up as a traditional living room, with a fireplace on the far wall, framed by an oversized couch in front of the bay window opening toward the street and a loveseat facing the couch. A large reading chair matching the one in the library closed the square around a large coffee table.

Tim Schroeder was on the couch. He lay on his back, arms and hands in a funereal position across his torso. Jack moved to the couch to make sure Tim was breathing normally, and not in any obvious pain. He leaned close to see if there were any obvious marks on his head or neck.

"It was a mild sedative, Detective Oatmon," Sasha said. "He will be out for a little while longer. I assure you he will be fine."

"Good. Then let's go put an end to this. Now."

She led him back into the library and closed the door again. "Are you sure you don't want a drink?" she asked.

Jack relented, only to make them feel at ease. "A small Scotch neat, please."

"Excellent," Victor said. He motioned Jack to the chair once again. "I will have one too please, Sasha."

She had obviously played hostess before, and the three were soon holding glasses of expensive single malt. "To the successful conclusion of our business," Victor toasted.

The three raised their glasses and drank.

Jack took a very small sip and placed the glass on the edge of the table. "So, how is it going to work?"

"I have a plan," Victor said. His posture changed to convey that he was now in charge of the meeting. "Frank DeMarchand, your partner's killer, is currently in the upstairs library making arrangements to leave with us at the conclusion of our business. Of course, he is unaware his plans will change, and will stay behind as a guest of the French and American authorities. Alexei Persoff, Magda's killer, is lurking outside the house to make sure you haven't set a trap for us. If he sees anything even remotely suspicious, and calls to warn me, both you and Mr. Schroeder will die immediately. Our escape routes have been meticulously planned, so it is in your best interest to conclude our business on my terms."

"You seem very confident of yourself and your plans," Jack said.

"I am indeed, Detective Oatmon. Do you have any idea where you are right now?"

"I'm afraid not," Jack said honestly.

"I am sure you know Craig Lawrence?" Victor said.

"The head of the United States Mission here in Paris," Jack replied. "He is fully aware of my status on the task force here."

Victor roared with laughter. "Of course, he is on the task force with you. You're sitting in his house, in his favorite reading chair. He said I could use it in an emergency, so I finally took him up on his offer. His wife and children are conveniently spending the summer with her parents in the United States, which makes it much easier for Craig to indulge his fascination with teenaged boys and girls, something I was able to help him with over the last few years. To save himself, he would protect me before you and the task force."

Jack said nothing.

"Are you shocked, Detective? Surely you had your suspicions."

"I knew the dirt went pretty high up but, so far, I only know he is not well liked," Jack said.

"Believe me, Craig Lawrence is the tip of the iceberg. Most of the rank-and-file inspectors, and *flics* in several arrondissements, are completely compromised. Daniel Covyeau was the one person we could never turn, one of the very few failures in my career. It is another indication to conclude our business, and for me to retire. Wasn't there a famous American football player or coach who believed it was better to retire a year early rather than a year too late? An athlete will only risk embarrassing himself with his declining skills. In my line of work, Detective, staying too long leads to much more serious consequences."

"So let's do it," Jack said. "What is the first step?"

Victor Ischenko spent ten minutes explaining the deal. It was simple. Ischenko would provide the task force with a complete description of Dante International's activities, in exchange for his freedom.

Jack agreed to everything. He desperately wanted to get himself and Tim out of this alive. He'd worry about everything else later.

"That's it then. See, I told you this would be easy." Victor stood and offered his hand.

Jack shook it. It felt like making a deal with the devil.

"I assume you came armed?" Victor asked, already knowing the answer.

"Of course. My service revolver in a shoulder holster and a small pistol on my ankle," Jack answered. There was no reason to lie now.

"Excellent. When the time comes and I ask for your service revolver, please hand it over. You will still have your back up pistol for protection until I give you back the revolver. I am afraid it will be necessary to keep Mr. DeMarchand from getting suspicious."

Victor went to the intercom on the wall next to the door leading to the living area. He pushed a button.

"We're ready," he said, then led Jack and Sasha into the living room.

CHAPTER FORTY-NINE

Frank DeMarchand heard the muffled voices from below as he finalized his escape plans. He had spent the evening accessing his bank accounts online and transferring the funds to new accounts. He knew this day would eventually come, and he had planned accordingly.

He accessed all of Dante International's accounts, plus Victor Ischenko's personal accounts, including the ones Victor had cleverly, but unsuccessfully, tried to hide from him. DeMarchand had devised a software program to spy on Victor's computer and Dante International's accounts, and was alerted any time Victor or anyone else logged into them. A disturbing new pattern of financial transactions over the last few days had made him highly suspicious of Victor Ischenko's motives and future plans. His boss, friend, and mentor for almost two decades was planning something big, and keeping him out of the loop. DeMarchand decided he wasn't going to stick around to find out; it was time to move on.

He transferred most of Ischenko's money to his own secret accounts. DeMarchand now had more money than he could spend in two lifetimes, and planned to enjoy it someplace warm, sip drinks with umbrellas, and watch pretty girls walk by in dental-floss bikinis.

At the time he killed Eric Schroeder in Los Angeles, he was truly convinced he would never be able to escape from Ischenko and his associates. The subsequent events of the last few weeks had changed his mind. A young, inexperienced couple, Rick Asher and Nikki Dunn, had eluded the professional assassin Alexei Persoff. They had been so successful in fact, that even now no one in DeMarchand's wide circle of contacts had a clue as to where they were. If Rick and Nikki could disappear so completely, he was convinced he could too. The money would make it so much easier.

DeMarchand was emboldened by how easily he had been able to spy on, access, and manipulate his boss's private financial world. His meticulous nature, attention to detail, and ability to foresee consequences far into the future would trump Ischenko's carelessness and arrogance. He couldn't wait to see the look on his face when Victor realized he and Sasha would be penniless, and possibly in the hands of the authorities. After Ischenko summoned him, he called Alexei.

"Get into position."

He shut down the laptop, stored the electronic gear in his shoulder bag, and checked to ensure the small automatic pistol in the pocket of his perfectly pressed blue blazer was loaded, with the safety off. He stopped at the door, looked back to make sure he hadn't left any incriminating evidence, turned out the light and walked downstairs.

ග

Alexei moved toward the house. Sasha and Jack had left the front gate open, and the two black Mercedes sedans were tandem parked in the gravel driveway, facing the street for a quick exit. Using the cars and the hedges along the driveway as cover, he slipped past the front of the house, and silently entered through the same kitchen door Sasha and Jack had used earlier. He positioned himself behind the closed oak door of the library, and waited.

ග

Nikki watched Alexei go through the gate. She was tempted to leave her hiding place and move closer, but decided against it. Her vantage point behind a tree a few lots down offered her a clear view of the bay window at the front of the house. Behind the sheer curtains she could see the faint outlines of several people moving around the room. She felt helpless not knowing exactly who was in there, or having a plan of action if it went bad.

But, Jack had been emphatic. She was only there as back-up in case things got out of hand. The gun in her backpack was little solace at this point.

She saw the light in the upstairs window go out, and a few seconds later an additional body moved behind the curtains. Okay, she thought, all the players are in place, whatever was going to happen would happen in the next few minutes. She silently wished Jack good luck, and hoped he and Tim would get out alive.

CHAPTER FIFTY

Tim Schroeder's mind slowly started to work again, and his eyes fluttered open for a brief moment. The scene he viewed with slightly blurred vision confused him. A familiar face sat at the end of a couch, but the rest were unrecognizable. The light from the lamp on the end table hurt his eyes, so he closed them and tried to concentrate. The pain in his shoulder from Leveque's hasty and clumsily plunged needle kick-started his brain. He remembered greeting Leveque at the door, their brief struggle, and hearing another voice before losing consciousness. It was that voice speaking again now. He kept his eyes closed and listened.

ೲ

"Everything is in place for our departure," DeMarchand said. He lowered his shoulder bag to the floor next to the leather reading chair and sat down. DeMarchand had barely acknowledged Jack and Tim's presence when he entered the living room, concentrating on Ischenko, the only real threat. Ischenko sat on the matching love seat facing the sofa and the bay window. Sasha stood next to the fireplace to Ischenko's left, her wary eyes on DeMarchand and the oak door leading to the library.

"Very good," Ischenko said. "I'm sure you have handled everything with your usual efficiency, Frank. However, before we leave tonight, I have made a concession to Detective Oatmon. You will deposit one million dollars of *your* money into my new personal Zurich account. I will give you the passwords and account numbers when you are ready. Once Sasha and I are safe, I will transfer the money to Detective Oatmon to be used to assist the families of Los Angeles police officers killed in the line of duty. It is a small price to pay for our freedom. You have several accounts with at least that much in them, so it shouldn't take you more than a few minutes. Sit right there, use your laptop and the secure wireless connection so conveniently provided by Director Lawrence."

"And if I refuse?" DeMarchand asked.

"Then you will die in that chair before you have a chance to move," Ischenko said. He pulled a small pistol from behind a cushion and pointed it directly at DeMarchand's chest. “Please turn on your laptop and get started, Frank; we don’t have much time.”

“What happens after I transfer the money? What assurances do I have that Detective Oatmon will not shoot me once the money is transferred?”

“You have no assurances. In the interest of fairness though, the Detective will relinquish his service pistol until we leave.”

He motioned to Jack, pointing to the coffee table. “If you please, Detective.”

This was the moment of truth for Jack.

Should he really trust Ischenko? He looked from Ischenko to DeMarchand, and then to Sasha standing next to the fireplace. Jack thought he saw her nod almost imperceptibly. He removed his revolver and placed it on the coffee table.

“I’ll hold it for safekeeping,” Sasha said. She carefully picked up the revolver, held it in her right hand along her thigh, pretending to be afraid of it. She moved back to the fireplace before anyone could protest.

It was then Jack realized that Sasha had positioned herself in the perfect spot. She was the only one in the room who didn’t have to move their head to see everyone, and she had a clean line of sight to the closed door to the library. He made eye contact with her, and smiled.

DeMarchand seemed satisfied with the arrangements, pulled his laptop from the shoulder bag, and booted up.

“Put the laptop on the edge of the coffee table so we can see what you are doing,” Ischenko said. “I don’t want any surprises.”

DeMarchand gave Ischenko a look of disgust, but complied. It was awkward for him because he was forced to sit on the very edge of the chair and reach almost arm's length to the keyboard. It put him in an awkward, vulnerable position, his hands far away from the gun in his coat pocket. He pretended to adjust his jacket to the new position, but in reality tried to move the pocket closer to his thigh for easier access. He hoped the move would fool Ischenko.

It didn't.

"Don't worry about the gun in your pocket, Frank," Ischenko said. "Keep your hands on the laptop where I can see them."

DeMarchand decided the charade had gone far enough. He had no intention of transferring money to anyone.

"I think it is time for us to renegotiate our deal," he said. He stopped typing, but didn't move his hands away from the keyboard.

"You are in no position to negotiate, or renegotiate, anything," Ischenko said. He stood up and towered menacingly over DeMarchand's crouched figure. "I run the show, so do as you are told and transfer the money. Remember, I have a gun pointed at you."

"I'm not the only one with a gun pointed at them," DeMarchand said. "My renegotiating skills have some facets you might have overlooked. If I die, you die." He looked toward the now slightly open oak door to the library, and all the other eyes in the room followed.

Alexei Persoff stood partially protected by the doorway, but there was no mistaking the automatic pistol aimed at Ischenko's head.

"Alexei, whatever he is paying you, I'll double it," Ischenko said. He turned back to face DeMarchand. "No, I'll triple it."

DeMarchand sneered in triumph. "I'm afraid that won't be possible. As of now, you and Dante International are penniless."

He closed the laptop, put it back in his shoulder bag, and stood up. He moved toward Alexei. "Victor, your arrogance and carelessness are no match for me. I have been the brains of this company for years now, and I plan to keep what is rightfully mine. I am taking everything of yours, too. It will be payment for your plans to double-cross me tonight."

A look of genuine surprise flickered across Victor Ischenko's face. He wasn't surprised at DeMarchand's money grab, but couldn't figure out how DeMarchand had smelled out the double-cross. He calmly sat back down on the loveseat, and smiled.

"Well, well, this is a strange turn of events. I really didn't think you had it in you to confront me, Frank. However, you are getting a little ahead of yourself. What was the name of that program you told me about, Sasha?"

"Double Steal."

"Ah, yes, another American sports term, and perfectly appropriate for our current situation. I hope our American friends on the couch will appreciate its use." He smiled at Jack.

"You see, my dear Frank, we found your little spyware program on our system and took measures to monitor and counteract any of your financial maneuvering. All of the transactions you performed over the last forty-eight hours were intercepted by the Double Steal program. The funds have been rerouted to a secret account elsewhere, somewhere you will never find them."

"That's impossible. I have confirmation numbers for every transfer," DeMarchand said. "You're bluffing."

"I assure you I am not," Ischenko said. The steel came back to his voice. "The confirmation numbers generated by our program will not work. If you don't believe me, sit down and try to access one of your new accounts."

DeMarchand hesitated, but said, "Remember, there is still a gun pointed at your head. I can assure you Alexei will have no problem putting a bullet in your brain. In fact, he would probably enjoy it now that he knows you were going to double-cross him, too."

"Remember there is one still pointed at you, too," Ischenko echoed.

DeMarchand reluctantly sat down again, retrieved his laptop, and turned it on. He saw no reason to use the coffee table, and silently watched as the computer booted up on his thighs.

CHAPTER FIFTY-ONE

Jack got distracted from the confrontation by a gentle pressure on his lower back. Thinking he was leaning awkwardly against one of the sofa cushions, he felt behind him with his right hand. He didn't find a cushion, but a foot, Tim Schroeder's foot. He sat back and stole a glance at the other end of the couch. He made eye contact with Tim, and gently squeezed his foot. Tim responded by blinking quickly and moving his foot again. Jack was relieved to see Tim was alert, but he still needed to get them out alive. He moved his hand away from Tim's foot and as close to his ankle holster as he could without arousing the suspicion of Alexei or De-

Marchand. Jack looked at both of them and realized his first priority was avoiding Alexei's gun. DeMarchand was totally engrossed in the laptop screen.

ẽ

Tim Schroeder almost felt normal again. Maybe all the workouts and naps had helped his body recover more quickly from the sedative. He hoped his signal to Jack had not been seen by the others in the room, because the element of surprise might be the only thing to save their lives in the next few minutes. His brief times with Jack back in Los Angeles, and in Paris with the task force, had convinced him Jack was good under pressure.

He tilted his head ever so slightly, opened his eyes as far as he would dare, and surveyed the room. He recognized Ischenko and DeMarchand from the CIA and police photographs, but didn't recognize the woman by the fireplace. The vague form in the darkened doorway was too concealed, but he could see the silenced end of the pistol still pointed at Ischenko. The last thing he did before closing his eyes again was check the slight bulge near Jack's ankle. He had seen Jack take the small holster on and off several times when he visited with him in Los Angeles for his brother's funeral. He felt reassured to know they might have some firepower.

ẽ

The look on DeMarchand's face said it all. He entered several confirmation numbers, and to his chagrin, none of them worked. There was no use in checking the others. He was sure the result would be the same.

He now had nothing.

All the years of risk and hard work were wasted if he could not convince Ischenko to negotiate. He decided to use one of Ischenko's own tactics and attack rather than compromise or retreat.

"Alexei, I think it is time to show Victor we are serious."

ꕥ

Alexei moved into the room, the muzzle of the gun still aimed at Ischenko's head. "Put your gun on the coffee table and give him the instructions to retrieve his money, or I will kill Sasha," he said.

Ischenko put his gun on the table.

Alexei turned to point the gun at Sasha, but it was too late. The bullet Sasha fired from Jack's service revolver slammed into his left shoulder and spun him back into the library doorway. Alexei screamed in pain, but the wound was not fatal. Sasha had missed his heart by a few inches. He rolled over his good shoulder into the darkened doorway, and returned fire. The bullets ricocheted off the stone fireplace sending razor-sharp shards spraying through the air. Victor Ischenko and Sasha took cover behind the loveseat, giving Alexei enough time to get through to the library and slam the door. Bleeding profusely from the wound to his left shoulder, he knew his best chance of survival was to flee.

He crawled to the kitchen and saw two sets of car keys hanging from a pegboard near the entry door. He had to put the gun down on the counter for a second as he slipped both sets off their hooks. Hoping everyone in the living room would think he was still behind the library door, at least for the next few precious seconds, he eased open the kitchen door and made his way to the back of the first car in the driveway.

He looked back, but no one was there.

Through the shutters of the library windows he could see the door to the living room was still closed. He only had a few more seconds. Using the cars as cover, he duck-crawled to the passenger side of the Mercedes nearest the street, his thighs and calves aching from the effort. The passenger-side door was unlocked, and as soon as he opened it the interior light came on. He couldn't worry about that now. He scrambled in, shut the door, and fumbled in the darkness with the first set of keys. He tried the obvious ignition key on the ring.

Bingo!

The big sedan roared to life. He jammed the car into first gear and floored the accelerator. The tires spun frantically in the graveled driveway, found purchase, and shot the car through the open gates. Steering and shifting with his one good arm, he took off for the safety of downtown Paris.

CHAPTER FIFTY-TWO

"Don't!"

Sasha thought quicker than Ischenko, and had the presence of mind to remember DeMarchand still had his gun. She caught him as he reached for it, the awkwardness of having the laptop on his thighs delaying his movements.

His hand stopped.

"Take your right hand away from your pocket," she said. DeMarchand complied, putting his hand on the armrest of the chair.

"Now take your left hand, thumb and first finger only, and *slowly* remove your gun. Put it on the coffee table next to the other gun. If I see any part of your palm on the gun, or a finger near the trigger, I will kill you."

DeMarchand believed her.

Moving deliberately, he closed the laptop, reached across his body, retrieved the gun, and placed it on the coffee table next to Ischenko's. The laptop slipped from his thighs, falling to the floor with a soft thud on the expensive carpet.

"Leave it!" Sasha instructed, before DeMarchand could make another move. "Put both hands on the armrests where I can see them."

Again, he complied.

In the short silence that followed, they heard the sedan in the driveway start and speed off the property. "You are all alone now," Sasha said. "Even a sewer rat like Alexei has abandoned you."

ઌ

After hearing the shots, Nikki ran back to the motorcycle, prepared to do as she had been told, get help. She would ride by the house, hoping to get a glimpse inside. She was fifty yards from the house when one of the sedans came screaming out of the driveway. In the light of the streetlamp she had a flicker of recognition.

Alexei!

He looked hurt.

Nikki didn't know what to do: go for help as instructed, or take the chance of losing Alexei by not following him. She drew even with the house. Through the sheer curtains of the bay window, she could see Jack's profile sitting on the couch, his head going back and forth like he was watching a tennis match. Thank God he was still alive, she thought. Acting on pure instinct, she decided Jack was safe for the next few minutes. She revved the small motorcycle to its maximum; the front wheels almost came off the pavement as she raced after the black Mercedes, its red taillights fading in the distance.

☙

In the few seconds of uncertainty caused by Sasha's confrontation with Alexei, Jack thought fast. He dropped down between the couch and the coffee table, smoothly removing the small pistol from his ankle holster. Pretending to protect himself and Tim he hovered closely over Tim's upper body.

"Don't move," he whispered to Tim.

Using his body to cover his movements, Jack slipped the pistol into Tim's right hand, guided it down to hide it under the edge of the couch. It had taken no more than a couple of seconds. Jack hoped none of the other people in the room would notice Tim's change of position.

Tim used his left hand to give Jack's forearm a reassuring squeeze, amazed at how cool Jack was under fire. A surge of gratitude swept over him, along with a feeling of calm. All he had to do was take his cue from Jack, and they would both get out of this alive. He moved his eyelids up a millimeter at a time. He could see enough to be ready.

CHAPTER FIFTY-THREE

"Excellent work, my dear," Ischenko said. "Now we must quickly conclude the business at hand." He stood up from the cover of the loveseat's armrest and moved to retrieve the two guns from the coffee table.

"Leave them!"

Ischenko stopped.

The vehemence and tone of the command shocked him. He turned to see Sasha pointing the gun at him.

"Sit down."

"Sasha, my dear, have you lost your mind?" Ischenko asked, complete surprise on his face.

"The mind you have used and abused for so many years?" Sasha's contempt was obvious. "At least Frank is right about one thing tonight. You are a complete fool. Now, *SIT DOWN* or I will shoot you without a second thought."

"You are making the biggest mistake of your life, Sasha," Ischenko said. "You will never make it without me." Even as he said this, he did as instructed, and sat down on the loveseat.

Sasha laughed with delight. "You really are a big, stupid fool, and I am sick of your bullshit. How could you have been so oblivious for all this time? Since the moment you kidnapped me twelve years ago, I have been planning this day. From the beginning when you continuously raped me into submission, then shared me with your friends, I knew I would find a way. You are an animal, Victor, not fit to be a human being. You have hurt too many, destroyed too many lives to deserve to live."

"I am a changed man," Ischenko said. A faint hint of fear crept into his voice. "I am giving it all up for us. We have a new life planned; don't throw it away now."

"You inconsiderate moron. Do you really think I am that stupid, Victor? That I could ever trust you? The only reason you would change is because you are forced to do so. You are a dinosaur, protected and coddled for so long you have no sense of reality. Your time has passed."

"You could never shoot me, Sasha," Ischenko said. "You don't have the guts. If you had the guts, you would have done it a long time ago."

"I wasn't going to leave until I could destroy you completely," Sasha said. "All those computer classes you made me take to help you with your business have proved quite valuable. Think real carefully. The Double Steal program was my idea. All the money DeMarchand thought he stole is now mine, safely tucked away in accounts no one will ever find. I am now rich and in charge of my own life, a life you took from me to suit your own selfish purposes. It stops now. It is over, Victor."

Victor got up.

"You will never pull that trigger, Sasha. You know it and I know it, so stop this nonsense. Let's get out of here before it is too late."

He moved toward Sasha.

"It is already too late," she said. "Rot in hell, you bastard!"

The gun exploded once more in her small hand.

Ischenko's forehead disintegrated. His large body crashed violently onto the loveseat, coming to rest in a half-sitting position. His brains sprayed over the back of the couch, blood dripping down to the seat cushions.

"Don't!" Sasha screamed once again to a shocked DeMarchand. She pointed the gun at his forehead. He had made a move to retrieve his gun from the coffee table. "Don't think for a second I won't shoot you too, Frank."

Sasha moved quickly and efficiently. She threw Victor's gun onto the loveseat next to his corpse, and picked up DeMarchand's gun in her left hand. She felt a lot more comfortable now that she controlled all the guns.

DeMarchand eased back into the reading chair and waited. "What now, Sasha? Do you have a plan? You seem to have your hands full, literally and figuratively," he said.

"Frank, you are almost as much of a fool as Victor," she said. "I once thought you could be salvaged from Victor's grasp, but I was mistaken. I despise everything you represent."

"You still haven't answered my question, Sasha. What now?"

"The plan remains the same, you idiot. It was my plan all along. You don't think Victor set this all up by himself, do you?"

Still pointing Jack's gun at DeMarchand's head, Sasha moved to a credenza on the far wall behind the loveseat. A large, elegant black leather laptop case sat on top. She put DeMarchand's gun in the side pouch of the case, looped the strap over her left shoulder, and pulled out a bulky manila envelope. She moved back across the room, the gun steady on DeMarchand, the eyes of all three men on her.

"You remember the deal, Detective Oatmon?" she asked.

"Yes."

"Excellent."

She placed the envelope on the armrest of the loveseat, inches away from the lifeless form of Victor Ischenko. She retrieved Victor's gun from the cushion and put it in the laptop pouch next to the other one.

"You will find as much information as I could remember in the envelope. There are names, addresses, dates, and the last known whereabouts of several hundred women around the world. I did the best I could, and I apologize because some of it will be outdated, but might help you in some other way. There are also names of many of the officials he has bribed and compromised here in France, and the United States, plus many of Victor's contacts in Poland, Romania, Bulgaria, Moldova, Ukraine, and other places. Some of the information is handwritten, but most of it is on disks. Victor's cell phones are in there, too, and they might be helpful."

"Thank you very much," was all Jack could say.

"Here is your cell phone," she said, placing it on the envelope. "I will return your gun when the time is appropriate. I still need it for a few more minutes."

"Sasha, why don't you stay and help us? We can help you, protect you. Think of how many lives you could save."

"You could never protect me as well as I can protect myself, believe me. However, I promise to honor the million-dollar commitment to your fund. I will stay in contact with you, but it will be from a distance, and on my terms. That's the deal, and it's not negotiable. I have lived up to my part of the bargain by delivering your partner's murderer to you. I am sorry I didn't kill Alexei, but he is badly wounded. That should be enough for now."

Jack didn't like it, but he understood. "Okay."

"Now I need you to live up to your part of the bargain, Jack. Don't try to stop me."

"I won't. I give you my word," Jack said.

Sasha opened the door to the library with her free hand, the gun still pointed at DeMarchand's stunned face, backed out of the room, and closed the door. She pulled the extra set of keys to the second Mercedes from a pouch in the laptop case, and went out the kitchen door. She slid into the soft leather driver's seat of the second Mercedes sedan, the laptop case on the passenger seat, started the car, and drove away.

CHAPTER FIFTY-FOUR

“Well, I will be leaving now,” DeMarchand said. He rose from the reading chair, and shoved his laptop back into the case.

Snap!

Jack wasn’t surprised to see the large switchblade knife DeMarchand held a few feet away.

“I wouldn’t be so sure of yourself, Frank,” Jack said.

“You don’t scare me, Oatmon. If you move I will slice you to pieces and leave your body parts for the stray dogs in the alley.”

"I don't think that is going to happen, Frank," Jack said. He smiled. "Are you familiar with the game Rock, Paper, Scissors?"

"A child's game. Besides, you have none of the three, and I have an extremely lethal weapon a stride away from your heart."

"How do you know for sure?" Jack said.

He raised his hands in front of his body to draw DeMarchand's eyes, giving Tim Schroeder the perfect opportunity to raise his hand from under the couch. He pointed the small pistol at DeMarchand.

"Drop the knife," Tim said coldly. He moved to a sitting position and had a momentary flash of dizziness, most likely the residue from the sedative, but recovered quickly. "I'll kill you as quickly and easily as you killed my brother, you fucking lowlife."

Jack stood up.

"Do as he says. We have every reason to want you dead, and nothing to lose at this point. Drop the knife, Frank. It's over for you, too."

DeMarchand decided he would rather die than spend the rest of his life in prison. He flicked his wrist so quickly Tim didn't have a chance to fire before the tip of the knife pierced his forearm. Tim screamed in pain and the gun fell to the floor. DeMarchand leapt at Jack and drove his head into Jack's torso. Jack had anticipated the move and used DeMarchand's own momentum to hurl him over the couch. DeMarchand flew over Tim and his bleeding arm. He landed with a crash at the base of the bay window.

Like a cornered animal, DeMarchand again chose to attack rather than defend. He was up quickly and back over the couch before Jack could retrieve the gun. Their bodies fell heavily on the corner of the coffee table, breaking one of its legs. It crumpled at an odd angle as they hit the carpet together.

DeMarchand proved to be a lot stronger than Jack anticipated, and had the early advantage as they landed in a heap, DeMarchand on top. He tried to maneuver his legs to pin down Jack's arms, but Jack was able to twist his torso away. Now on his stomach, Jack first moved onto all fours, then lifted up to a standing position. DeMarchand, now on Jack's back, had him in a firm headlock, doing his best to crush Jack's breathing passages.

It was working.

Jack didn't have much time before losing enough oxygen for his brain and muscles to respond properly. He turned his back to the wall of the library, crouched slightly to pull DeMarchand a little off balance, and back-pedaled hard toward the wall.

Jack heard a satisfying *oomph*!

The impact forced the air from DeMarchand's lungs and the men collapsed to the floor again, both gasping for air. Jack broke free and scrambled the few feet back toward the coffee table looking through clouded eyes for the gun.

ೞ

They had hit the wall so hard Tim felt the vibration on the couch. He pulled the knife from his now-useless, bleeding right arm, and looked for the gun. Holding the damaged arm hard against his body, he used his left hand to feel under the couch.

Nothing!

It couldn't have gone far, he thought. It had to be under the crumpled coffee table. He pushed the broken table as hard as he could with his left hand.

Thud!

The far side of the table hit Jack squarely in the forehead as he was looking from the other side.

Ughh!

That was all Tim heard as he watched Jack slump back against the corner of the loveseat, blood running down his face.

It was up to Tim now. The effort with the table had proved unfortunate for Jack's forehead, but it also produced the gun. Tim saw it near the broken table leg a split second before DeMarchand.

He grabbed it with his wobbly left hand.

DeMarchand launched himself in the air toward Tim with the ferocity of a starved wild animal fighting for food. He landed with his feet near Jack's prone body, the middle of his body over the damaged coffee table and his head and torso coming down on Tim's outstretched arm. Tim heard the sickening *crack* as the force of the collision broke his left wrist, involuntarily pulling the trigger.

ᔓᔕ

In his daze, Jack heard all the sounds, the screams coming from two different throats, and the muffled report of the gun. He struggled to his feet, almost passing out from the blow to his head. There was blood pouring on the carpet at an alarming rate.

"Tim!" DeMarchand's body obscured his view of Tim's face and torso. "Tim!" he shouted again.

DeMarchand groaned.

"Please God, no!" Jack could never live with himself if he lost Eric and Tim to the same madman.

DeMarchand was barely conscious when he rolled off of Tim's body, an ugly wound on his right side. Jack was so relieved to see Tim using his injured arms to push DeMarchand aside it almost brought tears to his eyes.

"Are you hit, too?" he said, moving quickly to Tim's side.

"No bullet wounds, but my right arm is bleeding like a stuck pig, and I'm sure my left wrist is broken." He grimaced in pain and looked at DeMarchand. "Is he dead?"

"I don't think so, but I might have to move fast to save his life. First, I'm going to help you."

Jack ripped off his windbreaker and wrapped it tightly around Tim's bleeding right forearm. He gently moved Tim to sit against the couch. "Neither one of these injuries is life-threatening. Hold both your arms close to your body, and don't move. I'll call an ambulance."

Jack looked to the loveseat. The envelope and his phone had been knocked to the floor in the scuffle. A quick look did not yield the phone so he ran to the library and used the house phone to call for help. It took precious time to communicate the emergency to the woman on the line. It was made easier due to the address showing up on her caller ID, and Jack only knew he was on Rue du Château.

He hung up and went back to the living room. He pulled off his cotton dress shirt, knelt, and pressed it against De-Marchand's wound.

"Don't die, you miserable piece of shit, I want to see you experience hell on earth by spending the rest of your life in prison."

CHAPTER FIFTY-FIVE

Chief Inspector Covyeau awoke from a half sleep with a dull ache in his right shoulder and a faint tingling in his arm and fingers. The cause for the lack of circulation was Chloé's weight. Her head nestled comfortably, for her at least, on his chest. Their energetic coupling earlier on the warm summer night had left them sweaty and spent.

Still naked, they lay entwined on the bed with no covers, enjoying the cool breeze filtering through the slightly open window. The bedroom remained candlelit, the small flames dancing shadows on the walls. He was at peace here and considered spending the night, but realized that might tempt fate a bit too much. Even with his wife out of town, he felt it prudent to return to his own apartment.

He was able to slip out of bed without waking her. He took a moment to marvel and appreciate the beautiful form sprawled across the soft, pastel-colored sheets. He didn't doubt for a minute his good fortune. To find such passion and enthusiasm at this point in his life was truly a blessing. He had no illusions or delusions it would last forever, but he was willing to take the risks to make her a part of his life for as long as possible.

He retrieved his clothes scattered about the bedroom, and quietly moved to the living area to dress. The faint light from the bedroom candles was not enough to prevent him from stumbling over his leather satchel propped up against the side chair. One of his cell phones spilled a few feet away across the hardwood floor.

"Merde."

He leaned over, turned on the reading lamp next to the side chair, sat down, and began to massage his sore toes. He heard a soft purring noise. He looked back into the bedroom, assuming it was Chloé's snoring, but she was breathing normally.

The noise persisted.

He righted his upended satchel and noticed the missing cell phone. His personal cell phone was there and turned on, his regular police phone turned off. The task force phone was not in the satchel. He searched on his hands and knees and found it on the floor under the window curtains, just as it started to vibrate again.

"Inspector Covyeau," he answered quietly, but heard nothing in response. He repeated his name.

No response.

He climbed back up, sat in the side chair, and looked at the phone. It was flashing he had a message, not receiving a call. He punched in his code for voice mail, and listened to Jack Oatmon's concerned voice asking him to call right away, regardless of the hour. He punched the preset number for Jack's phone, and waited. After four rings he heard Jack's familiar voice, but it was the pre-recorded instructions to leave a message. Chief Inspector Covyeau thought it odd to be asked to call immediately, and then get voicemail.

He called his office phone and heard the same message from Jack. Both messages were a few hours old, but left no other details other than to call. Covyeau sensed something was wrong, his detective training and intuition kicking in.

He dressed quickly, smelling his mistress's scent on his fingers as he buttoned the top of his shirt. It would be such a shame to never return here. Hoping the whole situation had not blown up in his face, he went to the bedroom, gently kissed his lover's forehead, ran to the door, and raced down the stairs two and three at a time.

CHAPTER FIFTY-SIX

As luck would have it, the house was only a few blocks from the American Hospital. Jack, down to his plain white undershirt, stayed with DeMarchand until the paramedics arrived. He had regained consciousness briefly, but Jack was unable to get anything from him at first.

As the sirens got louder, Jack pressed.

"Listen, DeMarchand, you have to know I think you're human scum without a shred of human decency, but I'm willing to make a deal. Tell me where Alexei is going and I'll do what I can to help you both. For once in your fucking miserable life, do the right thing."

DeMarchand said nothing. His eyes glazed over and Jack thought he was going to lose him. The paramedics were almost there.

"If you don't help me, I'll leave you to the mercy of the French authorities and walk away. Trust me, you don't want that to happen. I won't help you unless you help me, now where is Alexei going?"

"15 Rue de Mulhouse, apartment 12."

DeMarchand passed out.

That's where Rick was!

ꕥ

The ambulance pulled into the driveway followed closely by a small police car. It was strangely quiet as both sirens were silenced. Jack left DeMarchand and went to the door.

"*Ici, s'il vous plaît.*" After a few weeks in Paris he had learned only a few French phrases. He led the EMTs to the living room and the two injured men. They were followed by two *flics*.

"*Parlez-vous anglais?*" he asked.

"A leetle bit, yes," said the EMT who seemed to be in charge.

Jack was able to explain enough of the story to warn them DeMarchand was dangerous, and say that he and Tim were the good guys. The lead EMT translated to the two *flics*. They kept a careful eye not only on DeMarchand, but on Jack, too. He must have looked suspicious in his bloodstained undershirt and bleeding from the cut on his forehead.

Jack looked for his cell phone in the mess, explaining in a calm voice what he was doing. He found it under the library chair and showed it to the *flics*.

"I want to call Inspector Covyeau at Interpol," he said.

The EMT translated again. One of the *flics* nodded and ushered Jack to the foyer to give the EMTs room to work.

Covyeau picked up on the first ring.

"Jack, where are you!"

"You're not going to believe it," Jack began. His training took over as he gave a brief verbal report. "I'm at Craig Lawrence's house near the American Hospital. Ischenko is dead, and DeMarchand is shot but alive. Alexei Persoff is wounded and at large. He's headed to a safe house at 15 Rue de Mulhouse, apartment 12, it's in the 2nd. I have Rick positioned there now with my task-force cell phone. We need to get him help right away."

"You have a civilian involved?"

"I couldn't get in touch with you, so I had no choice; I'll explain why later. Right now we have to protect Rick, and apprehend Alexei before he does some real damage. Alexei is shot in the left shoulder and driving a large black Mercedes, possibly an embassy car. Can you get someone over to Rue de Mulhouse right away?"

"I will go myself. Keep talking while I get to my car."

"I tried to call you earlier; did you get my messages?"

"I picked them up a short time ago. Sorry I was unavailable."

"Where were you?"

"I will explain later, too," Covyeau said. "We both will have some explaining to do with all the gunshots and wounded. Make sure you mark the weapons as evidence, especially your service revolver, because it is not registered with Interpol or the French police."

"Well, you see, that's the funny part," Jack said. He could hear that Covyeau was not laughing. "I don't have that gun anymore. Sasha took it, she promised to send it back," Jack said, and laughed despite himself.

"Incroyable." Covyeau reached his car and Jack heard him start it.

"That's not the half of it. I never fired a shot."

CHAPTER FIFTY-SEVEN

Alexei didn't think he was going to make it. Every time he pushed in the clutch with his left leg, the movement sent a jolt of pain through the entire left side of his body. Waiting at a stoplight on Avenue de la Grande Armée, he reached over to the glove box and found a small package of tissues. He had to use his teeth and one good hand to get the tissues out. He pressed them to his bleeding left shoulder.

He had been lucky. The bullet passed through the flesh between his torso and his arm and exited out the back of his armpit. No vital organs were hit, but he was losing a lot of blood. It saturated his clothes and the fine leather upholstery.

He moved as little as possible to put the car into first gear, then drove through the roundabout at the Arc de Triomphe. He cursed the traffic, still heavy at this hour, but he only had a few kilometers more.

He had to get away.

No way was he ever going back to prison.

ᔕ

Nikki had no trouble following Alexei, the maneuverability of her motorcycle a distinct advantage in the heavy traffic. But Alexei knew where he was going, and she didn't. She had no idea what she was going to do once he did stop. He was driving fast, but not enough to draw attention. The route took them down the Quai des Tuileries, along the river, and then left as he headed past the Louvre.

Driving in the middle of the night with a dark visor certainly didn't help, but she tried to orient herself. A couple of hours ago she was looking at a large map of this exact area. It dawned on her Alexei might be heading to the Rue de Mulhouse address where Rick was stationed. She had no way to warn him. Then she remembered the phone she had taken from the man at the restaurant. She had to call Rick as soon as possible.

ᔕ

Alexei drove past Les Halles, angled left up the Rue Montmartre and then right on Rue des Jeûneurs. Traffic was thinner here on the narrow one-way street. The apartment had been chosen with care, in the building on the corner of Rue des Jeûneurs and Rue de Mulhouse. Both were one-way streets, with Rue de Mulhouse a dead end in the T of Rue des Jeûneurs. Anyone driving on Rue des Jeûneurs could only turn right onto Rue de Mulhouse. This gave Alexei a commanding view of all three parts of the T, and any pursuers would be forced to continue in one direction and make a time-consuming loop all the way around to the entrance of Rue des Jeûneurs to make another pass.

The apartment was also on the top floor with access to the roof, and the numerous escape routes Alexei had mapped out through other buildings. The routes brought him out to the busy streets of Rue de Cléry or Rue du Sentier, where he could easily blend in with passersby.

He wasn't worried about parking the car. He would abandon it now anyway. He didn't want to park too close to the apartment, but he had no choice in his weakened state. He had five flights of stairs to climb. At least the tissues were doing their job; the bleeding had slowed to a trickle. He felt a little stronger.

The street was too narrow to double park, plus it would bring unwanted attention. With his one good arm he parked illegally in front of a cloth merchant's shop driveway two buildings away. By the time anyone noticed in the morning, he would be long gone. He was only staying long enough to pick up the money belt stuffed with cash, the extra fake passports, dress the wound as best he could, and change clothes. He hoped the six Extra Strength Tylenol gel tabs he planned to take would help. Maybe he could rest for a few minutes, too.

CHAPTER FIFTY-EIGHT

Chief Inspector Covyeau sped up Rue du Louvre, ignoring the I. M. Pei pyramid off to his right. He pulled out his cell phone and called Rick.

He identified himself and told Rick he knew Jack had asked for his help. "Where are you?" he asked.

"I'm down the street from the apartment building. The two streets here are one way, so I should be able to see anyone coming by car or motorcycle."

"Are you well hidden?" Covyeau asked.

"I'm doing loops on my bicycle to keep moving. There's not much activity here this time of night, and I didn't want to be conspicuous by staying in one spot."

"Good thinking. That area has a lot of fabric merchants, so it doesn't have as many apartments as some other areas. I should be there in a few minutes. Keep riding around; I will find you." Covyeau wanted to get there quickly, not only to prevent more bloodshed, but to come up with a plan to keep Rick out of danger.

ᔓ

Nikki was a hundred yards behind Alexei when he stopped. She pulled in behind a large work van, probably used to deliver the large bolts of fabric for one of the area merchants. As soon as he emerged from the car she could see he was injured. He moved awkwardly up the street, punched in a code on the keypad, and disappeared into the building on the corner.

She pulled off her helmet and got the scrap of paper with Rick's phone number. She felt strange using another's personal item, but she had no choice.

Rick answered on the first ring.

"Where are you?" he said.

"How did you know it was me?" Nikki asked, stunned.

"Nikki?" Rick said, equally stunned.

"Yes, who did you think it was?"

"Inspector Covyeau. He called two minutes ago. The number looked the same," Rick said, confused. "Are you with him?"

"No, I'm by myself on the motorcycle. Where are you?"

"Near the Rue de Mulhouse building, I'm coming around again. Whose phone are you using?" Rick asked.

"It's a long story, I'll explain later. Alexei went into the building on the corner," Nikki said. "I'm on Rue des Jeûneurs about a hundred yards from Rue de Mulhouse. I'm parked behind a large white van."

"I've ridden by it several times already. Stay there, I'm on my way."

There was nothing Nikki could do except stay behind the van and wait.

ஐ

The walk up the stairs took a lot out of Alexei, but the tissues packed to his shoulder had held and the wound wasn't bleeding dangerously. He moved around the apartment and closed all the drapes before he turned on any lights. In the kitchen, he found the Tylenol, dry swallowed two, then washed down four more with a bottle of Vittel. He leaned against the counter and belched. The sharp shiver of pain that shot through his injured shoulder made him wince.

He went to the tiny bathroom, delicately removed his shirt, and peeled away the sodden tissues. The stinging pain brought tears to his eyes, and the wound immediately started bleeding again. He took a hand towel and packed the wound in front, using his teeth to rip pieces of tape to hold it in place. He found another towel, walked back to a chair in the living room, and placed it on the back corner. He sat down, pressed the exit wound against the towel, and rested.

He had never given this address to anyone, and the name on the lease matched a fake passport. He would be safe now, at least for a few hours.

He was wrong.

DeMarchand had followed Alexei to the apartment one night and learned the false name he used on the lease. DeMarchand sent the silk tie from Savile Row de Paris there as an emergency tactic to deflect attention away from him, and toward Alexei.

It had almost worked.

ꟹ

Rick reached Nikki in less than five minutes, breathing heavily from the sprint on the bike. He pulled in behind the van and dismounted.

Nikki didn't know how she was going to tell him about the confrontation at the restaurant, or explain why she abandoned Jack to follow Alexei.

"Are you okay? You're shaking," Rick said.

"I'm fine, just worried about Jack and Tim. It might be time to get help."

Neither one noticed the car pull alongside them and stop. The passenger-side window rolled down electronically, and the driver leaned into the opening.

"Get in, hurry," was all he said.

"I sure hope you're Inspector Covyeau," Rick said. He instinctively put himself between the car and Nikki.

Inspector Covyeau was familiar with Rick and Nikki from file photographs. Neither of them had ever met him.

"I am," Covyeau said as nicely as he could. "Please get in. We will draw attention at this time of night." He pushed a button and the doors unlocked.

Rick thought the odds this person was someone other than Chief Inspector Covyeau were astronomical, but he hesitated for another second anyway. He hadn't come this far to do something stupid that might cost them their lives.

"Please trust me," Covyeau said. "We are all in danger."

The tone of concern in Covyeau's voice was genuine. Rick looked at Nikki; she seemed to notice too. She patted Rick's arm for encouragement and they got in the car, Nikki in the back, Rick in front. If anything was wrong, Rick wanted to be the one closest to the danger.

Covyeau relocked the doors and slowly drove down the narrow street. "Which building is it?" he asked.

They were almost even with 15 Rue de Mulhouse. "The one on the corner," Nikki said, pointing to the right. "Alexei went in five or six minutes ago."

"You were helping Rick here?" Covyeau asked. He glanced at her in the rear view mirror.

"No, I was following Alexei on a motorcycle."

"A motorcycle?" Covyeau said. "From where?"

"A house near the Pont de Neuilly Métro station," Nikki said.

"You were backup for Jack?" Covyeau was incredulous.

"Yes, I followed Jack there. I was only supposed to go for help if things went bad. I heard some shots fired and recognized Alexei racing out of the driveway. I saw Jack through the curtains; he looked safe for the moment so I took off after Alexei. I wasn't thinking of the danger."

"*Incroyable*," was all Covyeau could say.

Rue des Jeûneurs sloped slightly upward after it passed Rue de Mulhouse. Covyeau drove up the incline as far as possible while keeping the front of Alexei's building in sight. He pulled in front of a garage door with a huge No Parking sign, lowered all the windows, and shut off the engine. He turned his body to see both Nikki and Rick.

"Your assistance in this operation stops right now," he said. "I know it has been a very strange few days for you since Magda's murder, but I can't have you involved anymore. The risk is too high. I know you mean well, but for your own safety, please stop. Jack and I will handle it from here."

"Are Jack and Tim okay?" Nikki hoped desperately that they were.

"Yes."

"Thank God," Nikki said. "What happened? I heard several shots."

"As far as I have been able to discern, Jack is uninjured, but Tim probably has a broken left wrist and a gash on his right arm. They are on the way to the American Hospital with DeMarchand, who has a gunshot wound. Ischenko was shot to death. I still don't have all the details."

"It seems like all the bad guys got shot," Rick said.

"Not all of them," Nikki said. "There's another one lying on the floor of the cave at L'Avenue Bar & Grill with a bashed-in head."

This time Covyeau and Rick turned toward Nikki in the back seat. If the situation wasn't so serious, the look on their faces would have made Nikki laugh. "Oh, all right, I'll tell you."

Nikki spent the next few minutes relating the events at the restaurant. "He tried to kill me, but I couldn't leave him there. I called for help before I left, but I took his phone and used it to call Rick."

She handed it to Covyeau.

"The number is very similar to yours, Inspector," Rick said. "When she called me I thought it was you."

Covyeau opened the phone. The small LED light cast an eerie glow in the dark space of the car. He pushed a few buttons, read the information on the screen. A look of deep sadness came over him, his shoulders slumped.

"Who does it belong to?" Nikki asked.

"It is as I expected," he said, unable to hide his emotion. "It belongs to my best friend, Inspector Leveque of the task force."

CHAPTER FIFTY-NINE

Alexei awoke with a start. The digital clock near the television told him he had dozed off for twenty minutes. His body definitely could use the rest, but he needed to be alert, too. He forced himself out of the chair, grateful to see the ministrations to his shoulder had stopped the bleeding.

He reversed his earlier actions and turned out all the lights. Standing at the corner window, he drew the curtains back enough to see up Rue des Jeûneurs.

Nothing out of the ordinary.

He methodically checked down Rue de Mulhouse with the same result. His eyes shifted back to the intersection, and then up Rue des Jeûneurs again. He released the curtains. In the split second before the room returned to darkness, he saw a twinkle of light from a car interior up the incline of Rue des Jeûneurs. He strained his eyes in the dim light provided by the street lights. It was too dark to see anything that far away.

He went to the sideboard near the front door, retrieved his high-powered binoculars, and returned to the window. The binoculars were too heavy to hold and adjust with his one good arm, so he used the top of the lower pane to steady his view. He zoomed in on the car.

Another flash of light drew his eyes to the driver's side. An LED display of a cell phone. He couldn't recognize the figure, but he did notice the other two people in the car. He zoomed in closer. The figure in the back seat was smaller than the other two. The front seat passenger turned toward the back seat. There wasn't much light, but it was enough for Alexei to recognize the face.

Rick Asher! That image was burned into his brain after being outmaneuvered and humiliated in Florence. How could he possibly have found him here? Maybe it was a coincidence, but Alexei didn't believe it for a minute. It was way too late in the game for that. He had no choice. He had to leave, and he had to do it now.

Working with only one good arm, it took him a few frustrating minutes to secure the money belt holding all his cash and extra passports. It took even longer to wriggle into a shirt; the effort left blood seeping through his makeshift bandage. He took an extra few seconds to put on a light windbreaker to cover any blood on his shirt and conceal the Beretta.

At the back door, he took his last look around. He didn't have time to be sentimental, but he would miss this apartment where he felt comfortable and safe for the first time in his life. He slipped into the back stairwell, climbed to the exit, and disappeared over the rooftops.

ᏧᏍ

The first ambulance had already left with DeMarchand, accompanied by an inspector and one of the *flics*. More officials arrived to secure the scene, so Jack helped the EMT lift Tim to a standing position, then out to the second ambulance. Still not fully recovered from the sedative, Tim's head pounded worse than any hangover he could remember. The EMT said the knife wound might have nicked a tendon in his right forearm, so he would need surgery on both his arm and wrist tonight.

"Can you make it?" Jack asked.

"I'll be okay," Tim said, trying to tough it out. "How are Nikki and Rick doing?"

In all the excitement, Jack had forgotten about Nikki. Where was she anyway? Had she gone for help? He didn't even know if she was able to follow him to the house.

"As far as I know they're both fine. I need to stay here for a little while. I'll be over to see you later. I'll have more information then."

"I would never forgive myself if they get hurt," Tim said. They hoisted him into the back of the ambulance.

"That makes two of us," Jack muttered. He already felt guilty about Tim's injuries. The ambulance left the driveway for the short ride to the hospital. Jack and the English-speaking EMT walked over to the official in charge.

"How many phone calls were received for this emergency?" Jack asked.

The EMT translated, listened to the response and turned back to Jack. "The one from this house only," he said.

That didn't necessarily mean Nikki was in danger. It was possible she was still somewhere around the Pont de Neuilly Métro station, unable to find him. One way to find out: call Rick.

CHAPTER SIXTY

"I don't care if you have to wake President François Hollande himself, get me someone who knows the layout and the entry code for this building," Covyeau hissed into his phone. "We need to move in the next few minutes, do you understand?"

He held the phone in his hand, turned again toward Rick and Nikki. "Both of you are not to move from the car until I get back," Covyeau said. "Do I make myself clear?"

"Yes," they said in unison.

"Bon."

It only took a minute before Covyeau's phone buzzed.

He spent the next few minutes rattling off instructions in rapid-fire French. Nikki missed some obscure terms, but understood enough to grasp Covyeau's plan of attack. One team of two would be positioned in the courtyard, preventing an escape to the rear. Covyeau and two other teams would make their move from the front, one team from the direction of Nikki's motorcycle and another up Rue de Mulhouse.

"*D'accord,*" he said, and disconnected. "We have the code to the door now. It should be no problem to surprise Mr. Persoff and end it right now." He got out of the car, adjusted his light sports coat, and checked his weapon.

"Stay here," he commanded one last time. He moved down the incline toward the rest of his forces making their way toward the front door.

As Nikki watched him go, her hand moved to her backpack. She found the reassuring grip of the Glock, just in case.

&

Covyeau whispered instructions to his four team members, punched in the code, and the five men deployed professionally into the building and up the stairs. They arrived at the door of Number 12 in a matter of seconds, and with a minimum of noise.

No one said a word.

Covyeau decided Alexei was too dangerous to be given a chance to surrender. He signaled the two largest men to hit the door with a battering ram; the other three would follow them and secure the room. It should be over in a matter of seconds. He took a deep breath, looked at each man for a nod of assent, and gave the order.

The noise was earsplitting, reverberating in the hallway as the metal ram hit the door right above the lock. The ancient door jamb splintered easily, released the door from its flimsy constraints, and slammed into the inside wall. The battering-ram duo was out of the way almost instantaneously. The other three stormed the room with guns drawn.

It was dark.

The only light was from the hallway fixture seeping into the obviously empty living room. The team members were well trained and quickly cleared the other rooms.

"*Pareil,*" one said to Covyeau. Nobody.

Another one stood next to the back door off the kitchen. He opened it and looked into the empty stairwell.

"*Idem.*"

"Check with the other team," Covyeau commanded.

The man used his shoulder mic to check with the team positioned downstairs.

"*Non,*" he shook his head.

"Merde!"

Covyeau knew Alexei had entered the building less than an hour ago. Since then he, Rick, and Nikki would have seen anyone exit through the front. Alexei had left by the back; it was the only logical explanation. He stood at the bottom of the stairs leading to the roof. He looked at the officer next to him, put his finger to his lips, and pointed to the ceiling. He motioned a second officer to back up the first. They silently crept up the stairs and opened the door.

Covyeau could hear them moving around above him. There were no commands, no shots fired.

In two minutes they were back.

"Rien."

Then it hit Covyeau like a jolt. Rick and Nikki were in danger again!

He told the battering-ram duo to stay put, ordered the other two to follow him. For the second time that night he flew down stairs taking two and three at a time. He didn't notice the shocked and frightened faces peering from behind chained doorways.

CHAPTER SIXTY-ONE

From the shadows of a storefront on Rue de Cléry, Alexei watched two of Covyeau's men move up Rue de Mulhouse. As soon as they were out of sight, he crossed behind them and turned left on Rue Poissonnière. It was a short block before he positioned himself on the corner, looking down the incline of Rue Jeûneurs. He spotted Rick and Nikki, their backs to him.

Alexei approached the car stealthily. Amateurs, he thought. Assuming the threat could only come from one direction, they had left themselves vulnerable to an attack from the rear. They looked anxiously toward his apartment, and he allowed himself a quick glance in that direction. The lights in his apartment were on, the curtains partially open in one of the windows. He had gotten out in time, and now he had to move quickly to get away.

"Don't move," he said. Through the open window, he pressed the cold steel barrel of the Beretta to the back of Rick's head.

Nikki turned at the sound and gasped.

"Be quiet, Ms. Dunn, or I will kill him right now," Alexei said. He knew from experience his calm, cold demeanor would come across as sinister and deadly.

It worked.

Nikki was obviously terrified. She clutched her backpack in front of her, as if to stop a bullet. He leaned closer to the window.

"We are going to make this real easy," Alexei said. "You drive." He indicated to Rick with silenced muzzle. Before Rick could move in the awkward seats, Alexei heard a commotion to his left.

Covyeau and two officers burst out the door at full speed with guns drawn.

"Rick!" Covyeau shouted.

But it was too late.

He saw Alexei with a gun to Rick's head.

"Stop where you are!" Alexei screamed, the sound echoing off the stone walls in the night silence.

"Don't do anything stupid, Alexei," Covyeau said from fifty feet away. "Put the gun down and surrender. You don't have a chance."

Covyeau and the two officers inched closer, guns still drawn. Alexei was exposed outside the car, but still out of range for a clean kill shot.

Alexei sensed his vulnerability. "I said stop!"

This time the three men stopped.

"Put your guns down, or I kill them both," he said. "Do it now!"

"Do as he says," Covyeau whispered. The three men placed their guns in the middle of the narrow street. "Call the other team to approach from behind him." He didn't know if they would get there in time.

Alexei was at another disadvantage, with only one good arm. He told Rick to open the car door from the inside and get out.

"No!" Nikki said.

"Shut up, bitch," Alexei snarled.

Rick got the door open and backed out. The gun never left his head until the last second, when Alexei brought the gun through the open window frame and back in position. Alexei used Rick's larger body as a shield, and with a quick hip movement closed the door.

Covyeau and his men inched closer.

"This is very easy," Alexei said, loud enough for everyone to hear. "We move to the other side of the car. Monsieur Asher will get in to drive. Do as I say and no one else will get hurt."

Nobody believed that, including Alexei.

He backed Rick around the car to the driver's side.

"Open both doors."

Nikki was eerily calm. There would be one opening for her. After Rick got in the front, Alexei would be vulnerable when he moved the gun around the door frame to get into the back seat. She made sure she had a firm grip on the Glock, finger poised on the trigger.

It had to end now. Nobody called her a bitch and got away with it.

"Let Nikki go," Rick said. "You only need me as a hostage. Two of us are a hassle."

Alexei didn't have time to consider it.

"No way. I'm not going anywhere without you, Rick," Nikki said. She would lose her opening if she was forced to leave the car.

"Goddammit, Nikki, leave if he'll let you!" Rick sputtered in disbelief. "Come on, Alexei, let her go."

"No!" Nikki said again.

"Shut up, both of you," Alexei ordered. "You both come with me. Get in the car, but don't start the engine until I am inside."

Rick glared at Nikki as he angled his body into the driver's seat.

She didn't notice. Her eyes never left Alexei's gun. The timing had to be perfect or they would both die.

Any second now.

Alexei still had the gun to Rick's head. He couldn't resist a parting shot to the three policemen standing helplessly in the street. "Don't follow us, or I swear on your mistress's tits, they both die."

He pulled the gun from Rick's head and moved to get in the back seat. There was a split second his torso was exposed, the gun pointed upward for his elbow to clear the open window frame.

BANG!

Nikki didn't pull the Glock from the backpack before she fired. The bullet ripped into Alexei's chest and blew him away from the car. His face wore a look of complete incomprehension. He staggered backward across the sidewalk and hit the stone wall of the building.

He was still alive, but barely.

Nikki didn't hesitate. She scrambled over the back seat and out the open door.

Alexei raised his Beretta one last time.

Nikki fired again.

This time she was deadly.

Alexei dropped his gun as he smashed into the wall and crumpled to the pavement.

Shot by a woman, an amateur.

It was the last thought he had.

The twisted wreckage of Alexei's body lay against the building. It oddly mirrored a dark urine stain that started at the bottom stones of the building and snaked down the sidewalk to the gutter.

Rick jumped out of the car and Nikki buried her head in his chest. Covyeau raced over, made sure Alexei was dead.

"*Mon dieu*," Covyeau said. He gently eased the backpack from Nikki's hands. "It's over, Nikki. It's over."

CHAPTER SIXTY-TWO

Jack sat in the waiting room at the American Hospital with Rick, Nikki and Greg. They all had been up for almost twenty-four hours, their fatigue apparent. Jack tried hard to be mad at Rick and Nikki for taking so many chances, but his heart wasn't in it. The mere fact they all survived with only minor injuries was a miracle.

"I can't believe we were here eight days ago," Nikki said. She rolled down the sleeve of her blouse. One of the nurses was kind enough to take out the few stitches from above her left elbow.

"It's been an eventful week," Jack said. "It should calm down now though. Maybe you can get back to some sort of normal life."

"Fat chance," Nikki said.

"You're probably right," Jack admitted.

Further conversation was interrupted by the appearance of a surgeon. Everyone started to get up, but he motioned them all to stay seated. He plopped down unceremoniously on a stray chair and faced them.

"I am Dr. Stephan Kozi. I performed the surgery on your friend. He is in excellent physical shape and I expect a full recovery. I will not bore you with medical jargon, but the break in his left wrist was clean, and I reset the bone easily. The tendon on his right forearm was only slightly damaged and should heal quickly too, with no complications. He was lucky though. A few millimeters in either direction, the knife could have damaged some important nerves, causing a lack of motion in his fingers, but, as I say, this was avoided."

The relief on everyone's faces was evident, especially Jack's.

"When will he be able to go home?" Rick asked.

"You should be able to come back this afternoon to get him. He won't be driving anytime soon with both wrists in casts."

"We want to be there when he wakes up. Is that possible?" Greg asked.

"Not really; he is in the recovery room still coming out of the anesthesia. I will tell him you were here. Why don't you all go home and get some sleep? You look like you could use it."

He looked at Jack with an odd expression.

"Are you injured, too?" he asked.

Jack realized he had a large bump on his forehead, and still wore his bloodstained undershirt and jeans. "No, I'm fine, thanks," he said. "I used my windbreaker on Tim's arm and my shirt on DeMarchand."

"You helped them both, I am sure," the doctor said. "I'll ask a nurse to bring you something clean to wear. We can save your clothes in bags in case you need them as evidence." He rose to leave, the group effusive in their thanks. "See you this afternoon." He turned and left.

ᔕ

After getting Rick, Nikki, and Greg in a cab, Jack regrouped with Covyeau in the nearly empty hospital cafeteria. Covyeau had been on his cell phone constantly, coordinating with his colleagues to secure the two murder scenes in two different arrondissements. It was shaping up to be a colossal bureaucratic nightmare. Covyeau had been able to take custody of Sasha's package, and Jack wanted to get a look at it right away. The potential to damage or even destroy the Russian operation was substantial.

Covyeau had also used his influence to bring in some of his own people to guard DeMarchand. They would question him as soon as possible, but he was still in surgery and wouldn't be available until much later in the day at the earliest.

"The first thing we need to do is talk to Craig Lawrence," Jack said. "I can't wait to hear him explain away his relationship with Victor Ischenko. I'm not too optimistic about getting straight answers, though. He can claim diplomatic immunity and leave the country, if he hasn't already."

Jack pulled his wallet out and retrieved the folded contact sheet from the first task force meeting. He found Lawrence's cell number and dialed it on his task force phone, returned to him earlier this morning. He hit the button for the speakerphone.

"Hello?" answered a groggy voice.

Jack identified himself. "Where are you, Director Lawrence?"

"I'm back in Washington," he answered. "It's 2 a.m. here. Can't this wait until later?"

"I'm afraid not, Director Lawrence. There's been a development in the investigation here. We need you to come back to Paris and help us by answering a few questions."

"What kind of questions?"

"Like why was Victor Ischenko using your house as an exchange point? Or why he claimed you were a frequent client of his varied services, and not only those of legal-aged women?"

Jack could almost hear him wince.

"This is outrageous!" Lawrence screamed. "How dare you accuse me of such things?!"

"I didn't accuse you of anything," Jack said calmly. "I'm saying Victor Ischenko did."

"Listen, Jack," Lawrence said, trying to sound reasonable. "I left Paris yesterday morning and haven't slept for two days. I have no idea how Ischenko was able to get into my house. There is no alarm system, and I'm sure he has his resources."

"Had his resources," Jack said. "He was shot to death in your living room a few hours ago."

This time Jack heard an audible gasp, then silence. "What about DeMarchand?" Lawrence finally asked. There was fear in his voice.

"He was shot, too, but he'll survive. Inspector Covyeau and I plan to interview him in a few minutes. We think he's ready to spill his guts to save his ass."

Jack enjoyed putting the pressure on. Covyeau had been listening with interest, but now motioned with his hands to tone it down a little.

"Listen, Craig," Jack said. "Answer me one question now, please. Why was there an embassy car in your driveway?"

Craig Lawrence's voice seemed to come from far away. "The car?"

"Yes, the big Mercedes sedan with embassy plates."

"Oh, I bought that fair and square from the French Embassy. After 9/11 all the embassies in Paris, including ours, began replacing their existing fleet of cars with armored limousines. The French didn't complete the transition until a few months ago, and a friend at their embassy got me a really good deal on it. That car would cost me twice as much here in the States. What could it possibly have to do with the task force?"

Jack was distracted and angry. The brave young military men and women in Iraq and Afghanistan were getting blown up and maimed in tanks with insufficient armor, while effete pissants like Lawrence and his political buddies were chauffeured around Paris in armored limousines. It made him want to weep with shame for his country. He forced himself back to the issue at hand.

"Let's just say it keeps turning up in strange circumstances, like in the disappearance of Svetlana last week. Did you have anything to do with that, Director?"

"Of course not. How dare you ask. I have no more time for these ridiculous questions. Goodbye."

Craig Lawrence disconnected.

"That went well," Jack said. "I'm sure the next time we talk to him, he'll have his lawyer present."

"I would imagine so."

They were silent for a minute, both deep in thought.

Covyeau's phone buzzed again. He got up and moved outside to the courtyard to take the call. Jack watched through the window. He couldn't hear what was being said, but he wouldn't have been able to understand the rapid-fire French anyway. It was clear Covyeau was frustrated. He abruptly ended the call and returned.

"An interesting development, Jack," he said. "Inspector Leveque has regained consciousness. He plans to file attempted murder charges against Nikki."

"That's ridiculous."

"Of course it is," Covyeau said. "I have known Hugo for a long time. It is his way of starting negotiations. I will go to the other hospital and take care of it."

"We need to keep DeMarchand and Leveque isolated. We can play them off each other," Jack said. "It won't take long before one turns on the other, because neither of these guys wants to go to prison."

"They are both going to prison, my friend; it is only a matter of how long."

CHAPTER SIXTY-THREE

Jack was in the waiting room of the American Hospital again, going over his notes. Yesterday, after Covyeau left to deal with Leveque and get Sasha's disks transcribed, he was overwhelmed by fatigue. The two-and-a-half months of work, grief, and lack of sleep since Eric's death finally caught up with him. He barely made it back to his apartment, falling into bed and sleeping like the dead. He slept all day, got up in the evening to check messages, turned off the phones, took a pill, and slept all night. Now, he felt almost human again.

Covyeau arrived to join him for DeMarchand's interrogation.

"Here," he said, handing Jack a single sheet of paper. "You might find this interesting."

It was a copy of an item from the *Washington Post*, printed from Covyeau's e-mail account.

TO: dcovyeau@interpol.paris.fr
FROM: bseacrest@dcfbi.us
RE: Craig Lawrence

Daniel:

Thought you might like to see this right away. Say hi to Jack. Talk to you later.
Bill

> Washington D.C. — Craig Lawrence, the Director of the United States Mission in Paris, citing personal reasons, requested and was granted a leave of absence, effective immediately. He recently returned from France after his wife of twenty years filed for divorce.
>
> Director Lawrence has voluntarily admitted himself to an intensive ninety-day program at the Life Serenity Rehabilitation Center in Maryland, citing a dependence on alcohol and prescription medication. He has asked the media to respect his family's privacy in this difficult time. He promises to make

EVERY EFFORT TO SAVE HIS MARRIAGE AND RETURN TO WORK AS SOON AS POSSIBLE.

ASHLY HAINES, THE MINISTER COUNSELOR FOR AGRICULTURAL AFFAIRS, HAS BEEN APPOINTED INTERIM DIRECTOR.

"Not much of a surprise," Jack said. "At least we know where he will be for the next three months. It gives us more time to build a case. What else have you got?"

"We are going over Lawrence's embassy car for evidence. There was blood on the driver's side. So far, it matches Alexei's blood type. The partial license plate numbers match, too. I think we can assume it was the one used to take Svetlana."

"Yes, but by whom?" Jack asked. "I've been going over my notes and doing some checking. It couldn't have been Lawrence. He was in Brussels that night at a meeting, his presence verified by others, and his wife and children had left for the States days before. The other night, Ischenko and the others seemed familiar with Lawrence's house, so it could have been anybody in Ischenko's organization. We might never find out."

"Maybe Lawrence hired someone?"

"I don't think so. I got the impression from Ischenko that Lawrence preferred young boys and girls. Svetlana was not his type. Maybe DeMarchand can help us."

ꟷ

The interview with DeMarchand was mostly unproductive. He was obviously in pain and dulled by medication. He professed no knowledge of the embassy car, had never set foot in the house before he arrived with the sedated Tim Schroeder. He refused to answer any more questions before speaking to a lawyer.

Covyeau could not resist a parting shot. "It doesn't matter, Monsieur. I have already had discussions with Inspector Leveque. It will be interesting to see how you respond to his accusations."

DeMarchand's response was a derisive laugh. "Hugo Leveque is barely human."

CHAPTER SIXTY-FOUR

Henri Toulon, Dante International's former Chief of Security, made his way across the Boulevard des Invalides to the Rue de Varenne and the entrance to the Musée Rodin. As always, he was meeting his contact in the gardens near the Ugolino sculpture, a peaceful setting Henri always enjoyed. Today, his contact was already there, sitting on the bench facing the Hôtel Biron. They never acknowledged each other or spoke directly to one another. Henri sat at the other end of the bench, and pulled a sandwich and an apple from his small briefcase, simply another visitor enjoying the surroundings on a beautiful summer day.

"This is our last meeting," the contact said from behind the day's edition of *Le Monde*. "Our association has been mutually successful, but it is time to go our separate ways."

"I agree," Henri said agreeably as he munched on his sandwich. "We survived this long by being discreet, smart, cautious, and a little lucky. Now it is time to move on. Good luck." Henri collected the remnants of his lunch and silently walked away.

ᔕ

Henri's contact waited for several minutes, reading the paper before wandering through the gardens past the white flowering bushes, the *Burghers of Calais* sculpture, and back out to the Rue de Varenne.

The secret apartment was back across Boulevard Invalides on Boulevard de La Tour Maubourg. Originally it had been two apartments, both purchased after the early collaborations with Henri proved financially rewarding. The renovation had taken over a year, but the result was worth every Euro. The master bedroom suite was large enough for a king-sized bed and boasted a modern bathroom, complete with a Jacuzzi tub big enough for two. The reason for the painstaking efforts to create this perfect love nest lay naked on the bed.

"You are back so quickly today," she said, looking up from her magazine and smiling. "Why don't you get naked and join me. I missed you, Sasha."

Sasha shed her clothes.

"I missed you too, Svetlana."

EPILOGUE

Paris

One month later

It didn't take long before DeMarchand and Leveque were implicating each other. Chief Inspector Daniel Covyeau and Detective Jack Oatmon were masterful in pitting them against one another. Along with the information provided in Sasha's package, they extracted a wealth of information about not only the Ladies Invited/*Femmes Invitée* operation, but rival groups operating throughout Europe and the United States. Thousands of girls were rescued, and the flow of trafficked women substantially reduced, at least temporarily.

Covyeau and Oatmon had no illusions about the future. There would always be those ready to exploit the innocent and defenseless, merely providing the supply for what seemed to be an insatiable demand. Their jobs would never be finished, but they would take solace and satisfaction in their successes, however small or insignificant.

"It is like pushing wet spaghetti up a hill," Covyeau said.

"Or herding cats," Jack responded.

They were in the shadow of the Eiffel Tower, sitting in canvas beach chairs on the grass of the Champ de Mars, the evening sun sinking over the treetops, the sky and clouds morphing subtly into various pastel shades of blue, orange, and red. They shared a bottle of wine Jack had brought back from St. Émilion.

Joëlle's going away present to Jack was a week in Biarritz, and enrollment in a wine class in Bordeaux. She insisted it would be a tragedy if Jack left France without a working knowledge of wine. The class, and the week, turned out to be fun and memorable, the way Joëlle planned it. They swam in the Atlantic, took long walks on the beach at sunset, ate fabulous meals, and drank some of the best wine in the world. They made love in the morning, in the afternoon after a swim and late lunch, then again in the evening, still flush with the tingle of the sun on their skin. Not every day of course, but there were a couple of times they pulled off the trifecta.

Jack was scheduled to leave the next day for his return to the United States and his debriefing with Bill Seacrest at FBI headquarters in Washington D.C. He had mixed emotions about leaving, but Joëlle had insisted.

"No matter how hard you try, you will never be able to make this work," Joëlle said. "We both need to find someone we truly need in our lives, not simply someone we want temporarily. It has been wonderful, but it is time for both of us to move on."

Joëlle and Chloé had joined them for this last evening, but took a walk to the Trocadéro on the other side of the Eiffel Tower, allowing Jack and Daniel some time alone to say goodbye, and rehash the experience one last time.

Two small boxes with no return address lay open between them. One contained Jack's service revolver, the other a cashier's check for one million dollars made out to the Los Angeles Police Department.

Sasha had kept her word.

"There was a time I thought it was you," Jack said.

Covyeau chuckled. "I know. I wanted you to think no one was above suspicion. Considering my concerns about my best friend, Leveque, and Bonnard, I needed to ensure your objectivity and perspective."

"You realize three of the four task-force members based here in Paris were working for, or compromised by, Victor Ischenko," Jack observed.

Covyeau gave him an odd look, but said nothing.

"I find that very curious, don't you?" Jack asked.

"As they say, keep your friends close, but your enemies closer."

Paris

Bastille Day

One year later

Everyone was there.

Katarina, now Kathy Schroeder in the witness protection program, came with Adam Reeves. They were now a couple living in an LA suburb, and did a wonderful job putting together the memorial service for Magda. On the first anniversary of her death they chartered a boat and sailed along the Seine in the late afternoon sun. There was no clergy, only Katarina telling the small group how she had met Magda shortly after her mother's murder, how Magda had taken her under her wing, and made sure she went to school, insisting she make the effort to learn English. Katarina would never have survived the first winter if not for Magda.

With the sun sinking behind the Eiffel Tower and in the cool, softening shadows behind Notre Dame, Katarina poured Magda's ashes into the murky, slow-moving water.

"Goodbye, Magda, we will never forget you," she said, choking back tears. "You did not die in vain."

Katarina took a moment to regain her composure, and turned back to the group. "Adam and I also are inviting you all back here a year from today. Not just for the second anniversary of Magda's death, but to our wedding!"

The group erupted into hugs, tears, and conversations.

Jack walked over to Tim Schroeder. His two wrists showed the small scars from the night a year ago. "We did justice to your brother's memory too, Tim. Like Magda, his death was not in vain."

"I know, Jack. We did the best we could, that's all Eric would have wanted."

"What are you going to do now?"

"I sold my interest in L'Avenue Bar & Grill to Greg and Nikki, which makes them equal partners now. The place brings back too many sad memories of my brother and Magda. I've been an expatriate for too long, Jack; it's time for me to go back home and do something useful. What about you?"

"I'm off to start my new ICU assignment next week," Jack said. "I'm moving to San Francisco to work with an FBI unit. For you, it was the restaurant, for me it was Los Angeles. Too many bad memories. I'm looking forward to starting over in Northern California."

ᔕ

Greg and Nikki invited everyone back to the restaurant, closed for the day in Magda's honor. Tables were set up in the courtyard for an authentic American meal of cheeseburgers, fries, and California wines. L'Avenue Bar & Grill had reopened the previous August and, as Greg had predicted, was the toast of Paris. The notoriety it received from the murders made for many curious customers, but Greg was convinced it was the great food, polite staff, and good service that brought them back again and again.

The group of male models who crashed the final dress rehearsal the previous summer became a fixture. More nights than not they were there until very late, preening, posturing, and usually becoming so loud they needed to be asked several times a night to quiet down. The staff affectionately nicknamed them "the animals."

"So, how is the book?" Jack asked. He refilled Nikki's glass with a wonderful cabernet from central California.

"I finished the first draft last week," Nikki replied. "Thank you so much for asking. Writing is such a solitary experience. I never knew it would be so hard, or that I would enjoy it so much."

To help her through the tough months after the deaths of Magda, Gorky, and Alexei, the FBI crisis counselor recommended Nikki write it all down. Very early in the process, Nikki became convinced fate had given her Greg and brought her to Paris. It was now her responsibility to bring

Magda and Katarina's story to the world. She started with a letter to the editor of the *International Herald Tribune*, which led to an article for *Vanity Fair*. A well-respected publisher in New York saw the article, tracked her down in Paris, and offered a small advance for a book. At first she was not sure she could do it, but Greg's encouragement was unwavering.

"Come on, Nikki," he said over and over. "You have to write it. No one can make up stuff like this!"

Printed in Great Britain
by Amazon